Exile

Jerry Canada

The Tales of Terrowin

Book One

EXILE

Jerry Canada

Cover design by Pamela King
Editing by Ashley Atkins
Published in the United States by aea Media,
Chapel Hill, North Carolina.

ISBN 978-0-9862908-0-0 ebk
ISBN 978-0-9862908-1-7 pbk

Printed in the United States of America

First Edition

aea Media and Jerry Canada support the First Amendment
and celebrate the right to read.

*In loving memory of my mother,
Joyce Henderson Canada,
a woman who still inspires me
and told me the word "can't" should never
be a part of my vernacular.*

WHILE EVERYONE ELSE WAS SOUND ASLEEP, Sultan Assassin Kass sneaked out of her room and went to Professor Xalvador's laboratory classroom on the academic side of campus. She would have to work quickly. The door was unlocked, and inside she found the barrel of experimental fire powder. Kass loaded as much as she could carry into a huge sack and heaved it over her shoulder. She was not your ordinary sixteen-year-old girl. She headed back to the Royal Residence Hall.

When she reached the front entrance, she looked around to make sure no one was watching. She cut a small hole in one corner of the sack, to allow the powder to flow out. Then she took off, running around the building as fast as she could. Kass was able to make three complete spirals around the Royal Residence Hall before the sack was emptied. She went back to Xalvador's classroom to collect more. There was a second sack hanging on the side of the barrel. Kass filled her bag once more, securing the hole she had made before so as not to spill any out until it was time. She also grabbed the second sack and headed back to the Royal Residence Hall.

This time she did not run around outside, she made her way inside the building and unpinned the hole in her bag, allowing the fire powder to again seep out. She moved through the first floor and secured the Primos' door shut with a hook on the outside. On to the other floors she went, dispensing the combustible and double-checking to make sure the suite doors were locked from the outside with additional hooks. She skipped the sixth floor for the moment. The seventh floor would be more challenging.

Since the Ascensions lived on the seventh floor and were next in line to inherit the throne, their suite always had two posted guards on the outside. Kass had planned this moment for months. Prior to this night, she began secretly seeing one of the evening guards. He fancied her, going a bit weak when he saw her, and she would often meet him so they could take walks together around the campus late at night. He would usually tell his guardmate an obvious lie, that he was going to the bathroom, and then return twenty minutes later as if nothing had happened.

She walked quietly up the stairs, he was more on guard for her arrival than anything that might have to do with protecting the Ascensions. There she was. And then she was gone.

"Hey, I'll be back, I'm going to the toilet."

"Yeah, man, hurry back, God knows what you do in there, it takes you so long sometimes."

Off he went, down the stairs to the Sultan floor to meet with Kass. She grabbed his hand and pulled him into a dark corner. She didn't say a word.

"Oh, this is new, will I finally get to kiss the great and beautiful Kass?"

She pulled him close and said, "Wait, take off my mask."

He smiled and put two fingers on her lips. He then moved his hands toward the back of her head to unfasten her mask. "Kass, you know I've waited a long time to kiss you," he whispered in her ear.

As he was about to undo the clasp, Kass thrusted a knife into his stomach, and up toward his heart. His body lurched forward and she had to catch him lest he land face first. She slowly lowered him to the ground. Her eyes were cold and the look on his face was of someone betrayed, tricked and dying. Blood trickled out of his mouth, he was choking as the internal bleeding sealed his fate. Kass mechanically removed the knife from his torso and walked back to the Ascension Suite. This time, she deliberately made stomping sounds so the other guard would hear her.

"Oh, you're back! Took you long enough," said the second guard upon hearing the footsteps coming toward him. "Come on, I have to go also, come watch the bloody door!"

But it was not his guardmate. It was Kass, in her mask and moving like a predator. As soon as his eyes could make out who it was coming out of the darkness, he was hit by a dagger in his neck. He made no sound other than his lifeless body hitting the floor. Kass stepped easily over his body with her two sacks and secured the door to the Ascension Suite using one of the hooks.

She made it back to her own suite and entered her room, gathered a few personal items and made her way back outside the suite to the Sultans' common area. She turned around, secured the final door with a hook and walked outside.

It was a quiet night, only a couple of hours before sunrise. With her sword in one hand, she swiped at the stone and created a spark, igniting the fire powder. A spiral ring of flames started blazing on the outermost circle, racing around the first circle she had made going around the building. Then it continued to the middle circle and to the innermost circle.

The flames grew higher as the fire burned longer. By the time the second loop was completed, the outermost circle had grown to over ten meters, and when the third circle was complete it was over thirty meters high and burning hotter. Then, the fire shot inside the Royal Residence Hall, right toward where the baby Primos slept quietly in their cribs.

Chapter I

Centuries before, the leadership of Terrowin rejected all notions of a traditional monarchy. For too long they had been governed by failed kings, whose only right to govern was based upon familial bloodlines. The queens they married were no less of a problem. Some kings married for love, only to be so blinded by love sickness that they neglected their duties to the people. Other kings married for political favor. These unions often failed because of a lack of trust, or betrayal by a headstrong queen and her lust for power. Terrowin history is also replete with scandals that rocked the country when a king's mistress or queen's lover was exposed. The press and tabloid papers were always snooping, even lying in wait, to find a lover creeping out of the palace late at night.

The king's leadership counsel also had its share of internal strife, corruption and incompetence. Key advisors were often selected by the king in exchange for political favor, debt, or— even worse—because they were related to the king. Bribery reached all levels within the government, which left the king both paranoid and exposed, and the people of Terrowin without adequate leadership. Finally, as with most countries, Terrowin had its fair share of assassination attempts on the king's life, most of which failed, but always putting the king and country at risk.

Therefore, during a time period following a plague, a devastating earthquake and an especially unfortunate wardrobe malfunction, when Terrowin was without a king or a queen, the wisemen of Terrowin gathered and decided to form a new type of government. One that, in their grand collective wisdom, would benefit Terrowin and bring prosperity and balance to all citizens. After weeks of debate, they proclaimed the following:

Every four years, starting on January the first at one full second past midnight, the first-born male child recorded within Terrowin shall be King of Terrowin twenty-four years hence. The first-born female child who follows the King on New Year's Day shall be said King's Queen, twenty-four years hence. The next-born child, after the Queen, shall be heralded as Vice King and Advisor of the King. The child born subsequently shall be declared the King's Protector. The next female child shall be deemed the King's Mistress, and following her birth the next male child shall be the Queen's Lover. After the Queen's Lover, the next born child of either sex shall be the Assassin.

Each of these children, hereafter known as Royals, shall be raised by the State and will assume their birthright positions twenty-four years later and shall serve for four years.

God save the King. Blessings be upon our Land and all the Peoples of Terrowin.

The wisemen of Terrowin, long intrigued by the idea of all sorts of -ocracys and wishing to make the history books themselves, believed that every child in the country should have an opportunity to become king or queen. They also reasoned that any child, given the right education, upbringing and training, could fulfill any of these vital roles. The Birthing Ceremony, as it would come to be called, would forever determine Terrowin's future King, Queen, Advisor, Protector, Mistress, Lover and Assassin.

The king, beloved and supreme leader of Terrowin, would marry the selected queen. He would assume the same duties as kings past and have the same power to direct the country according to his own wisdom. The queen's main duty was to serve the king and be a woman of the people, sharing her best cookie recipes, making lunch for orphans on the minor holidays and being a shining light in the fashion world. She would have warm loving qualities, always follow her king's advice and play the role of devoted wife and helpmeet accordingly. She would also assume normal queen activities such as attending and creating public fund-raisers. She would be raised to be a woman of the people, and like the king could expect to be adored by everyone.

The advisor would be the king's successor should the unimaginable—well, ok, it could hardly be unimaginable if such extensive provisions were made, but let's just indulge the wisemen here—should the unimaginable happen to the king while he was in office. But the advisor's primary role is to provide counsel to the king in a non-biased, objective, and bro-like way. Even if it was a girl. Maybe especially if it was a girl. He or she would be the king's counterpart, his most loyal and trusted advisor.

The protector's duties were to protect the king at all costs, even with his or her own life. Without hesitation.

The mistress and lover, well, the wisemen of Terrowin decided that it was acceptable, even necessary, for the king to have a mistress. So long as the queen could have her lover, in the interest of equity and -ocracy. The latter two positions were not thought of as providing illicit favors and distractions to the king and queen. But instead to provide both the king and queen one loyal and trusted and damn sexy person who would be completely devoted to them and their happiness. These trusted companions would be schooled in the arts of music, poetry, helpfulness and sculpted muscles, as the case might be.

The final position created by the wisemen is the assassin. The assassin's role is to try, in any way possible, to kill the king during his four years in service. This may sound horrific and wrong. You are probably huffing and puffing and *this* close to printing some bumper stickers about coexisting and all, and that's ok. But just think about it. When has there not been an attempt on a sovereign's life? No. Seriously. When? All those angsty and emo people with weapons and poison skills, thinking society expects them to subvert the dominant paradigm like it's their destiny or something. Yeah, you get it now. Assigning an assassin to each king is as elementary as cutting into a snakebite. Well, maybe that's not the best analogy but don't be such a pedant! If all the narcissists and other crazies know there is someone assigned to murder the most powerful person in the world, they cannot possibly convince themselves that God is speaking to them, telling them it is their mission to eliminate the king.

And so it was declared: the seven Royals would rule Terrowin and guide her future forever thereafter.

Chapter 2

Gabriel and Savanna lived modestly by common day standards in Terrowin. Gabriel, a blacksmith, made his living forging iron throughout the day. He was a sturdy man, hardworking and honest. He barely made enough to support Savanna in their small two-bedroom cabin set several kilometers outside of the Capital. But, it was enough to ensure that they were fed during the winter snows and could occasionally partake in some of summer's simple pleasures, like fresh cherries. Savanna's favorite. When cherry season was at its peak, he would often work longer hours and after work he would stroll by the growers' market near the Capital, looking for the darkest, ripest, most plump cherries for her. The thought of making Savanna smile filled Gabriel's chest with an achy but otherwise indescribable pride, and he enjoyed spitting out the pits with her after a late supper as they watched the sun sink behind the hills. She made an enthusiastic game of seeing how far away hers could land. It was no contest. And it never occurred to her to make it a contest between them, which made him love her all that much more. He always wanted to give Savanna just a little bit more, a new dress, a larger cabin or an upgraded carriage. But he knew he was a man with limited opportunities. Somehow he couldn't comprehend that he had so much more—an abundance of character.

Savanna knew Gabriel was not the type of man to bring her flowers or serenade her with his voice. She knew he would never be rich or romance her as the knights did in the novels she read as a child. Still, she couldn't help falling in love with him because of his kindness, courage and determination. Her heart was the only thing she truly trusted, and he had her heart. Gabriel was simply a good man. Well, he also made her feel things she was sure would shock the general public. He had worked at her father's blacksmith shop since he was twelve, when he stopped going to school and worked hours that violated the rather progressive child protection laws within Terrowin. But Gabriel and his family needed the money, and Savanna's father gave him the additional work hours under the table.

On the weekends, Savanna's father allowed her to join him at the blacksmith shop. She would see Gabriel and the other men working making horseshoes, metal ovens and cast iron pots, which her father sold at a handsome profit. She would bring lemonade (cherry lemonade in season) to the gentlemen (and Gabriel) who worked in her father's shop. Gabriel always reached tentatively for a glass. She later realized that he had been conditioned to move slowly because of his stature. Before taking a sip he would say, "Thank you ma'am." Even though she was clearly younger than he. Five summers of watching him mature and grow, and his voice—his voice!—which once sounded like a girl's, was now deep and full. All of a sudden—no, not all of a sudden, but it felt that way in an overwhelming sort of sensation—he sounded like a grown man, and one more "Thank you ma'am" was all it took. She knew she was in love.

When they were teenagers, he was often distracted from his work as he imagined Savanna on her way to stop by the shop with some fabrication about going to pick wildflowers. They kept their love for each other hidden, outside of her father's view. But he still knew somehow.

When she turned twenty-one, they took a picnic to her favorite field of lavender and Gabriel asked Savanna to marry him with the most delicate circle he could fashion from the scraps of iron he would never be accused of stealing. With her father's reluctant but sincere approval, they married that year.

Chapter 3

The Royal Ascension School is the boarding school for all Royal children born on January first. Its mission, to educate and prepare the future Royals for their four years of service in accordance with strict guidelines developed by the Terrowin Education Commission. The Royals live there for the first twenty-four years of their lives. They learn all the necessary disciplines to fulfill their ultimate duties, according to the position they assumed upon birth.

The School is set high in the mountains in a caldera on the north-west border of Terrowin. The mountains rise up abruptly from the ocean, which borders Terrowin's western coast. The shores are rocky, not suitable for swimming or playing at the beach. The mountains are high enough to stop most of the clouds from coming over to the eastern side. Thus, the caldera is mostly sunny, green and picturesque.

The School is a magnificent estate constructed by a former King of Terrowin, long before the idea of Royals was ever conceived. It was the largest estate in Terrowin. Its owner was more interested in architecture and opulence than any sort of patriotic duty. Long abandoned, the property was refurbished and made into a school that would educate the future leaders of Terrowin.

So, you might be thinking, a property that big, for only seven students in each class, what a waste of resources! Oh, but the wisemen were wiser than you or I. They wanted to raise kings and queens who were subjects of the people. So, as a consolation, those babies born on New Year's Day, but not designated Royals, gain automatic admission into the School. The wisemen considered a lottery for the additional seats, but thought, how foolish! A lottery for admission to the finest school in the land? No. Anyone born on January first would be allowed admission to the School. Most parents accept this invitation and non-royal children attend the school starting at age four.

The School is set up to have each class advance together as they mature. They are separated into six classes:

Primos—birth through three years;

Emperors—four through seven years;

Pharaohs—eight through 11 years;

Princes—twelve through 15 years;

Sultans—sixteen through 19 years; and

Ascensions—twenty through 23 years.

Chapter 4

Savanna's one wish for her life together with Gabriel was that they would have a large family. Lots of kids. She was raised in a large family and wanted to repeat the joy of noisy family dinners, tradition-soaked holidays and many birthdays with her own children. So, when Gabriel proposed to her, she paused.

"Gabby, do you want to have a family with me?"

"Yes, of course, baby."

She smiled, "How many kids do you want?"

"As many as you wish, love. Although, maybe not too many, college costs are rising every year! And you'll have me working in your dad's shop forever!" They laughed together at Gabriel's attempt at humor.

Savanna grabbed his hand, looked him in the eye and said in all seriousness,

"Do you want to plan the births of our children?"

Gabriel knew exactly what she was asking, but they had never discussed this before. He thought for a moment, trying to figure out what she really wanted, but he was in love and would do anything for Savanna. His final response to her was,

"We can have as many children as you wish, and when you wish."

This was an important discussion, not only for Savanna and Gabriel but for all parents in Terrowin. Many Terwinians believe that giving birth to the future leadership of the country is the highest duty a citizen can perform. Also, no one can deny that the swag is pretty sick. Families plan pregnancies with the hope of giving birth at midnight on New Year's Day, but Gabriel and Savanna did no such planning.

∞∞∞ ∞ ∞∞∞

After they married, Gabriel and Savanna hoped to start their family right away. Savanna became pregnant within a few months of their vows. Sadly, she was unable to carry the baby through the first trimester. Gabriel consoled his wife as best he could and held a private funeral service to bury their child. He placed a small bouquet of lavender in the casket and assured Savanna that everything would be ok.

However, as the years went on, Savanna's body kept rejecting the babies inside her womb. A pattern of pregnancies followed by funerals became life as they knew it for many years. After the sixth miscarriage, Savanna succumbed to the fact that she would never carry a child to full term. She grew depressed over the years. Her one wish, to have her own family, had not come true.

The Birthing holidays were something that neither Gabriel nor Savanna could ignore. They had been married long enough to see three Birthing holidays come and go. Their cabin rested adjacent to one of the main roads leading to the Capital. So, every four years hundreds of State-sponsored horse-drawn carriages passed by, carrying expectant mothers to the Terrowin Birthing Hospital.

The last Birthing holiday season was torturous for Savanna. She just had another miscarriage in November and was still recovering from her latest loss. When Savanna saw the first triumphant carriage pass her house early one morning, she ran inside and locked herself in the bedroom. Gabriel spent hours trying to coax her out. Finally, at lunchtime she was motivated to emerge and make him some sweet potatoes and cabbage, but neither of them could eat.

It only got worse as more and more carriages approached the Capital. The persistent percussion of horses' hooves beating past their cabin seemed to never cease. To Savanna, it was as though the baby gods were mocking her. Teasing her, testing her faith. Gabriel feared that she had lost hope. That night, while lying in bed, he promised himself that she would never go through this again. He planned that they would take a vacation, far away from the Capital, during the next Birthing holidays.

Chapter 5

The staff at the School is comprised of former Royals and non-royal professors. Every former Royal customarily becomes a professor at the School. It's an unwritten rule, tradition even, that all former Royals serve at the School for several years. Former kings and queens usually serve as headmasters or advisors to an incoming Primo class. Other former Royals teach courses before retiring to the countryside to write a book or going on public speaking tours for generous appearance fees.

Royal professors teach classes according to their experience and expertise (i.e., former advisors teach courses in Statistics and Policy.) Theirs is a higher status than the non-royal faculty and they comprise the leadership of the School. Non-royal professors teach the standard courses, from earth science to calculus. From time to time, the School invites famous Terwinians to serve as non-royal visiting professors for one or two years. This is an exceptional opportunity for celebrities to do something special for the kids and make a heck of a lot of money. One year, the fastest human in Terrowin, Speedy "Linguini" Puchini, joined the staff after breaking the 100-meter Terrowin record. He was known to consume enormous quantities of pasta with clam sauce right after every one his victories.

Chapter 6

Three years passed since the last Birthing holiday and during the first week of April Savanna and Gabriel celebrated the Spring Festival along with most Terwinians. The festival commemorates the culmination of planting crops. Over a breakfast of smoked pork, buttermilk biscuits and duck eggs Gabriel said, "Savanna, you know, work has been pretty good at the shop the past few months."

"Yes, dear, I know, you've been working so much lately." She smiled. "What are you having to work on anyway?"

"Oh, it's nothing. Just a little overtime. But, I've managed to save up some money." He paused. "I thought we could take a vacation."

"Gabby! A vacation? Really?"

Gabriel had been planning this vacation for three years and wanted it to be a surprise for Savanna. This was exactly the reaction he'd imagined.

She jumped up and wrapped her arms around his neck. "Where? When? What are you thinking?"

"Well, I was thinking we could go to Lake Meehi, and maybe bring your parents to celebrate the New Year."

He had already invited her parents to go with them to Southern Terrowin and enjoy a few days by Lake Meehi, where it was said the New Year fireworks were almost as beautiful as the Capital's.

"Yes, I think that's a wonderful idea!" Savanna suspected that Gabriel's motivation was to take her away from those horrible parading carriages. But, they also hadn't taken a vacation in years. It was fine with her either way.

That night, before they went to bed, she snuggled close to her husband. Her heart told her that she had married the right man. A man who would take care of her. A man who loved her and wanted to make her happy. She surprised him with a shy, sweet kiss before they went to sleep.

"I love you Gabby. Always."

"I love you too Savanna. No matter what."

Chapter 7

It was a few weeks after the Spring Festival. Gabriel went to work while Savanna tended the garden. The day was going to warm up so Savanna tried to get her weeding and watering done early in the morning. She hated to get too much sun on her face and shoulders. She was pulling weeds when she caught the scent of something in the air. The smell of frying bacon from her neighbors' breakfast. Savanna felt a strange sensation in her stomach and she started to feel very warm. She tried to run into the house, her hand over her mouth, but it was too far away. She stopped in her tracks. Up came her own breakfast. She vomited on the edge of the garden, right beside the sweet peas.

She went into the house, straight to the bathroom and looked at herself in the glass. She knew this feeling all too well. But it had been almost two years since she was last pregnant. She had long since decided that she was cursed and instantly submitted to the notion that she would lose this child, telling herself to be strong this time and not tell Gabriel. She continued with her normal routine of tending the garden and the farm animals, and vomiting out of sight of Gabriel.

Two months later, Savanna's secret was still intact. Then, at dinner one night, she told him.

"Gabby, I'm pregnant."

"Really? That's great. Maybe this time we will be lucky. I love you baby." He tried not to sound too excited, knowing their history. "So, you just found out, only a few weeks. Well, no more gardening for you. I'll take care of it." That was one of the doctor's orders every time Savanna became pregnant. Bed rest.

"No, I think I'm three months pregnant. Remember that night during the Spring Festival?" she said, with a trembling smile on her face, her eyes starting to fill with water.

"Three months!" Gabriel couldn't decide if he was angry with her for waiting so long to tell him, or excited because she had not carried a baby for three months ever before.

"Oh, my God Savanna. This is the one!" He stood up and went to hold her. Tears of joy were already streaming down his face. "This is the one," he said to her as they embraced each other in the kitchen. He kept repeating, "This is the one."

"I hope so Gabby. I hope so."

Chapter 8

The School campus design is similar to the top universities in Terrowin. There are buildings for mathematics, science, health and physical education and other academic disciplines. In addition, there are buildings for each Royal position, where advanced instruction takes place. There are football stadiums, tennis courts, a golf course, indoor gymnasiums, swimming pools, playgrounds with swings and slides, a few pubs for the professors, Sultans and Ascensions, soda and coffee shops, a theater, several smaller cafeterias and one main dining hall that seats all the students and staff.

Students play frisbee and hackysack on the quad. A greenhouse nurtures the beginnings of exotic plants found all across the campus. Young botanists earn course credit for forcing and transplanting crystalbush, Meehi trees, flowering cumulus, apple and cherry trees, Royal ivy, lavender, butterfly blossom, bolinflower and Terrowin roses, thus ensuring the grounds could be featured on the cover of any glossy magazine on any day of the year.

A stream meanders across the grounds, filled with fat white and orange goldfish, purple, red and green nightshade swimmers, yellow Inti fish, blue moonfish and a few rare pink flamestarfish. There are intricate bridges at various intervals, graffitied on the railings with the names of young lovers. When the weather turns nice the older kids tie their hammocks to the trees along the banks of the water. A massive willashine tree grows in the dead center of campus, close enough to the Queen's Building for the roots to cause some concern.

Installation pieces by advanced visual arts students add personality and enhance the campus spirit. Gazebos are scattered about, and at dinnertime if there are any empty seats in the dining hall it is safe to assume someone is holding hands and nuzzling in the pagoda, hoping not to be found before sunset. Pop-up concerts by the music students and flash mobs choreographed by the dance classes are a fun surprise from time to time. Non-royal students are encouraged to be participators and activists, so there is usually someone ready to ask you to sign a petition.

There are two dormitories. One, the Royal Residence Hall, is reserved for the Royal children and all Royal professors. This building is seven stories and resembles a small castle. Just inside the entrance is a large foyer with one spiral staircase going up. A sign on the wall features an arrow pointing up and the words, Professor Suites 2, Emperors 3, Pharaohs 4, Princes 5, Sultans 6, Ascensions 7. There is another arrow pointing down one corridor, directing people toward the Primos, located on the first floor. The other residence hall is for non-royal children and professors who attend the School. It is not as impressive looking from the outside as the Royal Residence Hall, but it is the largest building on the campus, housing the majority of students.

Chapter 9

The day after Savanna's announcement to Gabriel they went to see her doctor. Her regular physician was not in the office that day, but she was able to get an appointment with a younger doctor whom she had never seen before. He asked the standard questions and ran some tests while Gabriel waited in the lobby, trying to calm his nerves by reading the latest version of *Big Game Hunting in Terrowin* magazine. She returned and they both sat stiffly, waiting for the young doctor to return.

"Congratulations Ms. Percy! I've confirmed that you are indeed pregnant. About three months and everything looks normal."

Gabriel shook the doctor's hand vigorously and then turned to Savanna. She threw her arms around him and they hugged with intensity while the doctor stood there for a moment.

"But wait, there's more! Your baby might be a Royal! That's awesome! Extreme! Congrats! You two must be so proud!"

"A Royal?" said Savanna. The thought never occurred to her.

"Yes, a Royal. Your due date is December 27. I'm so excited to be the one to tell you!" Neither Savanna nor Gabriel showed any emotion. "Ok, well, I'm going to schedule you for another appointment in four weeks. We have to take care of our future king!" He patted Savanna's tiny stomach inappropriately. She pulled away. "Well, congratulations, and I hear that the Birthing Hospital food can be kinda tasteless, so keep that in mind when you're packing your bags." He smiled. "A Royal!" he said, as he walked away. "My first Royal!"

Chapter 10

All Royals (Primos, Emperors, Pharaohs, Princes, Sultans and Ascensions) are provided the best education and healthcare in the land. They are raised by the State in accordance with strict guidelines developed over centuries. These children are nurtured and loved and never want for anything, with the exception of the assassin. Classical music is played for the Primos at bedtime, early mornings and during feedings. Early on, Primos are exposed to the most advanced speech-language course of study in the land. Play is designed to develop both analytical and critical thinking skills. The School also ensures that Primos have the freedom and liberty to discover and explore their surroundings safely.

At the same time, Primos are not overly protected. Caregivers are instructed to allow them to fall, cry and learn from their mistakes. But the interactions between the children are always monitored and sometimes manipulated in order to develop the skills necessary for their positions and fulfillment of their future duties. The School developed its own teacher training program of behavioral modification and attitude adjustment techniques to ensure a successful ascension.

The headmaster appointed to each incoming Royal class remains with them until they ascend. He or she provides both a mother's gentle touch and a father's toughness. Discipline is never physical (well, except with the assassins) and Royals are neither yelled at nor told such things as "children should be seen but not heard." Headmasters encourage their Royals to question authority and respectfully debate all those around them. But mostly, the headmaster serves as the one constant counselor for the Royals in their assigned class.

Chapter II

Over the next few months, Savanna continued to work in the garden and tend to the animals over Gabriel's objections. The corn was sweeter that year than ever before, and she was able to put away a generous plenty for winter. She and Gabriel never spoke of the Birthing holiday. Their focus was on the day-to-day care of the child growing inside her, and they marveled at each new change they saw in her physically.

She was almost seven months pregnant and it was a miracle indeed. Her belly had swollen and she started walking with a wobble, much like a penguin. She was surprised at how big her stomach was and it was hard to keep her hands off it. The baby moved every day within her womb, and she shuffled as fast as she could to Gabriel every time the baby kicked to have him feel the movements. Her baby was strong! Sometimes too strong, and she would often have to reposition herself in an attempt to keep pressure off of her innards. He or she was an active one.

Chapter 12

From the moment Primo King David was taken from his mother, he lived a life of privilege. He was small compared to the other Primos and lagged behind in his physical development. He could never put on much weight, had a host of childhood illnesses and was diagnosed with asthma as a child. Some wondered whether he would even survive his early years. The School solicited the most advanced doctors in Terrowin to monitor his development and he had his own medical staff on standby. Yet, his asthma continued to be a problem and had to be addressed on almost a daily basis.

During playtime, none of the other Primos were ever allowed to hit or strike David. Now, we all know that toddlers get into skirmishes over their favorite red fire truck or stuffed bear. The School handles these situations according to guidelines developed over the years. For instance, one time toddler David was playing with his favorite model horse-drawn wagon. Toddler Tem, his protector, snatched the wagon out of David's hands and yelled, "Mine! Mine!" which left David crying hysterically. Upon observing this, one of the caretakers came right over to Tem, and in an intimidating voice said, "No! If David wants it, David can have it!" and snatched the wagon from Tem, returning it promptly to David. Little Tem was left alone sobbing.

Now, under the same circumstances, had Primo Queen Nara taken David's wagon, the caretakers would handle the situation differently. They might allow Nara to keep the wagon, if David was not crying or distressed. But, if he was, they would try to distract David and Nara by setting up a game for them both to play with each other "nicely." Thereby manipulating their play interactions in order to foster a growing husband and wife relationship. This type of deliberate interference by the staff continued until the children began to understand their future positions. Research indicates that the children begin to comprehend their separate roles during the Prince (twelve-year-old) stage of their development.

As David grew older, his curriculum was designed to ensure that he would be an effective leader. His studies encompassed all the traditional disciplines: math, science, fine arts, literature, languages, music and philosophy. He would also take classes in debating, social policies, negotiations, social psychology, statistics, persuasion, diplomacy and public speaking. Thus, by the time he left the School, Ascension King David would be ready to assume his role as King of Terrowin.

Chapter 13

Savanna and Gabriel enjoyed the Harvest Festival activities together—the hayride was always her favorite, but that year Gabriel convinced her to avoid the roughness of bouncing across the fields. And she managed to grow dizzy and a bit breathless partway into the corn maze, but Gabriel gently scooped her up and carried her back out against the flow of the crowd. Just weeks until her due date, they were in good spirits as the hopes of having a healthy child grew stronger with each passing day. She and Gabriel were finally going to have a child, a family. He was the perfect expectant father and started decorating the baby's room. A crib, bottles, stuffed animals and toys filled the second bedroom of their cabin. He was waiting to paint the room until after the birth, pink for a girl and sky blue for a boy.

After the Harvest Festival, in late November, the State sent notices to all potential Royal parents. On December first, Savanna and Gabriel received their official summons and notice. The summons was delivered via government courier, in uniform, riding high on a white horse. He was carrying hundreds of them, all rolled up. He handed one to Savanna. To Gabriel he said, "Are you the father?" Gabriel stepped in front of his wife, clenching his fists, rising up to his full height as though he could come nose to nose with the man on the horse. "Wait, no! It's just a formality," the courier said. "I'm required by law to ask, in case the father must be notified separately." He asked for both their signatures as proof of receipt. The summons read:

To the Gracious and Honorable Ms. Savanna Percy. Congratulations! Terrowin may forever be in your debt as your yet unborn child may be one of the Royals of Terrowin! You and your husband are hereby requested to join the other Honorable Mothers of Terrowin at the Terrowin Capital Hospital on December 26 as we await the birth of your child. All expenses related to birthing your child at the Hospital shall be borne by the State. The country wishes you, your family and your child the best of luck, and we hope that you may be blessed with continuing the legacy of Terrowin.

Signed, King Theodore and Queen Victoria

Gabriel applied his clumsy signature, but Savanna hesitated. Her mind betrayed her and she thought of the carriages over the years, traveling past her cabin to the Capital. The same carriages she thought were mocking her just four years before, would ferry her in just a few weeks.

"Ma'am, your signature please."

"Oh, I'm sorry." She signed the papers and her knees buckled as she felt faint. She swooned, but Gabriel was quick enough to pick his wife up before she hit the ground.

"Is she ok?" asked the courier.

"Yes, we will be fine. Thank you sir."

Gabriel carried Savanna to bed where she would remain. Bed rest. Doctor's orders.

Chapter 14

From the start, Primo Queen Nara was an interesting child. Despite the best efforts to interest her in dolls and playing dress-up (to develop feminine qualities) she wanted to play with the boys. At age three, she was the "problem child" of the Primos, constantly fighting with David, Tem and Cedric. (Brandon was never allowed to fight with Nara, as he would eventually be her lover.) This was unacceptable behavior for the future Queen of Terrowin. The staff re-directed Nara's attention to her appearance, her clothing and playing with "girly" things. Queens of Terrowin are glamorous individuals, oftentimes creating the latest fashion trends, and Nara's behavior had to be changed.

Around age six, after constant positive and negative reinforcement, Nara understood that the more "feminine" she acted, the more she could get away with. Especially with David. She started throwing temper tantrums and learned that this behavior was deemed acceptable and even encouraged. She finally learned that her appearance and cleanliness were divine and brought about great praise from the staff around her:

"Oh, little Miss Nara, how beautiful you are! Like a shining star," was a standard response from the staff when Nara dressed nicely.

But, if she were to get herself soiled, the remarks were to the contrary—standards developed by Terrowin scholars:

"Oh, dirty little Nara! Too dirty for anyone to see!" Staff would quickly walk her to the washroom and clean her up.

By the time Nara ascended she would be well-versed in literature, arts, persuasion, negotiations, public speaking, fashion, formal protocol and domestic and public policy.

Chapter 15

Bed rest was the last thing Savanna wanted. No longer able to distract herself with working around the house and in the garden, her thoughts turned to the Birthing holiday. The holiday started on December 26 and lasted until the New Year. There were many events designed to draw large crowds. The Procession of Mothers, The People's Choice Name Contest, Meet the Former Royals and several other activities. On a wall outside the Hospital all the mothers' names were listed along with their expected due dates, age, number of previous children, height, weight, whether they had any Royal children before and how many times they had been at the Hospital trying to give birth to a Royal.

Bookies took full advantage of the mothers' history, and betting of all types and odds was available for the people of Terrowin to participate in. Long shots were always the earlier and later due dates, as well as first-time mothers, whose labors could last a full twenty-four hours or longer. Mature women, mothers who already had several children and those whose due date was December 31 always received the highest odds. There was also a premium on being a woman from the countryside rather than the city. The betting was raucous and rampant, on everything from who would birth the king to whether the advisor would be a boy or a girl, and of course the given names for all the Royals was always a hot betting item. More than once, depending on the odds and combinations of wagers, several Terwinians walked away millionaires after the festivities.

All these events led up to the New Year's Eve celebration, which included the King and Queen's Tribute Concert for the Royals, the Fireworks at Midnight and the Presentation and Procession of the Primos. The carnival atmosphere was made complete with street performers like strolling magicians and balladeers, face painters and caricature artists. This was Terrowin's grandest holiday and everyone in the country participated.

Ҫhapter 16

Primo Advisor Cedric would have to be a leader independent of King David. David would eventually seek out Cedric's counsel before enacting any new public policy or laws. Therefore, Cedric would not be raised as a "yes" man or a suck-up. For too long, kings were surrounded by advisors who simply had no backbone or confidence to challenge or question a king's decision. Well, in part, this was for good reason. Historically, prior to the wisemen's declaration, many a king's advisor was tortured or punished for questioning the king's wisdom. This included being sent to the dungeon, flagellated, burned at the stake, flayed, racked and sometimes sent to the ox box.[1]

Cedric was the one person who could directly question or

---

[1] Flagellation is basically an act of being whipped. Flayed refers to literally skinning a person alive. Racking was used to pull a person apart by their arms or legs until dislocation occurred or the limbs torn apart. The ox box was a solid piece of brass cast in the shape of an ox, with a door that could be opened and latched. A person would be placed inside the ox and a fire set underneath, ensuring a slow and agonizing death.

contradict David. As toddlers, Cedric was encouraged to challenge David. If Cedric had taken David's favorite horse-drawn wagon, the staff might let David and Cedric work it out between themselves. Careful of course to monitor the situation so that Cedric would not harm or intimidate David, but allowing them to scuffle a bit. Staff might also create a conflict between David and Cedric in order to whisper into Cedric's ear, "Cedric, David is just wrong about his answer, and you should tell him he is wrong. You're a big boy, don't worry, no one will be angry with you." Prompting little Cedric to be in David's face, telling him when he was wrong.

Cedric would be learned in many different disciplines, quite similar to David. He would also take classes on diplomacy, economics, public policy, education, law, business, history, financial markets and agriculture. As the king's future advisor, it was his duty to know all the relevant facts and give candid and sound advice to David for the betterment of all of Terrowin.

Chapter 17

Every time Savanna and Gabriel heard hoofbeats the morning of December 26, they peeked out the window. Already carriages were passing their cabin on the way to the Hospital.

"Did you remember to pack snacks?" Gabriel asked her.

"Mmm-mm." Savanna couldn't think about food. She would just take her chances with the Hospital's offerings. How bad could it be?

"What about clothes? Did you pack enough outfits for the baby?"

She hoped with all her heart that the only thing their child would need was something warm and comfortable for the ride back home. But she had dutifully packed several presentation outfits for the baby, selected for every possibility ranging from Primo King to Primo Mistress. She and Gabriel had modest belongings, but when their parents found out she was pregnant with a possible Royal, gifts started pouring in from everyone. "Yes, love," she said. "I packed all the best clothes."

She dressed herself in a white frock with blue flowers, and

was pleased when she saw him in the crisp shirt, tailored jacket and slacks she set out the night before. He wore his best shoes.

When the carriage arrived it caught them by surprise even though they'd been waiting all morning. Savanna and Gabriel walked slowly toward it and entered. Savanna hating her situation. Gabriel silent, not knowing what to say to his wife.

Chapter 18

People started gathering early on the morning of December 26 in front of the Hospital, hoping to get a first glimpse of the expectant mothers as they exited their carriages. Hordes of them, densely packed, politely pushing each other to get the best view. Some people believed that the way a woman walked the stairs, or how round her stomach was or how healthy and pink her cheeks were could be an indicator of whether she might be carrying a Royal. Family members lined the streets holding up welcome and good luck signs. Bookies roamed the crowds, taking early wagers. Oh yes, this was one event most people came to see!

The carriages started entering the Capital around noon, with most arriving by eight o'clock in the evening. Between two and five was when most of the action took place, as this was the time that most carriages entered the city. The carriages would be spread out in a slow-moving traffic jam, as each mother was given a chance to walk up the Hospital stairs and have her name announced to the people. Yellow tape extended around the stairs as a barrier for the crowd. Every year, without fail, someone would breach the barrier and run up to one of the expectant mothers to hand her a rose or a note, or even try to touch her swollen belly.

The press were the only ones given direct access to the mothers, as it was their duty to take pictures and ask each woman the same questions. Some parents went so far as to take speech and acting classes in preparation for this reality event that was filled with made-for-news drama.

The top reporter in Terrowin, Elizabeth Von Karat, was made famous when she was an expectant mother just twelve years earlier. Many around the country can recall her entrance into the Hospital. The story goes like this: Bitsy, as she was known, exited her carriage in an elegant evening gown that would not have been out of place at a palace gala. She hardly looked pregnant from the way the shimmery bands of fabric wrapped around her body. The first reporter—sadly, no one remembers her name at all—came to her and asked, "So, what Royal are you hoping for Ms. Von Karat?"

To which she replied, "Look no further Terrowin, Primo King Matthew rests here!" At that point, two male attendants in coordinated tuxedos and sequins leapt out of her carriage, tugged at her shoulders and ripped her dress off with a dramatic flourish, exposing her in her underthings. The words "Primo King Matthew" were written in large letters across her ribcage, with an arrow pointing downward to her belly. The paparazzi took pictures of her and she was an instant success. She made the cover of *The Terrowin Times* the next day and the media fell in love with her, as did the rest of Terrowin. They followed her the entire time she was at the Hospital. Some people even cried when she did not give birth to a Royal baby, but her celebrity was cemented. Every ceremony thereafter, at least one woman tried to stage an act that might gain her some immediate notoriety. Most failed, but the event and their efforts were something not to be missed.

Savanna's carriage was now second from the Hospital. She and Gabriel were close enough to hear what was going on outside. The ride there had been longer than they expected, and Gabriel even remarked that they could have walked to the Hospital faster than riding in the carriage.

"Honorable Mother, Ms. Kathleen Donaghue!" the announcer said over the megaphone. The crowd let off a roar at the mention of her name. At that moment, Savanna's carriage lurched forward to assume the next position. They waited about three or four minutes and then they were greeted by one of the guards standing outside, whose job it was to open the carriages and assist the mothers as they stepped down.

"Welcome, you're next." He escorted Savanna out the carriage and waited for Gabriel to exit before leading her up the stairs.

"Honorable Mother, Ms. Savanna Percy!"

As Savanna walked up the Hospital stairs, the crowd was at a fever pitch, but she could not hear them anymore. She felt as if she was walking in slow motion. Both she and Gabriel shielded their eyes against the blinding glare. The Hospital, which she had seen so many times before as a spectator, looked strangely unfamiliar to her. It was the largest building in Terrowin, some twenty stories high, and took up an entire city block. It was a magnificent building, constructed solely for this purpose. Hand crafted stained glass and stone carvings of various Terwinian icons and symbols adorned the white granite building. The design ensured that the building would shimmer and sparkle in the winter sunlight. Just above the entrance was the Presentation Platform, where the Royals would be introduced to Terrowin as they were born. On this day there were people on the platform throwing confetti as the mothers walked into the Hospital. Savanna looked all the way to the roof, where stood the Flames of the Royals. Six torches that would be lit on New Year's Day, one for each of the Royals, and extinguished upon the birth of the last Royal, the assassin. The two up front and center for the king and queen, and two along each side of them for the rest. A sign above the hospital entrance read, "Welcome Honorable Mothers of Terrowin!"

Several photographers and reporters swarmed around them, each yelling and trying to get their attention. Flashes went off right in front of her, which startled her for a second. She saw spots and faltered in her step a bit, but Gabriel held her close and they continued walking up the stairs.

"Savanna, do you have a name for the Royal?"

"Which Royal do you want to have?"

"How was your trip here?"

"Are you nervous about this being your first baby?"

"Did you eat any special foods during your pregnancy?"

"What did you pack for your hospital stay?"

"Did you plan to have a Royal?"

"How do you feel about the Royal process?"

The questions came all at the same time and it was hard to discern any one. It was all just a cacophony of shouting. She kept walking, not saying a word. Gabriel held his hand up, said, "No comment," and walked his wife cautiously up the stairs.

They were greeted at the top by a host of doctors and nurses.

"Welcome Ms. Savanna Percy. Come, let's get you to your room."

With those words Savanna and Gabriel passed through the large stained-glass doors and into the Hospital. The doors shut firmly and the noise from outside disappeared. Gabriel looked back, shocked at the immediate silence in the lobby. He wore a puzzled look on his face.

"Oh," one of the nurses said happily, "the whole building is soundproof! We can't have that nonsense disrupting our mothers in here, now can we?"

Gabriel's face lit up. He was going to like this place. He looked to Savanna, expecting to see her smile in return, but she was staring straight ahead.

"Come, this way, let me take you to your room."

Chapter 19

As you have been told before, the protector's sole duty is to protect the king. This position might seem like he or she is raised to become a brute bodyguard, like someone hired to protect one of Terrowin's famous singers. No! This position goes much further than creating some bulked-up, testosterone-raged person ready to punch out anyone who approaches the king in a threatening manner. Primo Protector Tem was being raised to be the director of homeland security for the king. He would be trained to lead an advanced team to scout out any areas where the king might make public appearances. He would also get training in counter-terrorism and counter-intelligence techniques, as well as advanced fighting.

Tem's other primary duty was to ensure that the assassin would never succeed in killing David. The wisemen concluded that if there was to be an assassin, naturally there would be an antithesis to the assassin. Thus, the protector was conditioned to believe that giving up one's own life for the king was his or her destiny. An honor, the highest of callings. Death was not to be feared, but one should be deathly afraid of failing to protect the king.

The School coerced and developed these feelings within the protector as early as possible. As a toddler, during playtime, Tem would often be told to go help David. He was constantly preached to: "Tem, David is like your little brother. You must protect him." Other times, if David was in an argument with another child, staff would encourage Tem to "go help David, now!" or another standard response, "Tem, you must never let anyone hurt David."

Games were designed to further reinforce Tem's feelings of devotion toward David. In football, Tem and David were always on the same team (Cedric was always on the opposing team.) David usually played forward, even though he was not the best athlete and usually the smallest player, and Tem played directly behind David. If, during a game, someone pushed or tripped David or otherwise made him fall, Tem would be there as the enforcer. He often received yellow and red cards for his actions. But the staff made sure to praise him, so long as his efforts were to protect David.

Tem's formal education would revolve around honor and ethics, surveillance, history, art, philosophy, anatomy, management, interrogation techniques, psychological warfare, comparative politics and behavioral and social psychology.

Chapter 20

In most cases couples arrived safely and checked in to their assigned rooms at the Hospital. Actually, the rooms could be better described as suites, for they were as sumptuous as anything anyone in Terrowin had ever seen outside the palace. Bedding made of the heaviest silk and finest cotton. Lanterns with sweet beeswax candles. Veined marble floors worthy of a cathedral. Views of the rolling mountains or the rushing river. They spared no expense in providing a comfortable setting for the women.

A private doctor was assigned to every woman. Midwives and nursemaids, known as much for their beauty and decorum as for their caretaking skills, moved from room to room on silent slippers, their uniforms barely making a rustle.

Babies were born in their own suites. Mounted on the wall directly across from the mother-in-labor were candles placed in small wooden holders with the title of each Royal printed below the candle. Mothers were informed that when the candle in the room had been lit, that specific Royal had just been born, and when the six candles were extinguished, it would mean that the final Royal, the assassin, had also been born. Women who gave birth prior to January first would never see those candles lit in their presence.

As the days passed on, Savanna and Gabriel could hardly believe it as they watched several of their neighbors already departing the Hospital with their babies. Savanna partook in reading some of the magazines, even being so bold as to tear out an especially delicious-sounding recipe for yam casserole with spicy peppers. She made Gabriel tuck it far down inside her suitcase, and then felt guilty immediately after. Gabriel took some time to go over the information booklet that was given to each family.

"Savanna, do you know that they only give the Royal parents twenty minutes to be with their children before they take them away?"

She didn't respond.

"And, here, it says that you have to name the child within those twenty minutes. Well, we haven't thought of a name just yet, have we?"

She turned to him and said, "I don't want to talk about it. Ok?"

"Well, I'm just saying, but what if we have the Primo King? I would hate to not give such a child a proper name." Gabriel had become seduced by the thought of his son becoming the King of Terrowin. He said those words with a smile on this face and a kind of pride that only a father could have for his son.

"I said, I don't want to talk about it. Ok!"

"Ok dear. Ok. But what if she's the queen..."

"Gabby!"

"Ok. Ok. Ok."

ℂhapter 21

The king's mistress, Ava, would not be raised as a geisha or ditzy airhead who only knew of pleasure, fashion, make-up and mirrors. The wisemen agreed that any mistress to the king would have to be a woman knowledgeable on a wide array of topics. They understood that all too often kings of the past shared their most intimate secrets, fears and even advanced war plans with their mistresses during pillow talk, cuddled together late at night. Mistresses had direct access to the king's ear and would be another person from whom the king might seek counsel. Now, the way the wisemen figured, this person better have the best interest of the country at heart, lest she give the king foolish and unwise advice—or even worse, no advice at all. Therefore, mistresses were raised first and foremost to adore the king and later to develop the intellect and understanding of government and business workings within Terrowin. The School ensured that Ava would have the best interests of the country in mind when spending time alone with David.

Ava's early years were spent learning to simply adore David. As far back as she could remember, she was taught that he was "such a handsome boy" and that she should go and "bring him his favorite toy." All communications with her were focused on making sure that she admired David and everything he did. She even shared her first kiss with David at age three. One day, during playtime, the staff told Ava in a playful voice, "Ava, go give little David a kiss-kiss." She quickly wobbled over, smiling, hands reached out to him, and grabbed his head and gave David a kiss on his cheek. "Mmmmmwah!" Little David ran off crying to the caregivers, Nara punched her in the face, but Ava's lesson was complete that day. At the School, this type of behavior among three-year-olds was encouraged. Although, it is true that in more conservative parts of Terrowin Ava might have been arrested and charged with a felony. But the wisemen knew better.

Ava took to her training exceptionally well. By ten years of age Ava believed that she and David were destined to be together. She daydreamed that he would marry her (but she had no notion of wanting to be queen.) Oftentimes she would be caught carving "David + Ava 4ever" on her desktops or random trees around the campus. She followed David around everywhere he went. Yet, when she realized that David was to marry Nara, she was not disappointed. She was only more inspired to show David her complete and utter devotion. This in turn, caused for some resentment and bitter interactions between Nara and Ava, which was normal behavior for girls. As they aged, they would come to accept their roles.

Ava would be schooled in art, music, poetry, athletics, public policy, history, warfare, fashion, dance, cosmetology, massage and the culinary arts. Yes, cooking. The wisemen knew that although the king might have a bevy of cooks on his staff, there is still nothing more seductive than having a woman cook your favorite meal in the middle of the night and talk about the day's events with you until sunrise. Something the queen would never do.

Chapter 22

On the last day of the year, as the morning hours passed, the excitement grew within the Capital. Now this is very different from the champagne-popping, ball-dropping excitement you might be thinking of. This is a sort of trepidatious elation, and by noon it had filled the entire tower. In the Hospital, first-time mothers who hadn't started labor yet, who weren't dilated at least a couple of centimeters by then, started to lose hope. Women bearing subsequent children were more relaxed, popping in on the others, chatting easily, asking their men for something to eat and even betting on card games. They still had time.

Eleanor Right was walking through the halls, checking out the competition. Tamra was gripping her bedrails and breathing heavily. She would go before midnight. That was a good thing because she would have been beyond impossible to live next door to if her child were a Royal.

"Thatta girl, Tammy," Ellie called as she passed, in what she hoped was an encouraging manner.

She looked over her shoulder at her husband, Mortimer. He was a gifted investor and provided well, but he was such a worthless mouse of a man. She hated the thought of giving him credit for this baby, whom she was certain was a boy, and whom she was certain would come into the world at just past midnight. She liked to imagine him already wearing a crown in the womb. Mort was walking behind her with his arms outstretched, as if she might stumble and he would catch her. Idiot.

A reporter came around the corner, almost running into Eleanor. Shaken, she quickly composed herself and held up her pad and quill.

"Loretta Jones with The Daily Bugle," she said. "Mind if I ask you a few questions?" She did not mind at all. Eleanor had been in the newspaper five times and she loved it. "Not at all," she said brightly, looking around for a photographer before remembering with some disappointment that there were to be no photos until the presentation celebration, only a handful of State-appointed reporters. That evening's edition would sell like hotcakes.

"Is this your first child?"

"My fourth! I just know this one's royalty." She wished Mort would disappear, and hoped Loretta wouldn't ask him anything. "A mother just knows these things."

"What is your due date?"

"January the first, of course." Loretta's eyes grew large. "Look, honey, I'm no fool. I planned for this, charted my body temperature and my cervical—well, you probably can't print that in the paper. But I didn't just fall off the turnip truck yesterday." Ellie leaned over to make sure she was getting all of this down. "I know what I'm doing. A woman just knows these things."

"What will you do with the gifts? If your baby is one of the Royals, I mean."

Why, oh why, did the million-dollar floor not open up and swallow Mort? If he said anything about investing it or giving a tenth to charity she would have to beat him when they got back home. She had three other precious darlings who deserved the very best of everything. And, of course, she had needs as well. "I'm just trying to decide if my title will be Princess Mother or My Lady the King's Mother." She contorted her face into what she hoped was a beatific smile.

"And the child? Do you have names chosen already?"

"Well..." Ellie wasn't sure if she should be mysterious or accommodating. But she was rather proud of what she'd come up with. Pride won out. "I really like the names that singer gave her children, and I'm sure it's a boy, so he will be King Moses. But if it's a girl she will be Queen Apple."

Ellie noticed another couple walking up the hall. The woman had jet black hair and exotic eyes and looked like one of those painted dolls. She was tiny. His palm was as big as her face. The only clue to her being a woman and not a child was her enormous stomach and the deep sadness in her eyes. Ellie assumed from how they carried themselves, yes she could even tell from the way a nine-months-pregnant woman carried herself, that they were lowborn and lowbred. They were watching her and whispering to each other through quivering lips. The reporter spun towards them as Mort fell into step behind Ellie.

"Loretta Jones with The Daily Bugle," she said. "Mind if I ask you a few questions?"

The woman looked to her husband to answer for her. He took her hand and looked at Loretta. "Just for a minute," Gabriel said.

Loretta was not exactly schooled in subtlety. "Is this your first child?"

The couple looked at each other. "Yes," said Savanna.

"What is your due date?"

Gabriel wrapped his arm protectively around Savanna. "It was December 27," he said.

"And if your baby is a Royal? What will you do with the gifts?"

Fresh tears ran down the woman's face and she shook her head. "No comment," said the man.

Loretta pressed on, assuming incorrectly that her tears were tears of joy. "Well, have you settled on a name?"

Savanna straightened herself as best she could. "No," she said.

After the reporter left, Savanna was walking to her suite when she stopped. Her water broke. The first telltale sign that she was going into labor. Her nurse ran to her side and helped her to a wheelchair.

"Oh, my! It's time to get you back in bed and wait for those contractions," the sweet nurse said excitedly.

Chapter 23

If the queen's lover, Brandon, was going to turn out anything like his mother, Ellie, the staff at the School would be tested to their limits. Although, his mother's psychological profile and personality scored at the highest level for his becoming a lover for the queen. Yes, the School conducts psychological and personality profiles on both parents of any Royal. We are talking about the leadership of the country, after all! After the Royals are born, their parents are thoroughly vetted in order to develop a unique program for each child.

Now, the handbook for the queen's lover is much more complex than all the other Royals and has undergone the most revisions over the years. I mean, how can one man ever really satisfy a woman?

Over the years the School tried various approaches to develop the perfect lover for the queen. They built his physical stature, only to find that she became bored looking at a muscle man. They created a sensitive guy, who would be her best friend, only to find that she was attracted to the ripped sentry standing guard outside her sleeping quarters. They tried the artistic male, well-versed in all forms of visual art, dance, theater and music. Only to find that she was totally into the head of international affairs. But the wisemen were undeterred!

They decided, in their collective wisdom, that the queen's lover would have to be versed in all of these things. But, his physical appearance was a must and early on Brandon's training centered on sculpting his body. At the same time, his musical and artistic talents would be developed. Developing his intelligence would come as part of his later teachings. His one mission: to be the man the queen desired and her most faithful muse.

Chapter 24

Murmurs went around the hospital about those women who were going into labor or whose water had broken. Hospital staff tried as best they could to keep things private, but there were always leaks to the press. It was almost three in the afternoon, and women who showed early signs of labor had a good chance of birthing a Royal past midnight. The betting outside continued and the bookies tried their best to get inside information as soon as possible, even going so far as to bribe some of the staff.

Ellie was walking the halls, hoping to induce her own labor. She passed Savanna's suite.

"Good luck honey," she said, not really wishing the best for them but trying to hide her own disappointment that she may yet again not give birth to a Royal.

Outside the Hospital, crowds of people gathered in order to get the best spot for the Royal Concert and the Lighting of the Royal Flames. This also happened to be the best view for the fireworks. If the scene during the Procession of Mothers was a sight, the evening hours on New Year's Eve at Terrowin Birthing Square was an extravaganza of epic proportions.

The outgoing King Theodore and Queen Victoria made their requisite appearance at the Concert in honor of the Royals and said their customary farewells to the citizens of Terrowin. The crowd was whipped into a frenzy as they cheered them on. King Theodore gave his last public address, as did the queen. This would be their final night serving the country. After the concert they would be whisked away to have dinner with the Ascension King Javier and Queen Tiffany Rose and their incoming Cabinet. Then, at midnight, in a private and intimate ceremony, King Theodore would pass his crown to Ascension King Javier.

People in the crowd wore the costumes of their region, favorite past Royals or the position they most admired. Signs were abundant.

"Don't Push Yet Mommy!"

"Push for the Primos!"

"Assassins Kick Ass!"

"John 3:16"

"In Royals We Trust!"

"Royals Make Better Lovers"

"I Was Almost a Royal!"

As darkness fell upon the crowd, lanterns lit up the Square. The front of the Hospital served as the stage where all the top government officials were given a seat at the festivities. Past Royals, the Supreme Judicial Court and generals of the military were seated on one side. On the other were a band and orchestra that alternated playing sets. The host was none other than Von Karat, who kept the crowd energized with a parade of entertainment, including keynote speeches, famous musicians, spoken word poets, celebrity chefs, comedians, jugglers and lottery giveaways.

Vendors roamed the crowd hawking various vittles and the latest popular drinks created by some of Terrowin's top mixologists. They also sold balloons to children with fun designs, the most popular was the "I ♥ the Primo King" or "I ♥ the Primo Queen." As the clock approached midnight, the acts outside became more spectacular as the drama intensified within the Hospital.

With just one minute before midnight, Elizabeth Von Karat led the crowd in the Square in unison to sing the Terrowin national anthem:

O Terrowin!

Our home and favorite land!

True Royal love in all thy sons command.

With Primo births we see thee rise,

The True King strong and free!

From far and wide,

O Terrowin, we stand on guard for thee.

Please keep our Royals safe and free!

O Terrowin, we stand on guard for King.

O Terrowin, we stand on guard for Queen.

At midnight, fireworks lit the sky above the Hospital. A glorious display that one year had to be cut short because the king was born at two minutes past midnight, a record for the

Royal King's birth that still stands. Although, you can get great odds betting that a Royal King's birth will occur within the two minutes after midnight, and those odds become 1,000,000 to 1 that the Royal Queen will be born within two minutes. The bookies loved selling these odds to any sucker willing to bet on those numbers. This is where they made their money.

After the fireworks, the orchestra took over the performances, playing something soft and slow. The High Priest of Terrowin came out and said a prayer for Terrowin, asking for healthy babies and a more perfect union in the future. The newly crowned King Javier and Queen Tiffany Rose made an appearance, alongside the high priest. However, this was not their time to address the citizens of Terrowin. King Javier would give the inauguration address to the people after all the Royals were born.

The crowd lit candles, lifting them to the sky as a gentle tune played in the background, awaiting the first sight of the Primo King, which would be preceded by the lighting of the middle torch. Ms. Von Karat introduced Terwintonix. A five member group came on to the stage. They were the upcoming stars of Terrowin, having created a different sound with their voices, which also sounded like instruments. They sang the old Terrowin classic, *The Little Drummer Boy*:

Come, they told me, pa rum pa pum pum.
Our newborn king to see, pa rum pa pum pum.
Our finest gifts we bring, pa rum pa pum pum.
To lay before our king, pa rum pa pum pum,
rum pa pum pum, rum pa pum pum.

The inside of the Hospital was abuzz with no fewer than twenty women in various stages of hard labor. Nurses and doctors timed contractions and measured dilations. Husbands hovered over their wives, comforting and cheering them on. The race had begun. The first male child would be the future king, the newest Royal.

"It's ok sweetie, you can do it. It's all going to be ok," cajoled a husband before succumbing to his true nature and yelling, "Do it now! Push!"

It was as if the husbands were cheering for their favorite Terrowin football team.

"This is what we have worked for, come on, it's now or never!"

"Just do it!"

Some even talked to their unborn children.

"Come on out little one. We're waiting for you. You can do it! You can do it!" yelled one father, standing behind an elderly doctor and staring at the space where he expected any second to see the crown of his child's head. Crown! Even the very word excited him. "Baby! Push!"

The doctor looked over his shoulder in disbelief. He thought to himself how society had changed. Years before, it would be considered inappropriate, even classless, to race to have a Royal. Things were so respectful back then, with families wishing each other a safe and healthy child. At least publicly. After Von Karat's stunt all hell broke loose and it was mother against mother, father against father. He shot back at the man, "Excuse me, sir!" The father walked back to his wife's side, embarrassed for just a moment before cheering her on again.

Some of the women were simply not ready to give birth, yet they tried to push anyway. Nurses and doctors scolded them to stop pushing, lest they injure themselves and their babies.

"It's too soon! You're not ready," could be heard out in the hall.

"Don't tell me I'm not ready! Grrrrr... ahhhhhhh!" The woman grunted and pushed with all her might. The vessels in her head were pulsing, her face flushed red, eyes full of determination. She was an older woman and would not be denied.

"The head is coming!"

She pushed harder.

"Come on baby," said her husband.

"It's a boy!" cried the nurse.

"The Primo King is born!"

Chapter 25

Word spread quickly of the birth of the Primo King. There was a staff of nurses solely responsible for informing the entire Hospital of each Royal birth, but first notifying those women who were in active labor. The staff was to enter those rooms and light one of the candles mounted on the wall according to the designation of the Royal birth.

Upon seeing the Royal King candle being lit, some women were disappointed and relaxed for just a moment. Others took a deep breath and started again. Now, the first female child would be the future Queen. And, in Terrowin, the queen is as much adored by the people as the king! The race started again.

Primo King David was born at 12:16 a.m. Thirty seconds after he was born the first Royal Torch was lit on the roof of the Hospital. The crowd below let out such a roar that the noise could be heard for kilometers around, and while it couldn't be heard within the Hospital, the building shook from the vibrations caused from decibels of screaming. People hugged and kissed each other. Some cried after seeing the torch lit. Horns played in unison and people danced in the streets as streams of confetti rained upon them. Primo King David was born!

After David was dressed by his parents, he was brought to a staging room adjacent to the balcony. King Javier and Queen Tiffany Rose, having just assumed power minutes before, were awaiting his arrival. This was their first official assignment since taking office and they eagerly grabbed up the newborn, who was dressed in an outfit chosen by his parents.

"What's the little one's name?" they asked.

"David."

They posed to take pictures with David. "Ok, little David, let's go meet our country," said King Javier.

King Javier and Queen Tiffany Rose walked together to the balcony. The crowd below went wild as they saw all three.

"Terrowin! I present to you Primo King David!" King Javier yelled as he lifted little David up over the side of the balcony for all of Terrowin to see. The orchestra struck up a lively pop song and the horn players moonwalked across the stage. Well, you might think this was irresponsible of the king and queen to hold a baby over a balcony, but in all of Terrowin history no king has ever dropped a Primo. Although, one baby was especially active and almost slipped out of the king's hands years ago. Since then, all the Ascension Kings have been properly trained to avoid even a near-disaster.

Upon learning his name, the crowd chanted in unison.

"David!"

"David!"

"David!"

Primo King David was brought back inside and given to his parents. King Javier and Queen Tiffany Rose met with David's parents, as is customary, and took pictures with them as well, until they had to depart when the next Royal was born. As the king and queen left David's room, King Javier remarked, "What a small little bugger he is."

There was already talk among the nurses and midwives that David's mother's doctor had been far off the mark when calculating her due date. His birth weight was in the lower half percentile-wise of all babies born in Terrowin. Surely he had been born prematurely, perhaps as much as a month, and babies his size usually didn't see their first birthday. The doctors ignored this chatter, however, because professional codes of loyalty demanded they not question their colleagues' diagnoses, treatments and advice unless two or more of them were in agreement that egregious unethical or criminal misconduct had taken place. And a few of the more devout among the birthing support staff took it as a sign: if the Primo King's mother was in fact there by some error, wasn't it a divine sign that this boy was preordained to be king? They jostled each other to get close to him, clutching the hem of his garment, and even going so far as to save one of his soiled diapers.

By 2:36 a.m. Primos Queen Nara, Advisor Cedric, Protector Tem and the King's Mistress Ava were born. King Javier and Queen Tiffany Rose made their presentations and met with each of their parents. There was deep disappointment, even resentment, among some of the other couples as the first four babies born after David were all males and did not qualify to be Royals.

Chapter 26

In Ellie's room, upon seeing only the last candle unlit, she was more determined than ever. She went into labor right after David was born and her body, accustomed to bringing children into the world, was just about ready to give birth. She may not have claim to the king, but the queen's lover would be just fine. Anything but the assassin, she thought to herself. Ellie worked her feet across the bed, and with a great heave-ho managed to push herself up to a sitting position. She leaned forward to get both feet on the floor and walked over to one of the bureaus on the other side of her suite. Her attending nurses and doctors tried to restrain her. They wanted her back in bed. It would reflect badly on the entire Hospital if something happened to one of the Honorable Mothers, but they were afraid of causing her harm and she fought them off.

Ellie stood there, standing and bracing herself against the chest of drawers. Three or four doctors tried to pry her hands off, afraid she would topple it, but she would not let go. "Mort!" she yelled. "Get over here and catch this baby!"

Mortimer at first hesitated. He didn't know what to think or do.

"Honey, please come back to the bed." He pleaded with her, standing by her side.

"You better catch this baby now!" She turned to him, and if he hadn't known her for so long, from the look in her eyes he would have sworn she was possessed by demons. But this was his Ellie, his childhood sweetheart. Well, maybe not sweetheart, but when she was a knock-kneed girl with pigtails she'd announced to him that they would be married one day, and he soon found out that he would never be able to refuse her. So this was his Ellie, and he knew what to do. He dropped on his knees and put his hands down low to the floor, underneath her nightgown. Cupped together, waiting, as she yelled at the doctors and nurses still trying to pull her away from the dresser, "Get off of meeeeeeeeee!"

And out popped a yowling, plump, healthy baby boy, right into Mortimer's hands.

Her body slumped over, exhausted. The medical team helped her back to bed. She looked to one of them, "Is it a boy?" she asked.

"Yes, it is. A Royal! The queen's lover."

"Primo Lover Brandon. Brandon's his name. I did it," she whispered softly, then fainted into the arms of the doctors.

Chapter 27

In Savanna's room, the last candle was lit. She was in full labor. She continually looked up at the candles. All the others were born and now only the assassin remained unaccounted for. She kept looking at the candles, trying not to push. Her contractions were so strong. She wanted those flames to be extinguished. Gabriel was at her side, murmuring soothing words of support. He had never seen his wife in so much pain. But the strength she showed was inspiring. She had been in labor for more than twelve hours. She was tired and at times slept between contractions, only to be awakened by a stronger one. But she kept going. He worried whether her little body could take much more.

"Come on Savanna, it's time to push," said her doctor.

She looked at the candles. The tears, and sweat dripping in her eyes, made it hard to focus on anything more than a couple meters away. It was blurry, but she could still make out six distinct flickering spots on the wall. She refused to push, but her body's natural forces took over. "Here comes the head. Ok, relax and wait for the next contraction, and I want you to push with all your might. Breathe, you're doing great. This is nature. Just feel it come." She lifted her head to see the candles. Another contraction was coming on. She tried her best to stop it. Letting out a scream, her body was wracked by the strongest contraction she had experienced, complete with an overwhelming sensation to push right that instant.

At that moment, a nurse rushed into her suite and extinguished all the candles with one wavering breath. The assassin had been born. Savanna saw this, and still in the grip of the contraction she pushed, holding Gabriel's hand as tightly as she could while trying to remember to breathe. Her breath gave way to a low growl, then a roar as the baby came.

"A girl! It's a girl!" cried the doctor.

Gabriel leaned over to hug his wife, who was exhausted but overwhelmed with joy and relief. "You did it, baby! You did it." Savanna cried and hugged Gabriel. They sat, holding their embrace while the nurses cleaned the child.

They handed the baby to her mother. Her eyes were still closed, her rosebud lips formed a perfect pout and she had a head full of hair. Savanna looked at Gabriel and whispered, "Salil. Can we name her Salil?"

Gabriel could barely speak through his joy. "Of course, love," he said. "Her name is Salil."

They posed for a picture together in their room. Savanna was finally, truly content. She had her family. Gabriel wrapped his arms around her as she held on to their child, both of them just staring at her sleeping face.

No less than five minutes later, a flurry of Hospital personnel rushed into Savanna's suite. There was an intense urgency on their faces as they carried on a frantic conversation with Savanna's nurses that Savanna herself could not hear. One of the doctors looked at her medical charts. He spoke to a midwife, and she bobbed her head up and down, Yes. Gabriel, only slightly disturbed by all the activity asked, "Is there a problem doctor?"

"No, no problem at all. But congratulations. Your child is a Royal. Little Salil will be the Primo Assassin!" The doctors and the nurses all had smiles on their faces. But Gabriel and Savanna could not comprehend what was happening.

"No, this is a mistake." Gabriel scrambled to shield his little family with his own body. "Malpractice!" he yelled. "The light was out, the assassin was already born!"

"Yes, that is true, there was a child that was born before yours, but in spite of our best efforts, and to the parents' great dismay, that child was stillborn and could not be revived," the head doctor explained, trying to calm Gabriel.

"Your daughter was the next born child, and pursuant to our Constitution, she is the Primo Assassin. You must be so proud, a healthy baby and a Royal. Congratulations! Now, you will have twenty minutes more with her before she is to leave for the Royal Ascension School."

"No. No. There must be a mistake. Not my Salil."

"Twenty minutes," said Gabriel, in shock at the news.

"Yes, please enjoy this time, and we shall return in twenty minutes. Congratulations again. A Royal!"

They all exited the suite giving the Percys their final moments with little Salil. Savanna wept. She thought that the baby gods had cursed her once again. The irony of wanting to have a child, a family for so long, only to have that child taken away by the government to be conditioned as a sociopath and trained as a killer. Together they said a few prayers for her. The time went by faster than they imagined, and soon enough the doctors returned.

They took Salil away from her distraught parents, placing a small black mask over her face as they wrapped her in a black blanket, careful not to touch the Primo Assassin's skin with their own. Savanna just stayed in bed, weeping, and Gabriel, with tearstained cheeks, embracing his wife, watched them close the door behind them. And, with the final Royal born and ready to leave, the caravan of carriages began its journey to the School.

Chapter 28

Assassins wear their masks at all times and are told that their hidden identity is their greatest asset. Their schooling is the most challenging and encompasses a wide variety of physical, mental and psychological training. They are drilled in archery, swordsmanship, martial arts, poisons, deception, disguise, tracking, bribery, primitive survival skills and one hundred ways to kill a king. By the time they leave School, they are experts in all the skills necessary to become the most feared person in Terrowin.

Salil would have a very different Primo experience from the others in her class. Terrowin believes that it takes a highly intelligent and analytical person to successfully assassinate the king. But, they also know that person has to be cold, indifferent and calculating. So, Salil's environment was both stimulating and sterile.

The first step in developing a cold, heartless person is to deprive them of any human contact and love from any person. Ever. Assassin babies are never touched by anyone. No skin-to-skin contact. No one rocks them to sleep, or drives them around in a carriage for hours trying to soothe them with a rhythmic bumpy ride. They are taught how to hold their bottles as soon as possible and even fast-tracked to feed themselves before they are ready. Oftentimes, Salil was left alone crying in her crib with a full bottle of milk beside her, the staff encouraging her to reach for the bottle even though she was still too young to hold it on her own.

Assassin Primos are also punished, both physically and verbally, the physical abuse continues until they enter the Sultan class at age sixteen. The verbal abuse continues until they ascend. They are never praised for doing exemplary work. Instead, they are made to feel as if they should do better.

Often a professor could be heard telling Salil, "That was too slow. Again!"

Sometimes, this statement could be followed by a smack to the face.

When Salil fell or hurt herself, no one was there to pick her up. She had to do it on her own. A caregiver would simply walk out of the room if she started crying from teething pain, falling down or waking from a nightmare. She was never comforted. She was raised hard, with no love at all.

One benefit Salil received was advanced physical development and play training in hiding and deception. Every Primo Assassin was walking before the age of one, and by two they were doing front flips, back flips, pull ups. By four years old, Salil was able to climb every building and tree on the campus, without a rope or assistance.

Assassins are not given toys to play with, unless they are toy weapons. But, hide-and-go-seek is a game Assassins are allowed to play and master. As soon as they start walking, assassins are led around the School by staff to play hide-and-go-seek. At first, staff members help them find good places to hide. Eventually, they are allowed to find places on their own. But if found, they are penalized with a slap on the wrist from a wooden ruler.

Corporal punishment for assassins is doled out in accordance with the guidelines at the School. Around age four, when they are spanked, they are told not to cry. If an assassin shows any tears, professors respond accordingly:

"Stop those tears! You are so weak, you will never become an assassin!" or "If you cry, I will give you something to really cry about!"

By the time they ascend, assassins should have no feelings, no sympathy or empathy for anyone. They are loners, outcasts, living their childhood without friends, boyfriends or girlfriends, without love from anyone. They live apart from other students at the School, invisible students with one goal programmed into their consciousness upon graduation:

Kill the king, by any means necessary.

Chapter 29

Twelve years had passed since David's class (Nara, Cedric, Tem, Ava, Brandon and Salil) was born, and they were soon becoming Princes. You see, at the stroke of midnight on January first, every four years, each class at the Royal Ascension School prepares to move to the next floor. On this night, the School was abuzz with activity as the students prepared for their move.

The rising Ascension King, in his Sultan suite, was awaiting his own move to the top floor of the Royal Residence Hall. "My lord, here are the carpet and bedding samples to choose from for your new residence." One of his newly appointed servants spoke to him as several assistants presented various types of the finest cloths. There was satin, silk, velvet, brocade and cotton so sumptuous you would swear it had been spun and woven by angels. But he seemed bored and uninterested.

"Do we have to do this now? Have someone else choose! Just make sure no bright colors. And no silk. I can't sleep on that stuff. Away!"

"My lord, fabric for your new wardrobe." He was presented again with several clothing options and looked them over briefly.

"No."

"No, not that one."

"Fine."

He sighed and waved his hand at the rest. "Maybe," he said as he shooed them away.

"Are you all finished packing my stuff yet? Why is this taking so long?" he barked at the others.

"And who's packing my stuff? Be careful with my things!" The rising Ascension King's staff was scurrying around, trying to move his belongings swiftly and safely up to the next floor. It was good to serve the next king, although this one was a little more obnoxious than those before him.

"What's my schedule like for tomorrow?"

Finally! Something they could assist him in without a battle. "Yes, my lord," an attendant stepped forward. "Tomorrow, you have a breakfast meeting with your new economic and policy advisors, then a lunch meeting with the head of transportation, about a complaint regarding the treatment of horses. There is also a petition about making horses more efficient by feeding them higher-octane grain."

The liegeman paused and took a breath, waiting for the Ascension King to argue some matter. Surprised at the lack of confrontation from his charge, he continued. "You will be golfing tomorrow with the advisor and your protector. There's dinner with your queen. She wants to go over some ground rules regarding you and your mistress."

"Wait, dinner with the queen? To discuss my mistress?" His face almost turned red and he wore a very puzzled look. "Umm, let's cancel that one."

"Cancel on the lady? My lord."

"Yes, unless you'd like to be the one to talk with her about my mistress. In that case, do not cancel but plan to go in my stead. Really, who does she think she is? Ground rules! I don't think so. Besides, dinner meetings ruin my appetite."

He nodded and struck through a line on his notepad. "Canceled."

There was a decidedly different energy in the rising Ascension Queen's room.

"Well, how do you think this would look on me?" She spun about, two gowns billowing from their hangers. "You know I just hate anything too loose-fitting."

"My lady, you would look fabulous in this one." Her attendant held up a citrine satin frock.

"Yeah, you said that last time and had me looking like some big yellow bird! Just awful," she spat. "Who's packing my things? Please tell them to make sure they don't pack my dresses. They should remain on their hangers and be carried individually. Last time it took a week for my seamstress to iron out the wrinkles. And no wire hangers!"

She paused, changing the subject. "What will the king be wearing tomorrow for dinner? I'd like him in something blue. With a jacket. No tie. He looks so charming in blue. And dinner should be something light, not too heavy. Sauce on the side for me. Oh and make sure dessert is his favorite, chocolate buttermilk cake with fresh whipped cream. He just loves his chocolate cake. But don't give me too much. I want to make sure I keep my figure, we are to wed in four years you know."

"My lady, there is a message from your king. Tomorrow's dinner is canceled."

"Canceled? How dare he cancel on me! I bet he's thinking he's going to have dinner with that hussy! Over my dead body. You tell him that dinner is not canceled, and that I'll see him at seven sharp, in the private dining hall. It's tradition. The queen always gets the first night. And he knows it."

"Yes, my lady."

∞∞ ∞ ∞∞

On the fourth floor, the soon to be twelve-year-olds (rising Prince class) were beginning their own move to the fifth floor. This was a special transition for them. From Primo to Pharaoh, students' sleeping quarters are pre-furnished. When Royals turn twelve, Terrowin believes that each child should begin to develop their own personal identities, to express themselves. And so, members of each new Prince class are allowed to design living quarters to their own specifications and according to their individual whims. It is a rite of passage, and students spend days planning the function and design of what will be their living space for the next four years.

Professor Walden called the Pharaohs to him in the

common area on their floor. "Ok, children, gather around." It was late, almost midnight, yet none of them were weary eyed. They came, still dressed in their daytime clothing.

"So, at midnight, you will be twelve. First let me say happy birthday to all of you! This is a truly joyous occasion. Now, as you know, we will be moving soon to our new quarters upstairs, and you will be officially promoted to the Prince class. Your training will be different, markedly increased in challenge and intensity, and, I sincerely hope, even more stimulating. But more on that later. So, who wants to tell how they designed their new room?"

Nara's hand immediately went up. As usual, she was the first to speak. "Well, my room is simply adorable. I've asked for a pink canopy bed covered with white lace rose petals. The curtains will, of course, match the bed. And the wallpaper will consist of balloons and clouds of different colors, representing all the people of Terrowin! Oh, and let me tell you about..."

"Ah, ok Nara, I think we get the picture. It does sound lovely, and you obviously put a lot of thought into your new quarters. Well done." Walden hoped she was sufficiently placated.

Typical Nara, the future queen. No doubt. Ava just rolled her eyes during her effusive ramblings, having already heard her tell it several times. Brandon sat very straight and still, his eyes on her, intent upon taking in her every word. The future queen's future lover would get used to listening to her discuss all the minutiae of her life. He might as well get started early. And David just squinted at her as if he could not understand a word she was saying.

"Well, ok. Now you know that each of you will be assigned members of the school staff to help you move, all of you except Salil. So, let's make sure we are ready to go."

"Professor," Nara interrupted, "why doesn't Salil get her own servants to help her move?"

Salil, wearing her mask, was startled and turned toward Nara at the remark. It was unusual for anyone to acknowledge her, much less speak about her.

"Well, Nara, as you know each of you was born into this world for a reason. You to be our future queen, David our future king and Salil to be the assassin. This is how it has been for generations within Terrowin, and your schooling is designed to help you all be the best that you can be in your respective future positions. Future assassins have to be strong, intelligent and independent. And Salil has those qualities, but we will help her to develop them even further."

Salil smiled slightly under her mask. She was unaccustomed to having anyone pay her compliments, although Professor Walden had praised her before on occasion.

"Well, maybe so, but I still think it's unfair," Nara said.

"And that's what's going to make you a great queen, my lady. They will write ballads about your graciousness and generosity of spirit." There was a knock on the door to their suite. It was midnight. "Ah, the servants are here. Let's hurry along children." It was time to finish packing and make the move to the Prince quarters.

Salil rushed back to her room in the Pharaoh quarters. It was a modest space for a girl of eleven. The walls were grey, adorned with several paintings of former assassins in their fighting attire. All were portrayed wearing their masks, striking intimidating poses with their weapons of choice. Some held swords, some posed flying in the air whilst executing a flying kick, others held crossbows or battle axes. She had a small cot on one side of the room with a steely blanket and lumpy pillow. There were two bureaus and one table with a chess board, the pieces scattered about, a game left unfinished.

She had packed earlier in the day. It did not take long. She had no toys, stuffed animals, or any other worldly possessions one might associate with childhood. Only her clothes, practice swords and bow and arrow. Everything she owned was packed in a black chest light enough that she could carry it herself to the Prince floor. While the other kids were working and directing servants, Salil moved stealthily through the halls and up the stairs, alone and unnoticed.

Chapter 30

Salil's new room was located farthest away from the entrance to the suite. That was the chosen location for all the assassin's rooms, in the far back corner. She was not much of a designer and lacked the creative skills that Nara and Ava had. So, when asked how she wanted her room made up, she wrestled with the decision for weeks. She wanted to be the best assassin there ever was. She finally decided.

She wanted to start living as an assassin and requested that her floor be covered with fifteen centimeters of soil. Salil liked being outside, and feeling the earth beneath her feet was always a good thing. It would allow her to practice martial arts and other fighting skills alone in her room. She also requested that two practice dummies be made for her. One with cushions and the other similar to a win chung wooden fighting man.

Salil lit the lanterns in her room and looked around, thinking that this was way more space than she needed. In the far corner of her room were the two practice dummies as she requested. The walls were grey, stone with various handles going up the wall in random patterns for climbing. There were several pull-up bars to practice her strength work, a roll-out mat for meditation, a table and two chairs, as well as a cushion that would serve as her bedding with the ever-familiar grey blanket.

Hanging on the wall, right at the entrance of her room was Salil's new mask. One additional benefit Prince Assassins are given is that for the first time they are expected to design their own masks. The masks of the younger assassins are designed by the School, simple masks of black cloth that cover their entire faces. Eye, nose and mouth sockets are all that are provided, held onto their faces by two strings that tie in the back.

The mask Salil designed was a simple hawk-like mask. This represented her gymnastic, jumping and climbing skills. After looking at her mask, she dragged her trunk to the far side of her room. She found the mat and unrolled it into the middle of the room. She sat with her eyes closed, breathing deeply and slowly. Assassins had to remember details about places, people and things that they encountered. They may have one chance to case a room, or house, as they were preparing for their assassination attempt. They needed to be quick and thorough. Her professors would often quiz her: How many people were in the room? What were their names? How many paintings on the walls, and of whom? What were they wearing? The level of detail assassins had to remember was remarkable.

"Two silver pull-up bars spaced approximately three meters apart. Fifteen hand mounts going up on the east wall, fourteen on the west wall and seventeen on each of the north and south walls—no only sixteen on the north wall. And one new mask on the wall at the entrance, eye level," Salil thought to herself, trying to remember how the room was configured.

Next, she went to her trunk and opened it. There were her clothes, which consisted of several robes and martial arts gees along with sweat pants, a ninja outfit and a black yukata. There were also knives and throwing stars, a jar of black marbles, two ropes of different lengths, a couple of her favorite books and a single letter written by her parents along with a gift. Unopened and unread.

Chapter 31

Policy dictates that the parents of Royals release all parental rights in order to ensure that their children are trained according to the standards set by the Royal Educational Committee. However, Royal parents are allowed to give one gift and send one letter to their child during the time they are at the School. When Pharaohs turn ten, they are given the gift and letter from their parents.

The letter is usually written in the days after the Royals are born, before their parents make the journey home from the Hospital with all their gifts. Salil remembered the day Professor Walden gathered them in the Pharaohs' quarters on the morning of their tenth birthday. "Children, come quickly, I have something special for each of you." It was early, and most of the kids were still in their sleepwear.

"When each of you was born, there was a grand celebration in the Capital where all the people of Terrowin gathered." He told them about the Birthing Celebration in detail, then said, "Each of your parents was instructed to write a letter that would be given to you on your tenth birthday." He motioned to the letters, rolled up scroll-like, bright red ribbons around the centers, and their names in big cursive letters on the outside. "Oh, and they were allowed to send you one gift along with that letter." He selected a scroll and held it out. "David, here is yours."

David took his letter along with a big box wrapped in heavy blue and gold paper, a thick gold ribbon on the outside. It would rival the best Christmas gift.

"Nara, for you, little queen." Nara's box was swathed in layers of pink and red, with a complicated and shimmering silver bow. It was even bigger than David's box!

"Cedric, the wise." Clearly he had been given a series of books, befitting the future advisor.

"Tem, the strong man. Yours." Tem's gift was modestly wrapped.

"Ava and Brandon, for you two lovers." They hurried forward, Ava slipping on the hem of her nightgown at the sight of the pretty package. Brandon made a show of hefting his gift, first in one hand and then the other, as if weighing it.

"And last but not least, Salil." Salil's gift was the smallest of them all. Flat, skinny and square. The wrapping was unimpressive. It may as well have been fishwrap. In that moment she was grateful for her mask.

"Now, remember, what is written in those letters is for you and you alone. Happy tenth birthday, kids!"

All the children rushed to their rooms to open the letters and gifts. Salil ran to her room, anxious. When she arrived, she closed her door tight and paused for a minute to look at the scroll and package on her cot. She was taught never to take action when she was feeling any type of emotion. Emotions can betray and cloud your thinking, she'd been instructed over and over in class. As she looked at the letter and present, she felt a series of sensations she had not felt before in her life.

Salil stopped. She breathed deeply. Willing her mind to calm her body. David and Nara's parents must be proud, she thought, happy to have their child become king or queen. Everyone adores them. But who wants the assassin? Who wants a child who is taught to kill that which they adore and worship? Her parents must loathe her, wish they'd never gone through the ordeal of having her. They probably wished they could erase her from their minds completely.

On her tenth birthday, instead of reading the hateful words of her parents, she took the scroll and gift and hid them in the back of her bottom dresser drawer. She knew it in her mind but was not ready to be faced with the stark and unforgettable reality that her parents did not love her. The letter and package remained there, two years, until it was time to pack for her move to the Prince floor.

Chapter 32

Salil, now twelve, was once again confronted with the letter and gift from her parents. She took off her mask, since she was alone in her room. Her face held the beauty of a Cinderella just prior to dressing for the great ball. She was a cute twelve-year-old girl. A little taller than most in her class, and thin, but her muscles were starting to show in her arms. Her long black hair unfolded and reached down her back. She had delicate features, light tan skin, and her eyes were wide and brown. Assassin training had thus far done her well.

She reached in the trunk and pulled out the letter and gift, sat with her legs crossed on her mat in the middle of her room and placed them both before her. Maybe today she would open the letter and read the hateful words her own parents—the only people in the world who might ever have loved her—had surely written to their great disappointment of a daughter. Maybe today she would open the gift they had sent, not from a place of love but out of obligation to fulfill their duties to the State. It was the smallest gift given to any of them. She thought about hearing the other kids talk, saying how proud their parents were and the extraordinary gifts they had each been given. Her thoughts betrayed her once again, and she found herself feeling both hatred and loneliness. A feeling of being unloved and unwanted, disliking everyone around her and even cursing her very existence. She grabbed the letter and the unopened gift and threw them across the room, opening her mouth to a cry of anguish she could not help but release. "I have no parents!"

Salil couldn't remember the last time she had cried, and now her big brown eyes were beginning to swell with water and turn red. Her nose started to run. She did not like these feelings at all. Emotions. Assassins were taught to control such things. "Emotions cloud your judgment. Make you hesitate when action is needed, make you miss the mark, or give away your thoughts, position or strategy." It was a litany she recited to herself over and over. Feelings were an assassin's greatest liability, and she was being trained to bury such things deep inside and never let them out.

Salil gathered herself, wiped her eyes and tried to restore calmness within her body and mind. She took several slow, deep breaths. She changed her clothes and put the letter and gift back in her trunk. Then she tied her hair up and walked over to the wall where her new mask was hanging. Putting it on instantly changed her attitude. She was no longer Salil, the lonely and unloved twelve-year-old, she was Salil the new Prince Assassin.

She went over to the bar on the wall and began doing pull-ups. She did them until she could do no more.

"Thirty-four, thirty-five, thirr-th-ssss." She maxed out at 35, but tried to hold the last one as long as she could. She was taught this is how you build muscle and get stronger. Train your mind to instruct your body to go above and beyond what it is capable of. Try to do one more pull-up, when the muscles can do no more. Fight it, hold it for as long as possible. This triggers a message from the brain to the muscles, "This person is crazy! Thinking we can do thirty-six pull-ups, and she's going to try to do it again, so we better build more muscle!" Salil always tried to max out during her workouts.

Next were inverted sit-ups. She hung upside down from the bar and curled up, working her abdominal muscles. Again until muscle fatigue and exhaustion. She started to sweat and was thoroughly warmed up. A peace had washed over her and settled deep into her spirit. She was back. She rested a minute, meditating in the middle of the room. Her body still warm from her exercises. Then she started to stretch.

Salil was as flexible and nimble as any Olympic gymnast. She could perform all the full splits and contort her body into shapes normal people could not. Sufficiently warmed up after her stretching, she grabbed her swords, one for each side. They were older swords, worn out from practice while she was a Pharaoh, but she was deadly with both.

She started first performing a kata, which is similar to a dance routine, but with several martial arts moves, flowing together: kicks, punches, blocks. "Kiaaaa!" she would yell at certain times during the routine, with an emphasis on a special punch or kick that was meant to be deadly. She then incorporated her swords into her routines as the katas progressively increased in level of difficulty. Now she was performing her routine, adding spinning moves and jumping techniques. Spinning in the air, she would take out one sword and swipe up high as if attacking an imaginary enemy high upon a horse.

"Kiaaaa!" she thrust the sword forward, into her imaginary opponent's abdomen. Now, in full sweat, breathing heavily, it was time for her to work with the cushioned dummy, to get the feeling of stabbing or striking a real person. She worked on the dummy, performing a series of martial arts techniques: punches, kicks, knife-hands and palm strikes. Always accompanied with her trademark "Kiaaaa!" at certain intervals. By now her hands were numb to the pain of striking the dummy, many days she hit it until her knuckles or feet bled. After the beginning moves it was time to go to the advanced moves. Her clothes now drenched. Her hair not flowing anymore but sticking to her face, wet from her own perspiration.

She had almost forgotten about the scroll and the still-wrapped package as she performed a series of jump spinning kicks on the cushioned dummy. "Kiaaa!" as her foot landed on the side of the dummy's head. Now, for the hard part, her jump flying techniques. Assassins had to learn how to fly. Not literally, but her martial arts training included jumping techniques designed to kick a person off of a hypothetical horse. Salil had just learned these techniques and they were not perfected yet. From halfway across the room she got a running start, jumped in the air, turned sideways and led with her foot parallel to the ground, performing a flying sidekick to the dummy's head. "Kiaaa!"

After doing kicks with both feet, she took one of her chairs and tried flying over the chair while performing the same technique. This required a further running start. She took a deep breath, ran and jumped, flying through the air. Her arm extended with her leg. She had too much momentum. "Kiaaa!" Salil hit the dummy's head at the top, but her speed made her travel past the dummy, right into the corner of her room. She landed and felt something move slightly, beneath the dirt upon which the dummy rested. Thinking nothing of it—after all, this is a girl who requested that her brand new room be filled with dirt—she tried the kick again.

Once more, she ran fast enough to clear the chair but carried too much momentum and landed on the far side of the dummy. This time she could not shrug off the ground moving beneath her as she landed. Trained to notice her surroundings, Salil stopped and looked at the dirt on the floor there. She stood in the corner, took a wide stance and shifted her weight back and forth, from one leg to the other. There was an unmistakable wobble as she rocked back and forth.

"What's this?" she whispered, still trying to catch her breath.

Curious, she dug through the dirt until she had exposed the floor beneath, made of large, almost square, stones of uneven sizes, configured together in an unorthodox pattern.

The corner stone was fully exposed and Salil pushed on one side. It rocked a little. She started pushing down upon it, but it was firm and would not budge. Then she tried lifting the stone, which measured one meter by perhaps a meter and a half. It was heavy but only a few centimeters thick, light enough for her to lift. She raised the stone all the way and uncovered a dark hole, which appeared to go straight down. Her heart lurched a little and then began to beat fast.

"Knock, knock."

"Hello-ooo!"

"Salil, are you in there?"

It was Nara and Ava rapping on Salil's door. But her attention was focused on trying to see down the mysterious hole. Salil at first did not respond.

"Salil! Come on, open up! Let's see your new room!" This time she heard them.

"Umm, just a minute!" she yelled. She dropped the broad stone and hurried to replace the dirt over the spot in the corner and to cover her tracks.

"Come aww-on! Open uh-hup!" The new Prince Queen and Prince Mistress were tripping over each other in amusement as they sing-songed to her.

"I'm coming! One second," Salil said in an annoyed voice.

She placed the dummy back in the corner and walked to the door. She opened it slightly and stood there firmly, not allowing them to look in.

"Woah. Nice mask, Salil. That's so much better than that hideous thing you used to wear," Nara said. It was almost a compliment.

"Come on, let's see the new room," Ava was pushing on Nara, trying to gain some leverage to force the door open.

"It's really nothing." Salil steeled herself and swung the door wide, showing her room to them.

The look on Nara's face was one of shock and disgust. Ava just put her hand to her mouth and looked around. Nara was about to walk into the room, but stopped when she looked at the floor and saw all the dirt in the room, her foot in midair. "Well, I know they didn't want to give you any servants to help you move, but they could have at least cleaned up this place. Look at all this dirt! I hope you don't have to clean this up yourself. They work you assassins so hard at this School." Salil kept her guard up and took no comfort in her kind words.

Ava still holding her hands over her mouth in shock, finally spoke, "You will never get a boyfriend with a room like this."

"Quiet, both of you! The room is exactly as I requested. It's for my training." Salil shut her mouth abruptly. Had she ever spoken so many words at once? She thought the room was perfect.

"You actually designed this? With this, this, dirt on the floor?" said Nara.

"Yes. I did."

"Well, to each her own. But, you better wipe your feet before you leave this room, lest you track dirt everywhere in our suite!"

"Oh, you are going to have such ugly feet walking around

in this dirt. You'll need a pedicure every week!" Ava said this with some measure of sadness in her voice.

David, Cedric, Tem and Brandon came running en masse into Salil's room.

"Woah, look at this room! Cool!" said David. The Prince King was the shortest of the seven, the most immature and underdeveloped for his age. He had light brown hair and brown eyes and a frailness that belied his age.

"How deep does the dirt go?" David fell to his knees and started digging.

Nara just shook her head and rolled her eyes. "Boys." He was so immature, yet this was the guy she would eventually marry. She couldn't help but think, he's going to need a lot of work.

"Get up from there! Before you trigger an asthma attack! Who knows what kind of spores are in here." Tem picked David up with one arm. Tem was strong for his age, testosterone hormones kicked in early for him. But he knew his role: protect the king. Tem took his job more seriously than the other Princes and he was the strongest of them all.

"Don't hurt him!" Ava yelled with great drama and anguish, as she rushed to David's side.

"Oh, come on. I just wanted to see," whined David.

"Are you ok? Are you hurt?" Ava asked, as she started wiping the dirt off of him.

"Oh, god. He's fine," said Nara with obvious exasperation and perhaps a bit of jealousy in her voice.

On one side of the room, Brandon was doing pull-ups,

looking lovingly at his biceps when he finished. He started talking to his arms. "Gun one," he said as he kissed his right bicep, and "Gun two," as he kissed the other one, "All for you my lady." And he blew Nara a kiss in the air. Brandon was the athlete of the group. Shorter than Tem, he was both strong and quick for his age. But, he was far from the typical jock. He had a high degree of confidence and intelligence to go along with his already impressive muscular physique. The girls around campus adored him and would sometimes laugh and giggle as he walked down the halls going to his next class. The queen's lover was being trained to be the perfect companion for her. Although, Nara couldn't quite appreciate his beauty yet. In fact, she really couldn't stand him.

"Ok, everyone out!" Salil yelled. She was frustrated and quite annoyed by all the attention surrounding her room design, wanting to return to what secret lay under the floor.

"Ok, come on, let's go. You heard the little killer," said Tem. He disliked Salil and at every chance he would belittle her. They all walked out of her room and back into the common area of the suite, where they were met by Professor Walden.

"Ok little ones, back to your rooms. It's late and time to get some rest. Big birthday party for you all later tomorrow."

He walked to Salil's door and simply said, "Nice room Salil. Now get some rest please."

Chapter 33

It was well past two in the morning, yet Salil had not slept one bit. She stared at the corner of her room, toward the cushioned dummy, wondering what lay beneath. When she was sure everyone was asleep, she crept to the corner under the cover of darkness. She moved the dummy and dug the dirt away. Lifting the stone once again, she looked down into the void. But it was too dark. She took down one of her lanterns and brought it over to the hole. It went straight down, but she could not tell how deep. Salil worked her fingers through the dirt floor, imagining what Ava might say about her being in need of a manicure. She found a small pebble and dropped it down into the hole. One second, two... almost three seconds before she heard it hit the bottom. That's approximately twenty meters, according to the gravity calculations she remembered from her physics class. She reached for one of the ropes in her trunk, tied it to a metal pull-up bar and threw it down into the hole.

She lashed the lantern to her back and climbed down.

Upon reaching the bottom she found herself in a cavernous room, with one corridor leading out. She examined the space and found a mural on the wall adjacent to the exiting corridor. Salil held her lantern up to get a better view. It was a painting of an assassin in full uniform, a black ninja outfit, with a red dragon mask on. Swords drawn in both hands, arms apart, standing tall and intimidating. She knew this picture, she had seen it before. But from where? She thought. Oh! It had been taught in her history class, of the first successful assassin in Terrowin. Assassin Rigor Mortisis was a legend and hero. His ability and cunning were examples to be emulated, a great source of pride amongst assassins. It was his assassination of King Philips that ended the Great Depression and started the Renaissance age of Terrowin. Assassin Rigor Mortisis was given much of the credit for helping build modern day Terrowin. Beneath the painting was a quote:

"The Assassin's life is a lonely life. Assassins walk the Path alone. But only those chosen, who follow this Path, shall find salvation amongst the stars. Come... are you meant to walk the Assassins' Path?"

His name was written below the quote. Salil thought maybe he'd been the first to find this passageway, maybe he built it. It didn't really matter. There were several other assassins' names written below his, along with the year they walked the Path. They were all Prince Assassins. She looked at the bottom of the list, checking the last few signatures. She stopped and looked more closely. According to the last entry, no assassin had found this place in the last forty years.

There were thick cobwebs all around, and a passageway leading farther down. The path was narrow, going down below the ground, and seemed as if was simply dug out by hand years ago. The floor was packed dirt, as were the walls. It was a long walk, and soon Salil thought about heading back. This was way too far, and someone might notice that she was gone. But her curiosity told her to keep going. What was the "salvation amongst the stars" that was promised? She had to know.

The passageway started going up, at a fairly steep incline. She labored a little walking now, but she was still in the dark and there was still only one way forward. Up she walked for another thirty minutes. Finally, Salil could feel the fresh air moving on her face and swore she heard the sound of ocean waves. She had reached the exit.

The exit was located high on the side of one of the mountains surrounding the School, but facing westward, toward the ocean. Salil was about halfway up this particular mountain, in a cave that opened to a view of the waves. It was quiet, she was alone. She looked up, and the view of the stars was clear. Is this what the writing on the wall meant? This could be a place for her to get away from the School, from other students, from the pressure of being an assassin. A place where she could be alone. She looked around and found a rope hanging over the side of the cliff, mounted to a rock on the side. It was worn, but still had its strength. She tugged at the rope and thought about climbing down to walk on the rocky beach below. But, she'd forgotten about the time and worried she had been gone too long. The rope would have to wait for another night. As she walked back to her room, through the passageway, she felt a sense of excitement and also a slow, spreading pride. She had found this secret passage, a passage that only a select few had found before her. It made her feel special, part of something bigger than what everyone else knew her to be. She was starting to feel like she belonged to something. Salil lay in her bed, preparing her mind for sleep, but her thoughts were already on the next time she could escape down the passageway. She would bring some ink to write her name alongside the other assassins who shared her secret.

Chapter 34

On January first, the School hosted the largest birthday celebration in the land. Well, second only to the Birthing Celebration that was going on in the Capital. Still, the entire student body shared the same birthday, and the School made sure to have a party worthy of all the future kings.

The atmosphere at the School was carnival-like. Clowns, magicians and acrobatic performers moved about the campus performing tricks for all the kids. A woman handed out balloons after she twisted them into any animal the children could think of. There were stations set up around the campus for cotton candy, popcorn, candy apples, roasted corn on the cob, lemonade, corn dogs, chocolate covered fruits and every other treat a child could wish for.

The campus was transformed by the presence of several amusement park rides. No tickets were necessary, though any Royal could skip the line and go to the front—except the assassins. The rides included a speedy wooden roller coaster, a breathtaking ferris wheel, a merry-go-round where the children could choose to ride atop a dashing horse or nestled in the embrace of a giant chipmunk, zippy go-karts and a harmless looking but rather nauseating spinny tea cup ride. Music tinkled and banged from within each attraction and there was no limit to how many times the children could ride.

The Princes mostly paraded around together as a group, but without Salil. David's medical team was on standby, water boiling, just in case he had an asthma attack. The most advanced therapy to control a bout of asthma in Terrowin was to boil some water and drop in a special concoction of herbs and salts once the liquid reached temperature. David would then breathe in the water vapor with several deep breaths while someone held a cape over his head and shoulders. This created a tent to trap the medicinal powers of the steam, allowing him to get the most concentrated healing power into his airways. Until his lungs were cleared he would feel like he was drowning, and it was a terrifying experience for all. Though anyone watching would think it was most difficult for Ava, the way she swooned and sighed any time David had a spell. The staff was always behind David at events like this, just in case. And sure enough, after finishing a particularly jouncing ride on the go-karts, David started with the shallow breathing and sat down hard, but before he started gasping from a full-blown asthma attack he was carried over, tented and coached to breathe deeply.

Other attractions that the kids enjoyed were a haunted house, a strength test hammer and punching game, balloon darting, water-gun races and gypsy palm readers. Prizes were given out to winners, although the games were easy and most kids won something. A rock climbing wall scaled the entire side of the main academic building, and boys and girls participated in the challenge to see who could reach the top and ring the bell. There was no safety harness, only a net to catch those who fell and could not complete the journey upward. Salil was one of the few students who made it to the top that day. Tem saw her, and he immediately tried to follow. Although, he was not as good a climber as Salil and did not make it to the top. Bellowing and with his fists beating the air in futility, he fell into the net below. This put a smile of Salil's face as she watched from a distance.

Face painting sessions were popular with the girls. There were many designs to choose from: rainbows, butterflies, moons and stars. The very smallest children had to opt for a small design, since they were only able to sit still without fidgeting for a few minutes. But for the older girls the options were endless. One could even have her entire countenance transformed to resemble an animal's head, so naturally the School's grounds were soon turned into a menagerie. There were puppies, kittens and exotic birds. Of course Nara and Ava partook in this activity. Somehow, they both ended up as pink sparkling dragons, and when they saw each other neither was very happy about it.

An enormous pile of gifts was set up in the middle of the campus, piled high into the sky and assembled in a pyramid formation, with bright colors, in various shapes and sizes and with bows on all of them. The gifts were provided by the State to ensure that the students received the right things at the right time and to ensure that the Royals would be gifted appropriately according to their status.

Food tents were set up all throughout the campus that day. Many of the kitchen staff manned grilling stations offering everything from hot dogs, hamburgers and steaks to locally-sourced pheasant, rabbit and possum. Other choices included pasta stations, cold cut sandwiches, vegetable and fruit salads, french fry huts and make-your-own pizza. Drink stations offering iced drinks, fizzes, fruit smoothies and milkshakes were abundant. Ice blocks were brought down from the mountains and used to make ice cream, one of the most coveted treats of the day, with the most popular flavors being blackberry, honey-lavender and butter walnut. Miss Lisette from the laundry was furiously at work, pressing and rolling crisp, sweet cornmeal cones to scoop the ice cream into.

David, Nara, Ava, Tem, Cedric and Brandon went right to the front of the ice cream line and ordered their own favorite flavors. Naturally, David ordered first. He stepped right up and said, "Yes, I'd like the largest scoop of raspberry sorbet!"

Nara ordered next, "Just a small spoonful—half a spoonful, really, of blackberry in the bottom of my cone. On top of that please put a full spoon of butter walnut. Fill the cone almost to the top with honey-lavender. Then a heaping spoon of blackberry, and a big scoop of butter walnut on the very top." The server was rushing back and forth, making sure to get the order right. Nara made sure to know the most popular choices.

Once their group had been served, they walked away discussing what they should do next and just generally enjoying some good people-watching. As they happily licked their treats, Nara's cone seemed to spontaneously explode, splattering her face and dress with a runny, sticky mess. Her pink sparkly face paint streamed down her cheeks along with melting ice cream. She cried out in surprise, and then burst into tears. The others around her were laughing, and Nara ran away crying and screaming.

"Good riddance," Ava said, as she slowly licked her honey lavender scoop. She was just fine with that.

Brandon ran behind her, "Nara, don't worry, you still look good!"

David, Tem and Cedric looked up to the sky, down at their feet and all around at the nearby crowd, but they could not determine what had caused Nara's cone to explode. Cedric looking the most intently.

"It just doesn't make sense," he remarked.

David puzzled for a moment, but when the sound of the bumper cars caught his attention, he ran off quickly. "Tem, Cedric, let's go!"

Salil was not far away and saw the bizarre ice cream incident. As the other children dispersed, she walked over, looked around and studied the ground. There she found a small rock that was like nothing else in the dirt, hidden in the grass. A projectile, perhaps. She picked it up and looked toward the roofs of the campus buildings surrounding the celebration, attempting to ascertain where it might have come from. Then she disappeared.

Salil made her way through a music classroom, careful not to knock over the music stands or disturb any of the instruments. She pushed a window open and pulled herself up on to the roof. She was in stealth mode when she turned the corner, and there, over to one side leading away from the party, she saw a little boy with a slingshot in his hands aiming at his next target.

"Just a little more to the left," he muttered under his breath.

Salil smacked him hard on the top of his head with her hand. "Little Jimmy!" She grabbed him by the ear. "I should report you right now!"

"No, no. Please. I'm sorry, I'm sorry," he said.

"What are you doing up here?"

"Just practicing my hiding tactics. And getting some target practice in. I didn't hurt anyone!"

James, or little Jimmy as everyone called him, was the Pharaoh Assassin, born four years after Salil. He was small for his age and most people at the School already thought he was never going to be much of a threat. But, Jimmy was a quick learner and his ability to hide was impressive. He'd once been gone for so many days during his hide-and-seek game that the staff had to involve the entire School in looking for him. He only came out after the head principal threatened to "spank him until his butt cheeks were pink."

"Yeah, ok. But no more shooting cones. All right?"

"Ok, you won't tell anyone?"

"No," Salil said with a sigh. "You're ok." And she left to join the rest of the birthday celebration.

The gifts were distributed late in the afternoon while a grand "Happy Birthday" was sung by all the students in unison. "Happy Birthday, dear [insert your own name]! Happy Birthday to you!" Following the singing, fireworks were set off, illuminating the dusk for all the children to admire.

"Happy Birthday Walden!" said Professor Xalvador.

Walden responded, "A most happy birthday to you also. You know, these parties are not like they used to be. We never received such elaborate gifts, and look at all this stuff. I swear, they will spoil these children something rotten!"

"Come on professor, that's just your age talking. Times change, and sometimes for the better." He jumped back. "Children, please slow down!" A group of new Pharaohs ran past them both, almost knocking down Xalvador.

After the fireworks display, everyone gathered around a stage for the talent show. This was the main attraction of the evening, and students performed either in groups or individually to showcase their talents. It had morphed during the years into a competition where the Ascension King's Mistress and Ascension Queen's Lover dominated—and usually won—given their superior musical training.

Cedric had teamed up with four other students, including Ava. They were going to perform a song a capella, but not just the words. The students had practiced mimicking the sound of drums, guitar and bass, and together they sounded almost exactly like the song they were performing, without any musical instruments to accompany them. Cedric was a bass. They started their song, a popular one at the time, fast-paced with a chorus that stayed in your head for days. The students loved them. Girls screamed and swooned. Boys were a bit more subtle, with most opting for the cool rhythm nod and a few of the bolder ones making somewhat vigorous hand-horns. Even Professor Walden managed to move his body a little to the catchy sounds, smiling proudly at his Princes.

At the end of what they thought was the final act, Professor Wilhelmina came out on the stage. She was in charge of that year's Emperor class, and she waited patiently a couple of minutes for the crowd to finish applauding. As the noise died down, she took the megaphone. "That was Cedric and the Revolution! Weren't they wonderful?" There were a few calls and whistles, but mostly the crowd remained quiet as hers was a rather unorthodox appearance. "Happy birthday, everyone. Tonight we have a most unexpected surprise for you." Her manner was so calm, but her words! What could she possibly be talking about? The students turned and chattered amongst themselves. But it seemed no one had any foreknowledge of what she might be about to say. Professor Wilhelmina was acting as though she were incredibly excited herself. "Children, as a birthday treat," she gripped the megaphone hard and fanned herself with one hand. "As a special birthday surprise for you all," she turned her eyes to the sky and her lips formed an "O" as she inhaled and exhaled hard. "Everyone! I present to you, Levi Adams!" She dropped the mouthpiece and ran off the stage. Levi Adams was the most popular male performer in

Terrowin. As soon as the first chords were played, some of the girls passed out. It was his current number one hit. The conscious members of the audience raised their hands and jumped up and down and screamed. He then performed two of his all-time hits, one for the students and one for the teachers and staff. Then Levi Adams sent his band off stage and pulled up a barstool. Someone handed him a guitar, and he concluded the evening with a never-before-heard acoustic ballad dedicated to the future kings and queens.

The next morning, January 2, quite groggy and still a bit grimy, the children at the School started their new classes of the year. And the twelve-year-old Princes soon found out that the next level of coursework was much more intense than the classes they had taken as Pharaohs.

Chapter 35

Professor Xalvador taught Advanced Combustion, Fire and Explosives. He was a former assassin. Professor Assassins wore gold colored masks designed to resemble their favorite animals. Xalvador's mask was one of a king cobra, complete with puffed cheeks on both sides. His manner was authoritative, his voice commanding, and he often used a condescending tone when addressing his students. His class was open to all students who were in the Prince class and above.

He was dressed in a long black yukata, with two swords attached to opposite sides of his waist and a dark maroon sash as a belt. At thirty-six, he was in great shape. He made it his duty to keep his fighting skills better than all of his students, and he was the best swordsman, martial artist and fighter at the School. He also taught Master level fighting classes to assassins and protectors who were in the Sultan class and above.

Xalvador's classroom was dark, with high ceilings, and

resembled a dungeon more than a classroom. Charred animal carcasses hung from the ceiling around the room. Several birds, a cat, and even a horse carcass, burned almost beyond recognition from some previous experiment performed long ago but never taken down. In one corner was a pile of different types of wood, specifically labeled: smoke producing, starter, intense heat, quiet burn, slow burn and experimental. Opposite the stacks of wood were barrels of other materials, non-wood but combustible. Some items were labeled: fireworks, firecrackers, blockbusters and dynamite. Several small fires burned around the room on the floor, each started with a different material and smoldering different colors. Salil, Tem and Cedric were in his class, with about thirty other students. His assistant was Sultan Assassin Kass.

"So, class, who can tell me what these fires are, and why would you want to use them?"

No one in the class offered an answer, especially not Salil. Assassins were taught not to draw attention to themselves. None of them ever offered to give the answer in class, it was contrary to how they were raised. Besides, they were also taught that incorrect answers were met with some form of punishment.

"Anyone? Anyone? Kass, why don't you help them out?"

Her voice was very monotonal, as if reciting some rule of law. "The blue fire, it's the coolest, gives off almost no smoke when it burns, and burns slowly. The yellow fire, it's natural fire, such as burning wood. The bright red fire is coal, hot, intense. The black fire, it burns silently, quietly but quickly.

And, this darker red fire. I don't know what that is."

Smack! He hit her across her face with the flat side of his sword, so hard that her mask almost turned sideways. But Kass barely moved or said a word. Some of the other students in the class gasped when he hit her, while others thought to themselves that they would never raise their hand in his class.

"Of course you don't know. This is an experimental fire I have been working on. Highly volatile, quick burning, and very difficult to extinguish." He started pouring water on each of the fires. They all went out except the darkest maroon one, that one almost seemed to fight back as if it wanted to survive, stay alive. It ultimately burned itself out.

"Now, for your homework, I want each of you to think about and give me your recommendations on how one might create this type of water-resistant fire. You should also write down ideas for your own type of superfire and bring those recommendations to me for next class. Class dismissed." Xalvador shuffled some papers on his desk. "Kass, you stay after." The rest of the students hurried out to attend their next class. He shut the door.

"Let me see your face." He started to remove her mask. At first she turned away, as though she were angry with him.

"Oh, come on, you know I wasn't trying to hurt you. But, just because you are my special student doesn't mean we don't have to remain neutral in everyone's eyes." She didn't say a word and remained perfectly still as he removed her mask.

"Let me see that. Does it hurt?" He put his fingers on the red mark on her cheek. She flinched ever so slightly as he touched her face. Not so much from the throbbing pain she felt from the mark, but from the touch of his hand. It was an intense feeling for her.

"No. It doesn't."

He removed his mask, revealing his face to her. "You have such beautiful blue eyes, and your face, if you ever smiled you would look like an angel." He took her hand in his. "I'm almost done Kass, can't you see?" Her eyes lit up as he said this.

"How much longer?"

"Not long, I promise you. This will all work out as we planned. And then, we will not have to walk around wearing masks all our lives. The people of Terrowin deserve to see your face, your beauty. We will not roam this land faceless anymore. I promise you."

He embraced her. Her skin felt hot and it was almost as though something within her chest was swelling, about to burst. These were feelings that assassins were never meant to feel, and at sixteen the feelings Kass had for Professor Xalvador were intoxicating. They had known each other ever since he began teaching at the School four years earlier. Xalvador recognized something of himself in her and took her under his wing.

At twelve, Kass exhibited assassin abilities far beyond those students two classes, or eight years, ahead of her. She was a born killer. Athletic, strong and nimble. Kass was stronger than most boys her age, and her martial arts skills were, again, far beyond anything Xalvador had seen in a student her age. She was so deceptive! During her hide-and-seek games she would go missing for days, hidden someplace where it was impossible for a mere mortal to find her. She would be punished, but she learned quickly to ignore pain and neither one of them could remember the last time she had shed a tear.

Her best skill was sword fighting. She was deadly with one sword, an outright assassin with two in her hands. As a rising Prince, she was the best swordsman at the School. There was talk amongst the professors of her being one assassin who might actually succeed in killing the king when her time arrived. It did not escape anyone's attention that there had been the same talk about Professor Xalvador when he'd been a student at the School.

Chapter 36

Years ago, when Xalvador was a student at the School, his strongest skills were deception, disguise and acting. He watched his classmates, committing to memory how they talked, how they moved and how they acted. He honed these skills in his room, locked away late at night practicing in the mirror. He was patient and deliberate. For years, Xalvador perfected speaking like the Royals in his class, and by the time he graduated he could mimic any one of them.

Xalvador believed he had planned the perfect assassination. Upon graduation it would take three years to accomplish, but who said you had to kill the king immediately? Xalvador's assassination attempt would take place during a meeting between the reigning king and the Ascension King. It is customary for the Ascension King to meet once a month with the reigning King of Terrowin at an undisclosed location, different every time. These meetings almost always take place on a side road, where they both have the protection of their horse-drawn carriages and full complement of guards and security personnel. And the time, Xalvador had been able to discover the location of one of the meetings. He'd thought of everything. It was the perfect plan.

He was able to sneak his way into the Ascension King's coach, and he waited there until it was time for his trip to meet the king. As the carriage rode along, Xalvador subdued the Ascension King using a cloth soaked in a toxic extract of yew leaves and crystalbush bark designed to render a man unconscious. The caravan stopped at the designated meeting place. Evening had arrived and protocol called for the Ascension King to walk over to the king's carriage, enter and meet with the king. These meetings usually lasted only an hour.

Xalvador donned the Ascension King's clothing and wore a hood covering his head. He walked just like the Ascension King and commanded his security team with a perfect mimicry of the Ascension King's voice. No one knew it was him underneath the hood. He approached the king's carriage. The king's protector, standing right outside, greeted Xalvador by the Ascension King's name and opened the coach for him. As soon as he entered, he put one hand on his sword, underneath his clothing. Xalvador tried to control his breathing, he had waited his whole life for this moment. But the adrenaline flowing through his body was almost too much. He said one phrase to the king, "I've waited a long time to see you, Your Majesty."

But his voice, toward the end of the sentence, changed from the Ascension King's voice to his own, and the king immediately suspected that something was wrong and tensed his body. He lunged, but the king moved slightly to his right. Xalvador's sword aimed at his heart, missed the mark and struck the king in his left shoulder. The king called for his guards, the sword still implanted in his shoulder.

Xalvador was captured that night. He had failed to deliver the lethal blow and was subsequently tried in a public trial. He was exposed. A disgrace to all assassins, he was vilified by the public. Convicted, he was sentenced to spend the rest of his life in prison, in isolation. He obsessed about his failed assassination attempt. Replaying the evening over and over. His voice had betrayed him with his blade only inches away from its mark. He sat in prison for eight years, alone and despondent, driven mad from the repeated phrase in his memory: "I've waited a long time to see you, *Your Majesty.*"

"I've waited a long time to *see you, Your Majesty.*"

"Your Majesty."

"Your Majesty."

"Your Majesty!"

He could not get it right. Even in his own mind. The proper inflection escaped him, always beyond his reach.

Until one day, almost four years before, he was granted a pardon by the new incoming King Terrence. King Terrence was a kind man and wanted to show Terrowin that as a people they could be forgiving. He pardoned Xalvador and offered him a coveted professorship. Xalvador accepted and was released to start working at the School.

Even with his newfound freedom, the images still invade

his dreams and he often lies in bed, in the middle of the night, repeating the same phrase as he tosses and turns in his sleep, each time trying to say "Your Majesty" with the proper disguised voice, each time his voice betraying him:

"I've waited a long time to see you, *Your Majesty.*"

Chapter 37

Intermediate Cooking and Culinary Arts was taught by Professor Tinsley. He previously served as the Master Chef for several kings in the Royal Palace. Although not a Royal, he was well-respected, if a bit overly confident in his cooking abilities, and not afraid to express himself. Many of his previous students had gone to work inside the castle upon graduation, and just as many were thrown out of his class, never to return to the kitchen. His cooking was impeccable, but he was a tough instructor.

For Ava and Brandon this class was mandatory. One of many cooking classes they would take along with their art, music and theater classes. Ava persuaded David to take the class with her, for him it was a way to get a break between his rigorous core classes. Tem was there as well. Nara thought cooking was beneath the queen's duties and had decided not to take the class, opting instead to enroll in Formal Dinner Protocol and Proper Dining Techniques. Assassins and advisors didn't take such classes.

"Ok, class. Today we will separate the men from the boys, the women from the girls, the chefs from the cooks. Today you will have just thirty minutes to prepare a dish from the articles inside your baskets. You will be judged on savoriness, style and imagination. You are to make a meal fit for a king."

Each student in the class stood alongside a hot stove, water already boiling, and a countertop laden with cooking accessories. "There's a pantry over to the side, filled with herbs, spices and other staples you might need. Now, here are the items in your basket."

The door to the classroom burst open before he could continue. Nara walked in with several books in her arms, holding a piece of paper.

"Oh, is this Intermediate Cooking? Here, I just transferred one of my classes. Professor Walden said it was ok. I know it's past the deadline for adding classes, but he gave me an exception. And, no, I didn't take Beginner Cooking but how hard can this stuff be? A chop, chop here, and a cut, cut there. So, where do I sit?" she asked, looking around the classroom. Everyone was wearing white aprons and tall white hats. She spotted David as he tried to bow his head down, hoping she would not notice him.

"Ah, David, I'll take that station right behind yours."

Professor Tinsley took her pass, and Nara walked to the back of the room and settled in next to David. He shook his head in disbelief.

"Ok, as I was saying. You will have thirty minutes to complete your meal. Open your baskets! You will find pickled horseradish

dark chocolate sauce

fresh kale and

a live baby monitor lizard.

You have thirty minutes, your time starts... now!"

When the students opened their baskets, they were confronted with live baby lizards trying to escape. Nara peeked inside, not knowing what to expect.

"Oh, no!" she screamed when the lizard popped its head out and hissed at her. She quickly closed the basket. Several students were not so cautious. Before long, lizards were all over the classroom, scurrying about with students running after them. One girl, a non-royal, ran out of the classroom, chased by a lizard.

"Control your lizards, students! If you can't catch it, you can't cook it!" yelled Tinsley. In the first couple of minutes the room was in complete chaos.

With control of their lizards, several students ran to the pantry to grab things that might complement their dish. They reached for items such as olive oil, potatoes, onions, soy sauce, peppers, rice, polenta, rosemary, thyme, oregano. There was also an array of vegetables and fruits, including but not limited to tomatoes, corn, green beans, broccoli, celery, apples, oranges, and boysenberries.

Brandon, Ava and a few other students remained at their seats, deciding to conquer the baby monitor lizard, which had to be properly cleaned and prepped. Brandon, without any hesitation, chopped the head off his lizard and skinned the beast, exposing the most succulent portion, the two backstraps. He then grabbed Nara's lizard, quickly twisted its neck, and handed it back to her.

"For you my queen."

He filleted his backstraps and then went to the pantry.

Ava decided to go a different route. She knew that the tail of the lizard was just as delicious as the backstrap, if prepared properly. She chopped off the tail, and when Professor Tinsley wasn't looking she grabbed David's and started preparing his as well.

"Poor lizard," she said, finding time to put bandages on their tails before sending them off running wild in the classroom. Brandon looked over at her and shook his head. David just smiled, pretending to chop kale.

This was normal for David and Ava. In Beginning Cooking she prepared all his meals with Tem's help (in spite of his limited cooking skills he had learned how to slice and dice and be a good sous chef.) David made it through Beginning Cooking like this, and he would make it through Intermediate Cooking the same way.

"Oh, and class, the winner of this competition will get to create one meal at our annual Fall Festival celebration." This upped the ante. The contest was really between Brandon and Ava, although Ava would have to try to prepare two dishes in thirty minutes in order to help David.

Tem coarsely chopped a variety of onions and peppers. His first thought was to make a stew. He threw the live lizard in the boiling water (closing the lid very quickly) along with the vegetables and way too much oregano. Tem's favorite food was pizza, and oregano smelled like pizza. He liked to think of it as his signature spice. That was good enough for him, and it afforded him the time and energy to help Ava with whatever she needed.

Poor Nara. She didn't know a thing about cooking. Despite the frequent talk of queens sharing their recipes with the people, oftentimes they simply take the best recipe from one of the chefs on staff and present it as their own. The lifeless baby lizard disgusted her. She picked it up with two fingers at the thick part of the tail and squinted at it before dropping it back down at her station. What did they expect from her, really? Seriously, she thought, there has to be something deeply pathologically wrong with this Tinsley.

"Ay!" she yelled, as a lizard ran across her high heel shoes. She quickly grabbed her own lizard and did nothing but dash some olive oil on it, salt and pepper, then placed it in the oven. She turned the dial to broil, the highest setting, allowing the open flames to cook the creature. She peeked over at David. He was busy reading the latest edition of *Terrowin Football Weekly* with his feet up. She glanced at Ava, busy at work, a flurry of knowledge and activity, now chopping onions and vegetables. A frustrated Nara decided to mimic her, acting as if she, too, had everything under control.

"Ten minutes!" Tinsley was in his element. The bastard.

Ava looked over at Brandon, she was making better time. And preparing two dishes at once! Ava had cooked her tail to a chewy-tender delicious perfection. She decided to make kebabs. They were such a crowd-pleaser, who didn't like kebabs? She whipped up a marinade using the horseradish and completed her skewered creation with alternating colorful vegetables, mushrooms, onions and peppers. Ava put the kebabs directly over a grilling fire set up on her station for additional charring.

Brandon unleashed his ultimate cooking technique, the smoker. He used a handful of hickory chips and let them cook underneath a metal pan for a few minutes. Then he put the lizard backstraps directly on the hickory chips, covered them tightly and popped them back in the oven. He concocted two different sauces, one with the horseradish and one with the dark chocolate. With time running out, Brandon diced several apples and started plating his dish for judging.

Tem, as usual doing just barely enough to finish the assignment and pass the class, worked calmly, stirring his stew and tasting thoughtfully and adding a few additional spices. David just watched. Occasionally Ava would offer him a taste of a sauce and ask for his opinion. It was good to be king.

Nara on the other hand was completely lost. She was trying to figure out what to do with the kale and horseradish. She decided to mix the horseradish and chocolate together in a bowl. She forgot about her lizard! Smoke billowed from her oven, at first she didn't notice, but when the odor filled the room all eyes were on her.

"Oh my goodness!" She reached in with towels and tongs to get the burnt, stiff lizard out of the oven.

"Not to worry. No worries. Everything is under control."

Professor Tinsley came over to her station. Nara conducted herself as if nothing was wrong.

"Just perfect," she exclaimed. "Look at that charring!" Trying not to notice that he was standing directly behind her.

Tinsley rolled his eyes. "One minute left!" he shouted.

All the students hurried to plate their dishes. Ava had two perfectly symmetrical kebabs with vibrant colors and an attractive amount of charring. She used the chocolate to make a molé-inspired sauce to highlight the pungency of the horseradish marinade, which was set off to the side. She pan-fried the kale and added salt and pepper.

Brandon plated his filets, one marinated in a horseradish sauce, the other in chocolate sauce. The kale was blanched and accompanied by apples and walnuts to make a salad.

"Time!" All the students lifted their hands in the air, backing away from their plates. Nara dropped a heap of raw kale on her plate. Judging time.

The students presented their dishes in assembly-line fashion, one-by-one, to Professor Tinsley. Examining the first dish, he sliced open the lizard tail and looked inside. It was raw.

"What is this? You, come here. Did you prepare this meal?" A tall girl with long black hair approached reluctantly. "Yes, I did," she said.

"What, are you trying to kill me? Raw lizard meat? Raw lizard meat! I'm not eating this crap!" He shoved the plate off the table. Shattering as it hit the floor. Lizard, kale and sauce flying everywhere.

"Come here, you, what's your name?"

"Sally," she said, sobbing.

"Sally, don't cry Sally. Don't cry. Crying's not going to help. Come here. Come on, take off your apron. Let me have it." She looked up at him, trying to process what he might possibly want from her.

"I said take off your apron. There is no place in this class for anyone to serve raw lizard meat! There's the door, out! Out I said! Not in my kitchen! The king will have your head on a platter, you serve this bollocks!" Sally ran out the door, sniveling and wailing, leaving the other students in the class in shock. Brandon and Ava both smiled, knowing their dishes were properly prepared.

"Next."

"Well, my lizard is cooked all the way through," said the next student. "I also made cracklings from the skin to offset the acidity of the kale-horseradish slaw."

"Oh-ho!" Tinsley rubbed his hands together. This was an interesting turn of events from a minor non-royal over-reacher. Cracklings! But his pleasure and surprise were short-lived. "Where's the chocolate?" The student's face fell. "The chocolate sauce? You forgot it, didn't you?" Mr. Nobody nodded glumly and slunk back into oblivion.

Then it was Brandon's turn.

"Ok Brandon, what do we have here?"

"Well, let me tell you, I have a spicy lizard special, two ways. Yes, spicy, 'cause I like things hot. First, I smoked that bad boy with some hickory, ya know, to get rid of some of the gaminess, and to, uhhh, soften them up a little." Brandon gestured with his hands as if he were squeezing two tennis balls out in front of his chest. He turned his head to look at Nara and then gave Ava a wink. A few other girls in the class swooned a little at his words, and the boys chuckled.

"Then, I prepared two different sauces, one spicy, one extra spicy, just like I like my women." As usual, the entire room was his audience. Now, with the kale, well, I wanted to sweeten that up a bit, so I used some fresh firm apples, well, you get my drift. I may like my women spicy, but I'm a sweet kinda guy!"

"Thank you Brandon," Professor Tinsley could hardly cut him off soon enough. "Ok, let's see. Yes, I can taste the hickory, good combination. Good, but the danger with making things two ways Brandon is that sometimes one is just enough. I like the horseradish sauce, but the chocolate sauce just didn't do it for me. Not bad though." It was enough to make Brandon grin, nod his head and give a few fist bumps as he stepped back away from the front of the room. "Who's next?"

Ava pushed forward. "I am."

"And what do we have here, young Ava?"

"Well, I have a grilled lizard tail shish kebab. The lizard tail was skinned and cleaned and marinated in a horseradish brine. Of course I would have liked to marinate it longer, but with only thirty minutes, well, in any case it's complete with grilled red peppers, zucchini, white onions and shiitake mushrooms. Which makes for such a pretty color display! I made a red wine chocolate sauce for dipping. Now, on the side, for some added crunch, I fried the kale, in a small amount of oil. It's a new technique I read about in *Cooking In Terrowin* just last week!"

"Hmmm, interesting combination. I must say, the lizard is prepared perfectly. It's still moist, and the burst of flavors from the vegetable combinations is so perky. And, this fried kale. Well, I've been dying to try it and I must say, this just might make it on the Ascensions' dinner menu in the near future! Great job, my lady."

As she walked back, Ava stuck her tongue out at Brandon, and David gave her a high five, Terrowin style.

"And, what is this?" Professor Tinsley looked disapprovingly at a plate of burnt whole lizard, skin and all, still smoking, a black sauce dribbled on the plate with absolutely no inspiration whatsoever. There was a hodgepodge of raw kale on the side. His face contorted frighteningly as he tried to decipher what exactly he was looking at.

"Well, this is my interpretation of blackened lizard with a fresh kale salad!" Nara said, trying to act enthusiastic about her offering.

Now, professors are not allowed to yell at either kings or queens, and Professor Tinsley did the best he could at holding his tongue, because he was about to use words that a proper lady is never supposed to hear. Instead, he simply looked down at the plate and said, "Nara, would you eat this?"

"Uhhh, maybe?"

"Good, you can eat it, I'm not eating this. Class dismissed."

Chapter 38

Advanced Fighting is a mandatory class for the Prince King, Protector and Assassin. Ava and Brandon decided to take the class as well. Cedric had no time for advanced fighting, he was off learning about other things, more relevant to his position. Assassins would continue their training in Advanced Fighting Two and Three along with the protector. But this was one of the more popular classes, with well over forty students in attendance.

Professor Glinda was a previously unsuccessful assassin. A soft-spoken older woman who, despite her non-threatening looks, was rumored to have the harshest fighting class ever taught at the School. Her gold mask covered the top half of her face, with feathers woven into her greying hair, making her almost look like an eagle.

The classroom looked like a martial arts dojo (arena might be a better word.) Bars and rings were suspended from the ceiling, randomly placed about at various heights. In the middle of the room was a bridge that went the length of the room, with stairs going up on both sides. The bridge was approximately sixty meters in the air. There were various panels and handgrips affixed to the wall, going all the way up to the domed ceiling. Various weapons were attached high above on the walls: bows, swords, knives of varying length. In the middle of the room grew a single willow tree, reaching all the way up, with branches coming out in every direction and masking the ceiling.

So far, Salil had been the top fighter in their previous classes. Tem and Cedric hated that she always beat them in open hand and sword sparring. David was hardly a fighter, he didn't mind, so long as his medicine team would be ready at a moment's notice should his asthma act up. Based on past experience, this group was very much looking forward to Advanced Fighting.

Professor Glinda wore a bright red master's karate uniform with a gold sash and two swords tied at her sides. Two sixteen-year-old assistants were assigned to help her. Sultan Assassin Kass and Sultan Marcos, who was not a Royal. Kass and Marcos wore black karate uniforms with red trim. Their sleeves were cut off, exposing bulging triceps and biceps, and instead of pants they wore traditional-looking skirts. They stood behind Professor Glinda, hands clasped behind their backs, feet slightly apart.

"Let's start class."

Kass and Marcos brought their feet together and bowed their heads to the class.

The students bowed in return.

Kass wore a different mask for class. The School provides standard fighting masks to Prince Assassins and above. They are translucent, thin and soft, and while they distort one's features they do nothing in terms of providing any protection. They simply fit perfectly over the assassins' faces. Salil had her fighting mask on as well.

"Let us meditate," said Professor Glinda. She sat down and closed her eyes, breathing slowly. The students followed suit, legs crossed, eyes closed.

"Remember, empty your thoughts. Nothing around you exists. Hear, see, feel and smell nothing. Clear your mind of any doubt. The fighter's mind has to be free, free of fear, free of distraction, free of temptation. Breathe, inhale." She straightened her spine a little more as she inhaled. "Hold... and exhale."

Salil immediately liked the professor. Her voice soothed the class as they listened for other instructions. Advanced fighting, how hard could this be?

"Ok, little Salil, let's see what Professor Dmitri has been teaching you all down there in that beginner fighting class.

"Salil, up! Kass, up!"

Kass stood up immediately and took her position. Salil, not knowing exactly what was happening, stalled for a moment.

"Salil, here, come here, stand across from her." She obeyed, however reluctantly. Professor Glinda's demeanor had changed abruptly, shocking Salil and the rest of the class.

"Now bow to one another."

Kass bowed, and Salil bowed.

"Bow to me."

They both bowed to Professor Glinda.

"Assuming fighting positions!"

Kass, after executing several martial arts moves with kicks, blocks and punches, assumed a fighting position, arms in front, fist closed and in a deep stance. Underneath her mask, she had a smile on her face. Salil stood confused, putting her hands up as a boxer would. They didn't have any protection over their hands and feet. They didn't have the chest protectors they wore in Beginner Fighting. Her mind raced, trying to decide whether or not the professor was serious.

Professor Glinda grabbed Salil's shoulders and shook her. Her voice was sharp. "Now, listen, this is a fight, a real fight. Salil, protect yourself at all times."

Salil's adrenaline flowed, becoming a torrent in her body, and as best she tried she could not control her breathing. Did she hear the professor correctly? A real fight? She had been in several sparring matches with her classmates before. But, never a real fight. And standing across from her was this older sixteen-year-old killer who had done this before. Normally, she would be thinking clearly about what to do. But fear overcame her and she could not focus. She knew she was not stronger than her opponent who towered over her. Yet, here she stood, without armor, about to have the first real fight of her life.

"Begin!"

Kass advanced as if she was going to attack Salil. It was a

fake, to see what she would do. Salil moved back, put her hands up and circled around. Her foot movement was excellent, but this was more out of reflex than any conscious thought about defending herself. She was scared. Her feet remembered, never move back in a straight line, always circle. Salil circled back too far to signify any type of defensive posture. It exposed her fear and Kass knew it. While Salil was still trying to grasp the gravity of the situation, Kass visualized the techniques she could hit Salil with first.

Four years ago, Kass had been in the exact same position as Salil. She had to fight the sixteen-year-old male assassin. Yet, she didn't back away. She actually defeated him to the great surprise of everyone. It was rare for a twelve-year-old to beat a sixteen-year-old, and never in the School's history had a twelve-year-old female beat a sixteen-year-old male. But Kass was an exceptional student. It wasn't an easy fight for her, she suffered a broken nose, two black eyes, and couldn't walk for a week, but she didn't quit. The boy had suffered far worse.

I know what you're thinking: this is just cruelty! How could they allow children of such ages to fight, bare knuckles, to the tune of a broken nose and swollen faces? As discussed earlier, the School's mission is to prepare students for the world of Terrowin upon graduation. Assassins have to be tough. They have to be able to distinguish between being injured and simply being hurt. An injury disables you, allowing you not to fight anymore. Being hurt... well, boo hoo! Assassins have to know the difference. Just because you might get punched in the face, doesn't mean you are injured. Hurt, stunned, ok. But, you can still fight. Imagine if a mere citizen of Terrowin could defeat the assassin with one punch to the face. The School would be a mockery, and the citizens would not be pleased. This is how assassins have been taught for centuries at the School, and every Prince Assassin has to go through this initiation. Girl or boy.

After circling around, Salil—still with her hands up but not knowing exactly what to do—waited for the next move from Kass. Kass moved forward with a series of front flips and tumbles in the air, toward Salil, yelling as she executed the moves. When she was close enough, she jumped and twisted herself in the air, like an ice-skater performing a spin move, and at the last minute she let her arms fly out, her body in a letter T position, fists connecting with Salil's face, one after another, after another. Before she knew what was happening, she was hit three times. She fell to one knee and lowered her head in defeat.

Something warm was streaming down her lips, and a salty sensation overwhelmed her taste buds. It was her blood, now dripping on the floor beneath her. Fear was replaced by terror. She was afraid of Kass, and her nose hurt awful. The students in the room stood still, completely stunned at how hard Kass had struck Salil. Not to mention the technique and execution. It was something they had never seen before. Professor Glinda yelled, "Hold!" She went over to Salil and took her face gently in both hands, peering closely at her.

"Let me see. Oh yes, it's broken."

Salil was silent as she looked up at the professor. Her eyes swelling up with tears, both from the natural reaction of being hit in the nose so hard and the fear of a twelve-year-old child in a fight she no longer believed she could win. Salil knew this fight was finished.

"Are you alive Salil?"

Confused at this question, of course she was alive, she nodded her head yes.

"Can you continue?"

Salil knew there was only one answer. "Yes."

"Assume fighting positions!"

Kass took another aggressive fighting stance. Salil, in disbelief that she would be forced to continue, looked over at Professor Glinda with tear-filled eyes, hoping for some sort of relief, recess or even sympathy from the professor. None was forthcoming. The class remained silent, and Salil walked wearily to the fighting line.

"Salil, pssst," David whispered. She turned to him. He pointed to the wall and motioned her to go up. She looked at him, confused at first, and then it clicked.

"Begin!"

Kass came forward, ready to finish her off. Salil, still the best gymnast in the School, did a series of backrolls and jumped at the handles on the walls. She took off immediately, climbing up, higher and higher. At first she climbed as if her very life depended upon it. About halfway up the wall a familiarity came over her and her body, and she slowed enough to look down at Kass. Kass watched in disbelief at how quickly Salil climbed. Then she took off after her, like a lion chasing its prey.

"Go Salil!" yelled Ava.

"Come on, you can do it!" Her classmates cheered her on as she climbed higher.

Salil glanced at the weapons on the wall, swords, a shield, bow and arrow (the arrows had wood blocks on them,) a wooden sledge hammer and a rope with a solid wood sphere attached to it. They were all wooden. The School didn't want anyone getting killed. Salil saw one of the swords, grabbed it and jumped off the side of the wall onto the bridge high above the floor.

Kass followed right behind her, and she also jumped on the bridge. She had no weapon in her hands. Salil, running across the bridge to the other side, paused and looked back. Kass was unarmed. She remembered her own sword training and, thinking that maybe she had the upper hand, turned toward Kass and walked forward to face her. Her sword leading the way.

Kass did not back down, she walked closer and they met in the middle of the bridge, right where the big tree was located. Branches and leaves were right above the two of them, Salil held the wooden sword with two hands, firm, forgetting the pain in her nose. She swung wildly, not from the belief that she could actually defeat Kass, but trying to believe that she could at least fight her.

"Kiaaa!" Kass simply moved back to avoid the blow. Salil moved forward, hands high above her head, ready to chop down on Kass, "Kiaaaa!" but Kass simply stepped to the side to avoid the blow. Kass was just playing with her.

She swung at Kass again, still on the bridge. This time, Kass moved forward as Salil went to strike. Shortening the distance between the two, rendering the sword ineffective. Kass wrapped her arms around Salil's outstretched arms and lifted up. Salil's shoulder and elbow joints locked out, bringing immediate pain and forcing her to drop the sword. Kass then released her and kicked Salil so hard that she crashed into the railing of the bridge and tumbled over it, into the branches of the tree. Holding on to the branches for dear life, Salil frantically searched for a way to climb down. She looked back toward the bridge to find Kass. Kass was not where she had last seen her.

Salil heard a rustling in the branches. It was Kass. She was in the tree and continuing to pursue Salil. Leaves were falling to the ground, covering the dojo's floor. The students looked up in the tree to see what was going on. Their view obstructed by the leaves and branches. The tree shaking and swaying from above.

Thump.

Thump.

Salil dropped down first. Her uniform was covered with blood, she was still bleeding when she hit the ground face first. Kass was right behind her, landing on her feet. Her uniform clean, with barely a wrinkle. She stood over Salil, ready to deliver another blow to the back of her head.

"Hold!" yelled Professor Glinda.

Kass stopped in her tracks. Salil struggled to get to her

feet. Professor Glinda stood over her.

"Get up. Get up!"

Salil wearily rose to her feet and found her balance. She was exhausted. One of her shoulders slumped to the side. She couldn't put any pressure on her right foot.

"Can you continue?"

Salil did not respond.

"I said can you continue?"

"Yes. Yes I can," Salil said between deep labored breaths. She put her hands up in a fighting position and looked Kass directly in her eyes. She was no longer afraid. She had accepted her fate, and if she could not defeat her, she would at least be defeated with honor.

"Fight!"

With those words, Kass stood there and watched Salil. She moved closer. Salil, figuring she had one blow left in her, clenching her fist and waiting for Kass to close the distance. When she did, Salil threw the hardest punch she'd ever thrown in her life (at least it felt that way to her, but in her tired and exhausted state the punch moved in slow motion.) Kass turned her body, allowing Salil to hit her in the face. The punch had no effect, landing on the side of Kass's face. She just stood there, grinning at Salil.

"Time!" Professor Glinda yelled.

Kass shoved Salil just enough to make her fall to the floor. She had no more energy and collapsed.

"Get her to the infirmary. Class dismissed."

Classes in the Prince years were designed to be a

transition period for the Royals. In the beginning, the students were a little shell-shocked at the difficulty and intensity of the classes, but with time they adjusted. By summer, the classes they had taken as Pharaohs just seemed juvenile.

Terrowin Enquirer

FORMER KING JAVIER, QUEEN TIFFANY ROSE & DAUGHTER MYSTERIOUSLY DISAPPEAR—Foul Play Not Ruled Out

Former King Javier and Queen Tiffany Rose, who served as king and queen twelve years ago, vanished from their modest estate in Northern Terrowin. Also missing is their eleven-year-old daughter, Emilia. Neighbors solicited the police after not seeing the family for two days. Police sources informed the Enquirer that, "It seems like they just vanished. All their belongings were still at home, and a pot of coffee was left on the stove with two empty cups on the breakfast table." Police would not confirm that they suspect foul play, but an official spokesperson said they are considering all possibilities.

One neighbor, who wished to remain anonymous, stated, "They were the most unassuming couple. Quiet. He enjoyed fishing by the lake and she picked berries by the ravine in the mornings. And little Emi was so sweet. I can't imagine anyone who would wish to harm them."

Other folks speculated, "Maybe they left or were abducted by aliens, strange times we live in."

Police are asking any persons with information on the whereabouts of the former king and queen to please contact them immediately. King Javier and Queen Tiffany Rose last made headlines when after their reign they turned down a position at the Royal Ascension School, instead choosing to live out their lives in the quiet and unremarkable town. It was the first time in more than a hundred years that a former Royal declined a position at the highly regarded and historic School.

Chapter 39

At the summer solstice, the annual football games were to be played at the School's stadium. Each class, from the Princes upward, would have their intra-class championship game. Prince King David and Prince Advisor Cedric would pick teams and challenge each other in front of everyone. This was an event dating back to the opening of the School, and everyone made sure not to miss it.

David, though not the best athlete in the group, chose his team wisely enough. He knew he wanted Salil on his side, and she was his first pick. By default, Tem was already on his team. Cedric promptly picked Brandon for his team. To keep the peace, David put both Nara and Ava on his team. The rest of the players on both teams were non-royal Princes.

A day prior to the game, the School was abuzz with the upcoming match, and, given David's asthma, his team was declared the underdog. During dinner in the café, a reporter approached David.

"Prince King David, how are you going to deal with the

superior athletes that Prince Advisor Cedric has on his team?"

David was taking a bite out of a roasted chicken leg and was in no spirit to answer questions from a student reporter.

"Huh? What?"

"How will you win the game?"

"Well, we have the best athlete in the class in Salil. I'm sure she'll find a way to win the game for us. I'm not worried at all."

"Thanks for your comments. Prince Queen Nara, what is your prediction for the outcome of the game tomorrow?"

"Well, first, I'm hoping it doesn't rain, 'cause I'm not playing in the rain. All that mud, ewwww! Second, I hope the students have a wonderful time at the festivities. We should all be proud of everyone involved. Win or lose."

"Thank you my lady."

"Oh, and make sure you get a picture of my uniform tomorrow, it's divine! I had it specially created for this game. It has a border going down one side. And the shoes are sooo cute! With matching socks, of course. Oh, and, the hat—"

"Umm, thank you my lady. I will be certain to get a picture."

Cedric was over with his teammates, huddled together around a dinner table on the far side of the room. They were going over assignments and plans for tomorrow's game.

"Prince Advisor Cedric, a few questions for you?"

"Ok."

"How will you win tomorrow's game?"

"Well, I can't disclose all of our strategy right now. We will show it on the field. And hopefully may the best team win."

"Do you find it odd to be playing against your future king?"

"Not at all. If he's on the field, he's another player."

"Oh interesting, so does that mean you will tackle him if he has the ball? You will tackle the future king?"

"Yes, and anyone else that gets in the way of us winning."

At that moment, Tem walked by and heard Cedric's remarks. He paused and walked over. "You better watch what you say." Tem stepped up closer to Cedric, towering over him.

"Gentlemen, gentlemen, just a friendly game of football tomorrow. Shall we?" The reporter stepped in between the two.

"I'll see you and him on the field," Cedric shot back.

Tem walked away. Walking backwards, not turning his back to Cedric. He had a smile on his face, and his finger pointed in Cedric's direction. Let the games begin...

∞∞ ∞ ∞∞

The stadium was full and one could not ask for a more perfect day for a football game. Professor Xalvador sat next to Professor Walden in the staff section in the middle of the stadium. On one side of the stadium stood David's supporters and on the other side Cedric's. Usually the Prince King has more fans, but this year, with Brandon on Cedric's side, most of the girls were cheering for him.

David's team wore dark navy blue uniforms with gold trim

down both sides. "Kings" was written on the front of their uniforms in gold lettering. All except Nara, who insisted that she have "Queen" written on her uniform in a curly cursive lettering. Cedric's team wore cherry red uniforms and the word "Advisors" was written on the front. The two captains met in the middle of the field with the referees for the coin toss. David was joined by Nara and Ava. Cedric brought Brandon.

"Ok, you both know the rules. No roughhousing out there, or we will throw people out of the game. Remember, yellow card is your first warning, and after a second yellow card you are ejected from the game. Understood?"

"Yes."

"Yes."

"Ok David, you call it, heads or tails."

"Heads."

"Heads it is! Kings will receive the ball first."

David walked over to the rest of his team and tried to give some words of encouragement. "Come on, let's go out and have some fun!" he said, as his team ran onto the field and the crowd went wild with anticipation. Cedric's team followed, to even more applause.

David played the right forward position, with Tem just behind him. His medical crew stood along the sidelines, the water boiling. Cedric played keeper for his team, and Salil played keeper for the Kings.

The whistle blew. The game had begun. It was quickly evident that Cedric's team was superior as they controlled the ball and moved it down the field with ease. If not for Salil's cat-like instincts, they would have scored four or five goals within the first ten minutes.

The announcer said, "Salil makes another diving save! Oh, but she can't control the ball. A rebound. Goooooaallll! Goooooaallll! Goooooaallll!"

The Advisors struck first. Brandon scored on the rebound, an easy goal, then ran off to the side of the field into the far corner, his teammates chasing behind him. He did an airplane dive on the grass, chest first, sliding several meters with his hands apart. He lifted himself up, then peeled off his shirt and waved it around high above his head. Before his teammates could catch up to him, he was running alongside the bleachers, where all the screaming fans were. Brandon blew kisses to the crowd. Some of the girls in the stands went crazy, almost in tears as he passed them by. A few threw flowers to him. He picked up a yellow rose, then jogged over to Nara, took her hand and went down on one knee.

"That was for you my lady," he murmured as he held the rose out and kissed her hand. Nara, annoyed, grabbed the flower and pulled her hand away from his. But she had a little smile on her face, appreciative of the attention. The teams lined up for another start.

David was trying his best to control the ball and he passed it back to Tem on the right side. Tem looked over at Nara and Ava on the other side of the field, wide open. He kicked the ball to Nara. "Nara!" Instead of heading the ball, she moved out of the way and covered her head, running in the other direction.

Back came the Advisors, on the attack once more. "Near

the penalty box, he shoots! Save by Salil!" She kicked the ball with all her might, toward David. He was open and behind the defense.

"David receives the ball at midfield, Tem knocks down two defenders, and David has a free lane to the goal!" The announcer continued.

"It's David and Cedric one on one! He shoots! He scores! Prince King David scores! Goooooaallll! But wait. The referee's hand is up. Offsides! Offsides, says the official, no goal!"

David immediately ran over to the official.

"No way!" Hands on his knees, his breathing was noisy and labored. "No way I was offsides," he whined.

The official looked at David. "Excuse me my lord, what did you say?"

David replied, a bit breathless. "I said there was no way I was offsides. Bad call. Bad call." His voice cracking as he spoke.

The official blew his whistle. "Goal for the Kings!" he said. "Goal for the Kings!" The crowd went crazy. David ran over to get a quick breathing treatment from his handlers.

"Way to go David!" Salil yelled from her goal. Ava ran over to David to make sure he was ok and Nara did her best impression of a queen's wave to the crowd, acknowledging their appreciation for David's goal.

A furious Cedric ran to the officials. "He was clearly offsides. How can you change the call?" The referee simply walked away from Cedric. Play resumed, and Cedric's team was still in control of the game. A battle for the ball occurred at midfield, and one of the Kings was knocked down in the scrum. David cried from the other side of the field, nowhere near the action. "That's a foul! That's a foul, oh, come on."

At that instant, the referee closest to David blew the whistle, "Foul on the Advisors," giving the Kings a free kick. The Advisor player involved in the play protested and was promptly given a yellow card.

Salil took the free kick and kicked the ball into the penalty box in front of Cedric's goal. He came off the line and punched the ball away. A legal play. "Great save by Cedric!"

David, involved in the play, was simply overpowered and fell on the ground after crashing into one of his own players.

"Hey, that's a foul," David cried, as he picked himself up off the ground. The referee blew his whistle again, "Foul! Penalty kick!" Cedric fumed. He walked up to the official and started yelling at him. "Open your eyes! He got hit by his own player. Come on man, call it fair!"

Salil came from goal to take the kick. "Salil shoots, she scores! Goooooallll! And the Kings lead 2-1." David began to understand what was happening.

"Hey, he's out of bounds," yelled David. The whistle blew. "Out of bounds!"

"Hey, that's our ball, he touched it last." The whistle blew, awarding the ball to the Kings.

When the Advisors scored an obvious goal, David was having none of it. "Hey, um, offsides? He was offsides?" he said cautiously to the official closest to him. The whistle blew. "Offsides! No goal!"

Cedric had seen enough. He ran from his goal and confronted David. "David, you stop this right now. It's not fair."

"Leave me alone. Play your own game." Tem ran to David's side and the other kids on both teams ran toward each other at midfield.

"Cedric, back off!" yelled Tem, standing in between David and Cedric.

"Tem, butt out! David knows exactly what he's doing and it's not fair!" He poked his finger into David's chest. Tem's instinctive reaction was to punch Cedric and then jump on him. Everyone else joined in and in an instant there was a melee in the middle of the field. Nara and Ava stood to the side, watching the free-for-all. Brandon quickly walked over to Nara.

"I shall defend your honor! Ummm, be right back," and he ran toward the pile of bodies and jumped on top. Salil walked from her goal and was also at mid-field, but she just stood there. One Advisor player saw her and was about to attack. But Salil, still wearing her mask, simply looked at him and shook her head. No, No, No. He thought better of attacking an assassin and turned to find an easier target. A mass of bodies was piled up, kids grabbing and kicking at each other. David crawled out of the scrum unharmed and went directly to his handlers for his medicine, to prevent an oncoming asthma attack.

The referees tried to break up the fighting boys and girls, but they mostly ignored the blowing whistles. It wasn't until

Xalvador and Walden walked from the stands that the students understood that they went too far. "Children, stop this madness! Stop we say!" At Xalvador's words the kids stopped.

"This game is over! Forfeit by both teams. And, I want the Royal Princes to immediately go to your rooms," said Walden. The Princes had never seen Walden so upset.

"But, we didn't do anything," protested Nara, pointing at herself, Ava and Salil, who did not participate in the fight.

"I said everyone!"

"Aww, ok."

The crowd was leaving the stadium. Xalvador found Kass amid all the chaos and walked beside her. "It's time, my dear," he said. She kept moving and did not respond, but she understood what he meant.

Cedric, still upset by the game, bumped into David, which prompted a shove from Tem. They went to their rooms looking haggard, sweaty and still angry.

Back in their suite, Professor Walden called the Princes together.

"Now, children, what was today's lesson?"

"Wait, are we in trouble?" asked Ava. "Cause, really, me, Nara and Salil didn't do anything."

"Well, let's see how we all stand after this discussion. Although, right now, only one of you is not in trouble."

"Hey, wait, just one person? That's totally not fair," said Nara.

"We will get to you later my little queen. Now, what did we learn from today's lesson?"

Cedric shouted, "That David's the king and he will cheat to win a game!"

"Will not!"

"Will too!"

"Shhhh. The both of you."

"But, I didn't do anything. The refs made the calls, not me," protested David.

"Yes, that is true, you did not do anything. But you said more than enough," replied Walden.

"Yeah, all he had to do was whine and the refs gave him all the calls!" Cedric puffed.

"But they made the calls. I just suggested to them what the calls should be," David countered.

"And you wanted to win, yes?" queried Walden.

"Yes, of course. For the team."

Professor Walden sat up, and his voice got quiet. "David," he said, "it is a most powerful position you will one day assume. Thousands of people will do exactly what you tell them to do, and when to do it. This type of power can be very dangerous. It's seductive. Many a king has succumbed to the seduction of power. Power corrupts, absolute power corrupts absolutely. You have a responsibility to see past your own desires and be fair to all the people in Terrowin. One day, you will command our armies, dictate the path of our people, and you of all people in the Kingdom must be fair, even at your own personal expense."

"Yes, Professor. I'm sorry. I just wanted to win."

"I know, but sometimes a king can lose, and lose with

honor and grace. Today's events were a disgrace, and that must never happen again."

"Ok."

"Now, Cedric the wise. Can someone tell me whether Cedric's actions were proper and befitting the future advisor?"

"Hell yeah! Oh... I mean, heck yeah," shouted Brandon, sporting a swollen and red face. "It's about respect, you gotta get respect out on the field, and Cedric showed he ain't no punk. My man!" He tried to give Cedric a fist bump, at which point Walden took out his staff and whacked Brandon's hand away.

"No, no, no. Anyone? Anyone? Cedric?"

"Well, maybe I shouldn't have poked David, which then allowed his bodyguard to come attack me!"

"Cedric the wise, you are learning so much so fast. You were right to protest David's actions. He was being unfair. But you protested out of anger and emotion. You thought about winning the game, instead of thinking about everyone around you. Cedric, just as important as policies and economics is learning how to communicate with David. You must be able to help David see the light when his own judgment might be clouded. And most importantly, you must know how to communicate with him."

Cedric nodded his head in agreement and Walden continued. "You can pull him to the side, in private. Perhaps over dinner. Sometimes you can even raise your voice to him, but never in public and never with anything other than respect."

"I understand professor," Cedric said as he lowered his head, knowing he had failed this test.

"And you, Tem. Let's talk about you."

"What? I was only protecting David, as I've been raised to do."

"Yes, protect him you must. And protect him you will. But, sometimes you need to know the difference between David needing someone to protect him and David needing someone to give him a kick in the butt. Cedric is the one person who can do that, who will have the wisdom to do that. Tem, sometimes you must stand aside."

"So, if Cedric wants to beat up David, I should let him?" Cedric's head lifted up at this question, still angry with David.

"Hmm... Yes. I mean, no. What I'm saying is that you will have to learn to stand down and let these two work it out sometimes." Cedric stuck his tongue out at Tem.

"Now, Ms. Nara and Ava, let's talk about you two."

"Well, we were just standing there, while the boys, um, did what they do," Nara explained.

"Yeah, I mean, we didn't fight, God forbid." Ava agreeing with Nara.

"Ladies, ladies. Yes, and being such the proper ladies you both are, not engaging in the fight was the right thing to do." They flashed smiles at each other and nodded their heads.

"But, Nara, as future Queen of Terrowin, you also have a duty to the people of our country. And when David is out of line, or makes a mistake, it will be you who can also correct his ways. You my dear are the people's inspiration, and they will look to you and David for leadership and direction."

"Yes, professor, I understand. Next time I'll just bop him on the head!" Nara looked angrily at David. Professor Walden laughed.

"Ava, you also, although you might be David's lover one day, you will also have the ability to reach him, to counsel him. You are more than just a pretty face for him to look at and admire. You too have a responsibility to the people of our country, to help guide David to the right decisions." Ava's eyes widened as she listened to Walden's words. She had no idea! Feeling important, she sat up a little straighter. Walden continued, "Some days, it will be tough for him to discern right from wrong, but it is also your duty to help him through these times."

He looked to Brandon and then around at the group. "Does anyone know what Brandon did wrong today?"

"Yeah, jumping on top of the pile," said Tem, rubbing the base of his neck.

"Hey Professor Walden, I was just defending my queen's honor," Brandon responded with a touch of arrogance in his voice.

"Wrong again!" and he struck Brandon's hand once more.

"Brandon, your job is to defend her honor, but you have a duty to counsel and provide advice to her as well. You could have gone to her and told her that David was being selfish and her own honor was at stake. She is as much a part of this kingdom as David. Instead, you decided to join in the fracas and subsequently embarrassed this entire Prince class. A simple disgrace from all of you!"

"What about Salil?" shot back Tem. "She wasn't Ms. Perfect now was she?"

"Let's ask Salil. What were you thinking while all this was going on?"

She hesitated. And then she spoke.

"I was thinking how easy it would have been to kill David while they all were distracted."

∞∞ ∞ ∞∞

That night, following the football game, Salil returned to her hidden passageway. She needed some time to reflect on what Professor Walden had said. Gazing upon the stars on the clear summer night, she thought to herself more and more that the other Princes were a force that would only get stronger as the years passed by. Which meant that she herself had to become stronger as well. She now knew that they all would be working together to prevent her from her ultimate duty. One against six. "Assassins Walk the Path Alone," she read those words every time she journeyed down her secret corridor. Each time believing she gained a deeper insight from the words of Rigor Mortisis.

Chapter 40

On the following night, while everyone else was sound asleep, Sultan Assassin Kass sneaked out of her room and went to Professor Xalvador's laboratory classroom on the academic side of campus. She would have to work quickly. The door was unlocked, and inside she found the barrel of experimental fire powder. Kass loaded as much as she could carry into a huge sack and heaved it over her shoulder. She headed back to the Royal Residence Hall.

When she reached the front entrance, she looked around to make sure no one was watching. She cut a small hole in one corner of the sack, to allow the powder to flow out. Then she took off, running around the building as fast as she could. Kass was able to make three complete spirals around the Royal Residence Hall before the sack was emptied. She went back to Xalvador's classroom to collect more.

This time she did not run around outside, she made her way inside the building and unpinned the hole in her bag, allowing the fire powder to again seep out. She moved through the first floor and secured the Primos' door shut with a hook on the outside. On to the other floors she went, dispensing the combustible and double-checking to make sure the suite doors were locked from the outside with additional hooks. She skipped the sixth floor for the moment. The seventh floor would be more challenging.

Since the Ascensions lived on the seventh floor and were next in line to inherit the throne, their suite always had two posted guards on the outside. Kass had planned this moment for months. Prior to this night, she began secretly seeing one of the evening guards.

She walked quietly up the stairs, he was more on guard for her arrival than anything that might have to do with protecting the Ascensions. There she was. And then she was gone.

"Hey, I'll be back, I'm going to the toilet."

"Yeah, man, hurry back, god knows what you do in there, it takes you so long sometimes."

Off he went, down the stairs to the Sultan floor to meet with Kass. She grabbed his hand and pulled him into a dark corner. She didn't say a word.

"Oh, this is new, will I finally get to kiss the great and beautiful Kass?"

She pulled him close and said, "Wait, take off my mask."

As he was about to undo the clasp, Kass thrusted a knife into his stomach, and up toward his heart. Her eyes were cold and the look on his face was of someone betrayed, tricked and dying. Blood trickled out of his mouth, he was choking as the internal bleeding sealed his fate. Kass mechanically removed the knife from his torso and walked back to the Ascension Suite. This time, she deliberately made stomping sounds so the other guard would hear her.

"Oh, you're back! Took you long enough," said the second guard upon hearing the footsteps coming toward him. "Come on, I have to go also, come watch the bloody door!"

But it was not his guardmate. It was Kass, in her mask and moving like a predator. As soon as his eyes could make out who it was coming out of the darkness, he was hit by a dagger in his neck. He made no sound other than his lifeless body hitting the floor. Kass stepped easily over his body with her two sacks and secured the door to the Ascension Suite using one of the hooks.

She made it back to her own suite and entered her room, gathered a few personal items and made her way back outside the suite to the Sultans' common area. She turned around, secured the final door with the hooks and walked outside.

With her sword in one hand, she swiped at the stone and created a spark, igniting the fire powder. A spiral ring of flames started blazing on the outermost circle, racing around the first circle she had made going around the building. Then it continued to the middle circle and to the innermost circle.

The flames grew higher as the fire burned longer. By the time the second loop was completed, the outermost circle had grown to over ten meters, and when the third circle was complete it was over thirty meters high and burning hotter. Then, the fire shot inside the Royal Residence Hall, right toward where the baby Primos slept quietly in their cribs.

In the Prince suite, everyone was fast asleep as smoke curled into the common area, rising in slow motion toward the ceiling. Tem was the first one to wake, confused by his sense of smell. Was he dreaming? He smelled smoke, but not the smoke of wood fire or grilling meat or anything else familiar to him. He sat on his bed and rubbed his eyes a little too hard with the knuckles. "Ow!" He cried out a little in spite of himself and sniffed the air. No, definitely not dreaming. He opened his bedroom door to find the suite filled with smoke from eye level to ceiling. He grabbed his sword and secured it at his waist.

"David! Professor! Everyone! Wake up! Smoke! Fire! Fire! David!"

Tem quickly went to David's room and woke him up. Cedric was the first out of his room, along with the professor. They both were tall enough that the smoke filled their lungs as soon as they opened their doors. They coughed deeply.

Nara, Ava and Brandon were the next to leave their rooms.

"Children, stay low, come quickly to me." Walden tried to yell, but his voice was rough and cracking. He bent low so he could breathe cleaner air.

Salil came out of her room last. She had her mask on and was fully dressed. Assassins learned to be always dressed, even at bedtime, so that at any moment they could move on from wherever they might be. She had her swords tied at her sides. The other kids were dressed in their sleepwear. They huddled with Walden, just outside his room.

"Now listen, and do not panic. We are going to get out of here. I promise you. But everyone must stay calm." He looked quickly at each of their faces to make sure he had their attention and understanding. "Cedric, I want you to go to the sink and soak some towels in water. Hurry, child! The rest of you wait right here. And stay low!"

Professor Walden moved quickly to the exit door of the suite and placed his open palm against it. It was hot to his touch, but nevertheless he decided to open it. It was locked! He pushed and pushed with all his strength, but somehow it was secured from the outside. He raced to the window and pushed it open, only to be met with a screaming wall of flames, burning the right side of his face. They were trapped.

The Princes were huddled in the corner, choking on smoke and choking back tears, when Cedric returned with the soaked towels.

"Where's the professor?"

"He left us! He just left us here!" It was never a good sign when David whined.

"We're all going to die!" Ava started to cry.

"No! We're not. The professor will get us out of here," Cedric said.

David, Ava and Nara cried, smoke was filling the room and they had to be in a seated position, as the only fresh air remained just above the floor.

The professor returned. His expression gave no confidence to the children. He looked scared. Their faces fell and Ava, Nara and David burst into a fresh round of tears. Brandon did his best to stay calm and cool, but he was afraid also.

"Cedric and Tem, I need you two to help me push down

the entrance door." He paused, making sure there was no panic and that he had their attention. "Listen to me carefully, because we are going to have to do this standing up. You will stay low a few moments longer and take a couple of deep breaths—exhale fully, inhale completely, and repeat, filling your lungs to capacity with this good air—and then rise and follow me." He checked their faces for comprehension. It seemed to be all good. They were good boys and would be good men. He indulged himself just a moment to love and admire them, then he continued speaking. "I will give you a count, one-two-three, and on three we will all push the door together. Just two times only, then we have to get back low to take a breath. Ok? Do not breathe in the smoke."

"Ok, got it."

"Yes, professor."

"The rest of you, put these wet towels over your heads and if it gets too smoky, breathe through the towels." He was speaking to some point on the wall between Nara and Brandon. He could not look at their faces. If there was fear or, worse, panic, he might not be able to go through with his plan to save them. "We will be right back. Everything is going to be ok."

The three of them went off toward the suite door, hearing other Royal students yelling for help. Ear-piercing, stomach-turning sounds. The sounds of people trying to escape death.

Salil knew they were doomed. There was nothing and no one to save them. On her hands and knees she crawled toward her room.

"Where are you going? The professor said stay here!" cried Nara.

"Salil!" But it was too late, Salil disappeared into the smoke.

Chapter 41

Outside the Royal Residence Hall, students, staff and professors came running, awakened by the sounds of screams in the night. Some stood and cried, others yelled for water. Impenetrable walls of fire surrounded the building, shooting almost to the roof. Three rings of fire blazing straight up like something from a nightmare. They saw students, still inside, opening windows and crying out for help. Just brief glimpses, as the flames were too hot for any of them to look out for more than a few seconds. They saw smoke pouring out open windows. One woman carrying a Primo baby ran to the front entrance, swathed in towels. She paused, right before the flames in the doorway and made a run for it, protecting the Primo baby as she ran. She'd by some miracle made it through the fire in the Residence Hall, but as she reached the innermost spiral of flames their bodies disappeared. Incinerated instantly.

On the penthouse floor, the Ascensions tried to lower a rope made of bed sheets knotted together. They threw the line out their window on the top floor, but as the rope reached the bottom, flames started climbing the line to the top. The Ascension Assassin tried to lower himself down the rope as the fire raced upward. The flames were faster and reached him only a few meters outside of his window. He could hold on no longer and fell to the ground, dead upon impact, his body quickly consumed by the fire.

There was an emergency fire squad on the campus, and they rushed to the building in horse-drawn wagons with several large barrels of water and began setting up hoses with hand-drawn pumps. They gathered in front of the Royal Residence Hall in a line. At the command of the captain, they began to pump water onto the flames.

"Focus the stream on the front entrance! We have to get inside," said the commander of the fire rescue squad. "Everyone, ready, now!" Heavy streams of water came out of the hoses, all focused on the front entrance. There were eight firefighters holding hoses, and they focused their streams of water several feet apart from—and parallel to—each other. Trying to break the wall of fire. To no avail. "We need more power! Come together, all streams together!" yelled the captain. At once all eight hoses focused their streams of water on one spot. This seemed to be working, creating a small gap in the fire.

Another fireman, dressed in full protective gear, ran toward the small gap. "I'm going in!" he yelled.

"No, wait!"

He ran at the first fire wall, the small gap where all the

water was focused, right into the center of the water. His courage, that of a true hero. He made it through the first wall of fire. But surprised to have made it through, he stopped, confronted by the second wall of fire. There was no place to go. He looked back at the gap he had run through, but it was gone. Just a solid wall of fire once more, same as the one before him. He felt the heat of the flames eating away at his protective gear. He gathered himself for another sprint. He could do it, make it inside. He took off running, head down, but couldn't make it through the second wall of flames. His body disappeared in a flurry of ash and smoke.

The firefighters on the outside kept trying to put more water on the fire, but it just wasn't working. They'd never seen anything like this. It was as if the fire was only burning hotter. They tried for over an hour, using up every last drop of water. One stubborn firefighter even yelled, "We need more water!" The chief paused for a moment and looked around at his young men and women doing their duty. He looked at all the children and adults, staff members and non-royal students, gathered around the building, crying, holding each other, turning their heads away. Some had formed a train line, carrying buckets of water to refill the barrels. His men and women were sweating, some were being treated for burns from having gotten too close to the flames. The captain's mind scanned the entire scene, to him it felt like everything was happening in slow motion. He looked back up at the Royal Residence Hall. It was consumed with fire. There were no more screams. Fire and smoke billowed out of every window. The night was bright with the flames from this magnificent inferno. There was nothing more that he could do, he knew when to admit defeat.

"No, that's it," he said, his voice breaking as he tried to maintain his composure. "Halt with the water. Cease pumping." He cleared his throat. "Cease pumping!" he commanded.

"No! We have to try to save them, we can't give up!" came a voice from one of his officers.

"No. We have to make sure the flames don't spread to the rest of the campus. Let's form a line and dig a trench around the building. I have no idea how long this fire will last. This isn't a rescue operation anymore, it will be recovery after the flames recede."

The crowd and the firefighters could not believe what they heard. Everyone was gone. Some people fell to the ground, overcome with grief and shock. Others came together and hugged each other. Some just stood, watching in disbelief. The future of Terrowin wiped out in one night.

Chapter 42

Salil took a deep breath, stood-up and walked right into the smoke, ignoring the professor's advice about staying low. She reasoned that she could reach her room fastest by walking, and her memory would serve her well. When she reached her room, the smoke was starting to fill the entire space, but she walked directly to her chest and grabbed a small pouch. An emergency pouch that she was taught all assassins should prepare and have ready at a moment's notice. She grabbed the letter from her parents and the unopened gift and placed them inside her pouch. She then dropped low to the floor, her face almost touching the dirt, to take in the last of the breathable air. She stood up and returned to the other children huddled together inside Professor Walden's room.

"Salil, you're back!" Nara's face, for a brief moment, had a smile on it, but she soon returned to the understanding of their situation. David was in the corner of the room, crying, saying he didn't want to die. Ava and Brandon sat quietly trying to comfort David. Salil didn't respond. She looked around the room quickly. "Where is everyone else?" she said.

"Gone! They left us here to die!" cried David. At that moment the professor, Tem and Cedric returned. Their faces were covered in soot from the smoke-filled air and they were both sweating and coughing. Their body language was telling. They had failed to open the door.

Professor Walden tried to comfort his charges. "Children, you must listen to me."

"No, listen to me," Salil said in a commanding voice. "I have a way out. But we must go now! Take hold of each other's hands and follow me. We have to run, there is no time left!"

Salil grabbed Nara's hand, who grabbed David, still cowering in the corner. The others followed suit, the professor took up the rear. Salil had spoken with so much confidence, even he believed her. They all ran to Salil's room. As they ran, they heard screams of children on the other floors. Salil lowered the rope down the passageway as she had done many nights before. No one could actually see what she was doing in the dark, but they knew she was doing something. She paused and lit a lantern, exposing the secret passage to the others.

"Ok, listen, you will have to climb down this rope to the bottom, it's not that far."

"Oh, my, I can't climb that, I'll never make it," cried Nara.

"Yes, you can, or stay here and die," was Salil's only response.

"Nara, my little queen. You can do it, just go ahead and think about David. He's the smallest here and I'm sure he's ready to go." The professor spoke, trying to give both Nara and

David some comforting words.

"Let me go first my lady," Brandon said with newfound courage. "And if you fall, I will be there to catch you." Nara smiled at Brandon's chivalry. Quickly securing the lantern to his back, he went down first, followed by Nara, David, Cedric, Ava and Tem. Salil and the professor were the last two.

"You go little Salil. And remember, stay strong and protect this group. You all are the last of the Royals, and you must survive."

"Professor, what's going on, what do you mean?"

"I think someone is trying to kill the future leadership of Terrowin. And they may have succeeded. Get your classmates to safety, and get out of Terrowin. Head south. Do you hear me? Head south beyond our borders and keep going."

"Professor, aren't you coming with us?" Salil did not fully comprehend what he was telling her. Emotions filled her body once again, and her voice broke as she pleaded with him to join them.

"No, I have to try to save who I can. Go child. Go! And remember, head south! Get out of Terrowin! Find a place called Provins, you will be safe there. Provins! Go!"

Salil made her way down the rope, pausing to look up to see if the professor had changed his mind. He was not following her. He went back to the suite entrance and tried once again to break down the door. She heard a loud bang. And another one. And one more accompanied by a loud growl from the professor. That was the last one. Then, silence. She looked up and saw flames above her. She lowered herself faster, understanding that her rope was not flameproof. A few meters from the ground, the rope snapped, and Salil fell to the bottom and crash-landed, the singed rope tumbling down after her.

When she reached the bottom, all the Princes were accounted for. There was a sack that had been thrown down by Salil before she went back to fetch her classmates. When she left them the first time, she not only went to her room, but also to everyone else's rooms, to grab the few articles of clothing she could carry. She packed them up and threw them down the hole.

"Where's the professor?" asked Tem, looking at Salil suspiciously.

"He's not coming with us."

"What do you mean, he's not coming with us? What did you do to him?"

Tem thought this fire must be the work of an assassin. Maybe Salil herself. He stepped closer to Salil, towering over her now. "So, you lure us down here, in your secret passageway, how convenient, and now what? You gonna kill us all down here in your assassin hideaway?" Tem drew his sword on Salil. In return, Salil drew her sword and assumed a defensive position.

Tem lunged at her with his sword, and with one move Salil dislodged it from his hand and held her sword to his neck. "You can die here if you wish," she said in a calm voice. Tem stood still and looked her in the eyes. Cedric ran between them.

"Tem, enough. If she wanted us dead she would have never come to retrieve us. This fire was not her work. It was probably designed to kill us all, her included." He took a breath. "Salil don't kill him now, maybe later, ok?" Cedric said with a wry smile, trying to diffuse the situation.

"Someone wants us dead," Ava cried. "What did I do to deserve to die?"

David started gasping for air, he was having an asthma attack.

"David, are you all right? Give him some air, give him some air!" yelled Tem, pushing everyone away from David. Nara ran to his side and gave Ava a stern look not to interfere.

"Relax David. It's going to be all right. Breathe, slowly. Relax." After a couple minutes, David managed to regain his composure and control his breathing.

"So, now what? What do we do?" asked Nara, still holding David close to her.

"We go south, the professor said to leave Terrowin and head south." Salil tossed the sack into the middle of the whole lot of them, turned on her heel and acted as if she was about to leave. "Change your clothes, and carry what you can."

She had grabbed whatever clothes she could in the short period of time. David's clothes consisted of semi-formal attire, a dress shirt, brown pants and a blue blazer-type jacket. Cedric also had a brown blazer, pants and a green sweater. Tem had jeans, along with a polo shirt, while Brandon had a button-down shirt with oversize collar, bright, with many patterns. Ava had a white dress with long sleeves, and Nara a longer dress, heavy and made of expensive satin.

As they dressed in the strange cavernous room, Cedric said, "Ok, so, where are we going? Just south?"

"Provins. The professor said go to Provins."

"Provins, never heard of it." Cedric looked around the group. They were exhausted, and all dressed up.

"Not exactly traveling clothes," he remarked as they walked down the narrow passageway toward the exit on the mountain.

Chapter 43

The sun was rising at the School. The firefighters and students dug a trench a meter deep and three meters wide around the entire Royal Residence Hall. They succeeded in containing the fire, which burned for a few more hours. They were exhausted, and many of them took seats within the trench, waiting for the fire to go out so they could begin recovery of the bodies. Students, staff and professors came, bringing food and drinks. They also brought flowers, and a shrine was beginning to form in front of the building. Handwritten notes and signs read: "Lost but not forgotten." "Gone too soon. May you rest in peace." "We will always have you in our hearts, minds and souls."

Kass and Professor Xalvador appeared and came running toward the smoldering building. People approached them in disbelief. "You made it out! You're alive! Are there others with you?" cried people from the crowd, happy to see some survivors.

"What happened here," Professor Xalvador said in a

strong commanding voice. "Who's in charge?"

"Sir, I am," the fire chief stood and walked toward them both. "There was this fire, walls of fire. A fire I've never come across before in my life. It burned so hot. We tried, we tried water, we tried to save them—" He broke down and started crying.

"Save who? Tell me what happened. Control yourself."

"All of them, sir. All of the Royals."

"Who did this? Who's leading the investigation?"

"We were just about to go inside and do recovery. The fire has just about burned itself out."

"No! No one goes inside that building until I check things out, you understand me? Have your men wait here."

"Yes, sir."

"Kass, with me."

They entered the smoldering remains of the Royal Residence Hall, Kass following her instructor. Once inside, they removed their masks and headed toward the Primo sleeping quarters. "The fire worked just as planned," Xalvador said. "Did anyone see you?"

"No. I watched it from a distance. It burned really well. There was no stopping it."

"Did anyone escape?"

"Not that I saw."

"Ok, we have to make sure that all the Royals are accounted for. There are some crafty individuals here, so we have to be thorough. Come, let's count the bodies. Royals only." He paused. "I'll go check the Ascension floor, that's the most important group. You start with the Primos. And remember to grab the hooks from the doors. We have to cover our tracks."

Kass walked to the Primo section and noticed that the door was completely burned away. The fire had eventually reached inside the room. The hook lay on the floor and she picked it up and put it in her bag. Looking around the room she saw nothing but charred items. She found a stack of burned bodies in one corner of the farthest closet. A big twisted mass piled high, in the form of a dome. She removed the bodies from the pile. Some bones, arms and legs, burnt to a crisp, broke off completely as she tugged at them. The smell was overwhelming, but Kass remained true to her duty. As she pulled the remains off the pile, in the middle were several white towels that had not been burned, covering a smaller mass. She removed the towels, one by one, to uncover the Primo babies. Their bodies completely intact and the color within their skin remained. They looked like they were all just sleeping huddled together. No burns. But no life remained inside them. They had expired from smoke inhalation. Kass counted six of them, remembering she saw one carried out by a nurse and consumed by the fire.

Xalvador reached the Ascension Hall on the top floor. Outside the suite he saw the charred remains of the two guards Kass had killed. He walked into the suite to count the bodies. They were all gathered around the Ascension King. One body was missing. He walked over to the window, looked down to the ground and saw the Ascension Assassin's body at the bottom. His bones were cracked and in a distorted position, nothing of his flesh remained. He died from the fall, but his body was post-mortem mummified by the intense heat from the fire.

As they each made their way through the separate floors, counting bodies, they met at the Prince suite. "All accounted for thus far, except one Pharaoh," said Kass. "But, I'm sure the little one didn't make it."

"Little kids have a tendency to panic in these situations, his or her body could be anywhere, or even simply disintegrated. The fire did burn hotter than expected," Xalvador replied.

He walked into the Prince suite. "Such a shame, I liked this Prince class, that little Salil showed such promise." His voice sounded as he might have felt some regret over killing them. Kass, however, was clearly annoyed at the compliment Xalvador gave Salil. "Let's see how they died," she said as she walked past him to further investigate.

They found Professor Walden's charred remains on the floor, next to where the door had been burned completely away, the hook by his body. There were burned towels in the corner of his room, but no sign of any other bodies. They walked from room to room in the suite, searching the corners and closets. Still, no sign of any of the Princes. They made their way to Salil's room and in the corner found her secret passage.

Xalvador looked down the hole. He had never seen this before. "Salil, you little devil, you," he murmured. "Go down and find out what's there, then kill them."

Kass searched for something to lower herself down the passageway with. She tied several unburnt bed sheets together and went down. Xalvador impatiently waited for her return. When she came back, he asked, "So, did you find them?"

"No, there's some sorta tunnel that goes very far down, there were clothes in the main room down there, but no sign of them," Kass stated, matter-of-factly. "I think you should see what's down there," she added.

"Later, we don't have time right now. I have to figure this out."

He stood for a moment and thought. "Ok, here's what we will do, gather all the bodies we can find and assemble them on the first floor. Let's cover up this passageway with this, this dirt. We will tell everyone that we found all the bodies there were, that everyone else was completely incinerated. The entire Prince class, the only body we could find was Professor Walden."

"Ok. But what about them?"

"When the time is right, you will hunt them down and kill them. We have a lot to do, let's get started."

"Yes, sir."

"Let's get the bodies downstairs."

They worked together, quickly enough so as to not arouse any suspicion from the fire chief and others gathered outside the entrance awaiting their return. Finally, all the charred remains were assembled in the front entrance. They walked outside together, toward the fire chief.

"Is there anyone alive in there?"

"No, they are all gone. We gathered the bodies downstairs, some are unrecognizable. Some were completely incinerated and not recoverable." The fire chief shook his head back and forth and held it low. He then said, "May I ask, sir, where were you and my lady tonight?"

Upon being questioned, Xalvador quickly smacked the fire chief on the side of his face and took a step closer to him, towering over him.

"How dare you ask me a question like that at a time like this. I just lost my friends and colleagues, not to mention the children who perished."

"I'm sorry, sir, I understand."

"But if you must know, Kass was doing some advanced training under my direction last night in the forest. It's an assassin tradition, way above your pay grade. Understand?"

"Yes, I understand."

"Now you do your job, and find out who did this."

"Yes, sir."

"I must dispatch word to the Capital about this tragedy immediately. Kass! Find me the Royal messenger!"

Chapter 44

It was early dawn when the Princes reached the cave opening. The sky was a dark orange as the sun was rising, clear except for a few charcoal smudges of cloud scattered about. As they made their way down the rope onto the beach they could see a wall of black smoke still rising from the direction of the School.

"Do you think anyone survived?" asked Nara.

"I don't think so," replied Cedric. "Come on, we must keep moving."

They traveled south, along the rocky shore, in single file. Tem and Cedric leading the way, with Nara, David, Ava and Brandon walking single file behind them. Salil took up the rear, mostly because she felt that she was not wanted but also because she had no interest in small talk with the rest of the group. They walked for hours, past noon, keeping a pace slow enough for David to keep up.

"Are we there yet? I'm hungry!" David called.

"David! Keep your mouth shut, we have to keep moving."

Cedric never had patience for the Prince King's whining, but especially not today.

"Hey, give him a break. We've been walking for hours and we need to start thinking about food and shelter for the night," Tem answered for David.

"Well, look around at where we are," Cedric said. "I don't see a café with a buffet laid out for us right now." He spread his hands out dramatically and then dropped them to his sides in a huff. "Just keep walking." They had made it past the rocky outcroppings and onto the sandy part of the beach. It was sparkling black volcanic sand, reaching all the way to the mountains off in the distance to the east.

"What are we going to do for food? Water?" Ava flapped her arms about. "We're going to die out here!"

"Calm down, we are not going to die," answered Cedric, in an attempt to sound convincing.

"Ok, well, you're the genius of the group, Mr. Advisor." Ava wiggled her fingers in his face and he swatted her away. "What should we do?"

Salil stood off to the side, silent and still.

"Well, ummmm, there, we have to go to the mountains, there must be a cave or cliff somewhere up there where we can rest," Cedric said, although he did not quite believe it himself.

"Here, have some of this, this is all I have," Salil interrupted and stepped forward to offer a dry, thick cracker to David. It was something all assassins learn to make, from water, millet or barley flour and salt. They call it "molar bread," because it is so hard you can't bite it with your front teeth. Molar bread is far from delicious, but a few mouthfuls would satisfy any hunger for almost a full day. Salil's emergency pouch had enough molar bread and water to last her about three to five days if she were alone.

"Thank you Salil!" David gave a sly smile to Cedric as he bit down on the hard cracker.

"Oh, so you're holding out on the group now? Let's see what else you have." Tem reached out to try to grab the bag, but Salil moved backwards. Cedric grabbed him in a bear hug before he could take another step. "Let go of me Cedric!" shouted Tem. "If we are the last of the Royals, then we all know that David is our king, and we must protect him." Even when he should have been exhausted and confused, Tem still put David first. "It's our duty, it's my duty, to keep him alive. No matter what! You understand me? And if she has food and water to keep him alive, I'll take it from her—or anyone else in this group!" Tem pushed Cedric aside and drew his sword, placing the tip against Cedric's neck. "You do your duty, and I'll do mine." He pressed the sword ever so slightly, but enough that a bead of blood emerged at Cedric's throat.

"Stop you guys, please! Stop this now," cried Nara, tears running down her face.

Salil stood there, without making a sound. Then she spoke, "Here, have some water. I don't have much." She held out the canteen to Tem. Tem walked over and snatched the water from her hand. He gave it to David, who was still busily chewing on his molar bread, oblivious to all the drama surrounding him.

"Oh, thanks, this stuff is sure dry," he said, with a wad of saliva-laced bread in his mouth. He grinned and pointed to the ocean. "Man, look at all that water! What I wouldn't give for some... see-food!" he said, and then opened his mouth, revealing the half-chewed cracker bread in his mouth.

"Ewww, David you're so disgusting!" yelled Ava.

"Oh, come on man! Really!" said Cedric.

But David had broken the tension in the group, and Tem withdrew his sword, laughing with Brandon at David's little antic. David took a drink from one of the canteens Salil had and passed the water first to Nara, who then passed it to Tem. Cedric, Ava and Brandon all had a turn. Salil was last to drink, and only a few drops remained after they all had their portions.

Cedric looked around. "Come on, we must keep moving to find shelter for tonight."

"Yeah, and maybe some see-food!" Ava yelled, as she showed her mouthful of chewed molar bread back to David.

"Oh, yuck!" David seemed both delighted and offended.

"That's sooo not ladylike. Gross." Nara blew out a loud breath and continued walking.

They walked toward the mountain cliffs to the east, still maintaining a southern heading. Cedric led the way.

The energy provided by Salil's offering allowed them to continue until almost dusk. They reached a rocky outcrop at the base of one of the mountains. Walking along the rock line, they explored each corner, crevasse and cave in search of an adequate place to sleep for the night.

"Finally! Hey, guys, I think this will do." Cedric had found a cave nestled in the mountain boulders. It was dark, but it was dry, with no sign of bats or snakes. It seemed as if there was enough room to fit everyone inside comfortably. Upon taking one look inside the dark space Nara started, "I'm not going in there."

"Me either," Ava answered quickly.

"It will be fine." Tem was being uncharacteristically patient with the girls, but he knew David would not be safe unless they all stayed together as harmoniously as possible. "Nara, Ava. Watch, I'll show you."

"Hey, I'll show them," said Brandon, pushing Tem aside and trying to be the first to enter the cave. They jostled back and forth for a moment and then went inside together, disappearing around a curve.

"See, nothing in here, it's just dark. Come on ladies, it will be fine." Brandon's voice echoed from within the cave, deep enough inside that neither boy could be seen.

"Arghh! Help me!" yelled Tem. They heard a flurry of footsteps and everyone on the outside took a few hurried steps backward.

"Ayyy!" Tem came running out of the cave first. Brandon was right on his heels.

"Run! Run!" Tem bellowed.

Just then, two giant mighawks came flying out of the cave, screeching as they circled the entrance in a menacing manner. The wingspan of each bird was almost five meters wide. Tem kept running and was halfway to the beach, not looking back.

Brandon stopped to watch with the rest of the Princes. Then, right behind the birds, toddling clumsily, was their baby, who had not yet learned how to fly. The adult mighawks swooped around and dove down right at the entrance of the cave, landing in front of their baby. The birds towered over the children, the baby was a little smaller than David. They both squawked together. The mother approached the little one from behind and gave her a nudge. The father looked hard at the baby and then took off again. The baby flapped its wings as best it could, hopping back and forth from one leg to the other, trying to take off, mom nudging her closer to the edge of the cliff.

Meanwhile, Tem was still running down the mountain, slipping on rocks and soil and working hard to stay upright, not knowing what had followed him out of the cave.

The mother took off circling the cave entrance, and both parents squealed in the air in unison, as if again calling. Two more tries, and then baby took flight, unsteady and unbalanced, but airborne.

"How cool," David said breathlessly, but in a good sort of breathless way. "Radical!"

"Totally," Ava said in agreement. They all looked around then and saw Tem still running toward the beach.

"And he's your great protector?" Nara said to David with a perfect drawl and eye roll. The other kids burst out laughing.

"Brandon," Cedric said, "Go get him. Please?"

"Tem! Tem!" Brandon took off down the mountain.

"Salil, do you know how to make fire?" Cedric was not one

to be distracted from the task at hand, even by the unexpected and thoroughly entertaining display he had just witnessed.

"Yes."

"Great, we can gather some firewood. Ava, will you go find some bedding for us, and David and Nara, you can go with her if you like. Leaves, and any grass you can find. Hurry, please, before it gets dark."

They all rushed off, and reconvened back at the cave. Salil and Cedric brought kindling and firewood and built a fire just outside the entrance of the cave, while the others fashioned bedding from the brush and pine needles. Ava and Nara found some purple flowers to decorate their beds, and measured distance with hands and feet to ensure each was sufficiently spaced apart from the other.

"Well," Cedric started in with his pointy-headed Mr. Reasonable tone. "I think it might get a little cold tonight, and we may need to sleep closer together." Nara curled her lips and widened her eyes, but he continued. "To conserve our body heat. I think we should push these closer together."

"Ewww! I'm not sleeping next to David, or you or any of you boys!"

"Suit yourself Ms. Queen, I'll keep David warm tonight," Ava said, as she gave a smile to David. Still trying to one-up Nara when it came to David.

"My queen," Brandon reached his hand out to her. "I will protect you and keep you warm tonight."

Nara folded her arms across her chest. "Over my dead body."

"Oh, yuck," David's voice cracked and wheezed ever so slightly. "I'm not sleeping next to a girl."

"Ok, ok," Cedric knew when he was defeated. "I just hope we don't freeze to death."

Salil tended the fire and the group settled in for their first night alone, outside the comforts of the School. Beds of leaves and grass lay around the cave, with the light from the fire illuminating the inside. Cedric joined Salil outside when the others went to sleep.

"So, how's the fire going? Do we need more wood?"

"No," Salil said bluntly.

"Hey, listen, I'm not against you here. We need to stay together. You saved us, and I just wanted to say thank you. So, who do you think did this? Why did they want to kill all the Royals?" At that moment, a weary looking David came walking up and joined them around the fire, instinctively holding out his hands to warm them.

"I can't sleep, what are you two talking about?"

"We were just talking about why someone would want to kill everyone," said Cedric.

"Well, I've been taught that in our history, someone always wants to kill the king. So, that's why we have assassins, that's why we have Salil. To take away the desire of any people who might think they should kill the king. So, it has to be someone on the inside." He said it matter-of-factly, and sounding rather intelligent. For David.

"But everyone was in the Royal Residence Hall when the fire was started. As far as we know, all the other Royals were killed in the fire," Cedric said, scratching his head like his fingers were a rake, trying to figure out the puzzle before him.

David continued, "Well, I'm sure by now King Richard and his advisors are trying to figure out who did this and what the next steps are."

"Yes, but we don't know. We don't know anything yet. So, we just walk south like Professor Walden said." Salil's words were short and cold. Her manner abrupt as always. She stood up and walked away. David hurried after her.

"Salil, your secret cave was really cool! Thanks for showing us," he whispered to her. Salil did not respond.

The boys returned to their beds, David was placed between Tem and Cedric. After a few moments, he whispered to Cedric, "King Richard is a wise king, I'm sure he will know what to do and then we can return home," as he turned to fall back asleep.

Cedric sighed in the dark. "I hope so, David. I hope so."

Chapter 45

The fire chief and his workers were busy walking around the Royal Residence Hall, collecting evidence and taking samples. Doors were burned, windows blacked out and the stones of the building themselves were sooty and singed. There was a rope around the building to keep people out, and you could see the three charred spiral rings on the ground circling the building. The rings were darker than the surrounding area, sinister-looking and clearly visible. Around noon, the bodies of the dead Royals and their professors were being carried away on stretchers and blankets. Groups of people gathered outside with flowers and signs. Xalvador was there with all the other students and professors, doing his best to console them, telling them he would find out what happened and that no stone would go unturned.

Kass went to Xalvador's classroom to return the hooks and burn the sack she used to carry the fire powder. The slight residue on the leather made that a rather exciting little task! But that was just her nerves, the classroom had remnants of every sort of fire already: twisted scraps of metal, charred wood cinders, and even some blackened pottery shards. She looked around the room to make sure nothing was out of place. The barrel of experimental fire powder was tucked in the corner. She replaced the lid and returned to Xalvador, who was still outside masterfully consoling students, staff and administration.

As soon as Kass was at Xalvador's side, and before she could even breathe a sigh of relief, a messenger from the Royal Palace approached the front entrance gates to the School.

"News from the Capital! News from the Capital!" the messenger shouted as he rode his horse impressively through the front entrance. Terrowin skimped on nothing, and even the official messengers did not disappoint. He glanced briefly at the charred, smoking building, but he was just a messenger. He hopped off his steed like a gymnast and walked to the front of the Main Academic Hall. "News from the Capital!" he hollered, and a crowd formed around him as smoothly and inexplicably as ants, wondering what news could be forthcoming from the Capital.

"Hear ye, hear ye. All those present. Last night, King Richard and Queen Isis were assassinated as they slept. The advisor, protector, King Richard's mistress and the Lady Isis's lover were also murdered in cold blood. Assassin Leonardo, implicated in their deaths, was found dead outside the castle walls! From this moment forth, Ascension King William and the entire Ascension class shall assume their rightful responsibilities as rulers of Terrowin, and they are to accompany me straightaway, back to the Capital, according to the Terrowin Constitution."

The crowd stood in silence, not believing what they just heard. Murmurs, then wails, then screams came from those assembled.

"Haven't you heard, all the Royals are dead?"

"We have no king!"

"God save Terrowin!"

"The king is dead!"

"There's no one to lead us now."

"Is there anyone left?"

"Whatever shall we do?"

Xalvador was on. He lived for this shit. He just sank to his knees and dramatically put his hands over his mask. Kass placed a hand on his shoulder, the other cupping his elbow, and helped him back up. He took a slow, deep breath and addressed the messenger.

"Good herald, sir. All of the Royals perished last night in a fire whilst they slept." He swayed a bit as though his knees might buckle, Kass steadying him. "There is no Ascension class," a sob caught in his throat. "There are no Royal classes left." He let out a pitiful yowl like a kitten might make.

At first the messenger seemed confused by what he heard. He had been told to collect the Ascension class and ferry them to the Capital as soon as possible. He was neither prepared nor equipped to deal with any other contingency plans. He looked again at the smoldering building, and Xalvador touched his chest and spoke with authority.

"You shall take me back to the Capital in two days. As is plainly evident, I have a responsibility first to look after the students and oversee the investigation of this tragic fire. Once I have tended to my duties here, I shall ride back with you to the Capital and we will figure out how to proceed."

"But, I'm not sure that's protocol."

"Is there any protocol for this situation?"

"I, ummm, I guess not," the messenger stammered a bit before remembering his position. He straightened himself fully, even throwing his shoulders back with extra emphasis. "Sir, yes sir, in two days we shall return to the Capital."

Xalvador then returned to the center steps to address the ever-growing crowd. "Students, staff, administration. Today we have experienced the single greatest tragedy in Terrowin history. Let us bow our heads for a moment of silence."

Xalvador was not sure how long a moment should last, so he recalled a memory of Leonardo's kitchen the night before. There was a counter beside the sink, an island in the middle of the room, and a rolling cart by the pantry door. All the surfaces were covered with freshly prepared sweets. Cherry tarts, lemon squares dusted with sugar that looked like snow, egg cream smelling of lavender, a cake—oh yes the cake had been rum-soaked and generously adorned with coconut, little brown sugar drops for sucking, vanilla cookies that would melt in your mouth, tiny pies filled with pecans, something banana, what could that have been? Oh, surely that was enough time for a moment of silence. He lifted his head and continued to speak.

"Our reigning king, along with all of the Royals here at the School, has been killed. As of now, I shall assume responsibilities here and will return to the Capital in two days. School is suspended and will be closed until further notice. Please let us take tonight to remember our fallen heroes with a candlelight vigil in their honor." Xalvador was such a statesman. No one questioned him at this moment, people still in shock from the dual tragedies. That night, around the blackened remains of the Royal Residence Hall, people gathered, lit candles and shared stories and tears in honor of their fallen comrades.

The Terrowin Times

KING RICHARD AND QUEEN ISIS ASSASSINATED!
All Royals Killed in Superfire at Royal Ascension School

Last night a double tragedy struck Terrowin. King Richard and Queen Isis were murdered as they slept at the Royal Palace. Protector Sheila, Advisor Malcolm and the king and queen's lovers were also killed last night. Police are still conducting their investigation, but inside sources indicate that the killings could only be the work of Assassin Leonardo, who was also killed last night, apparently by one of the king's guards.

Allegedly, Assassin Leonardo had been working as the Royal Palace Master Pastry Chef for the past two years, under the assumed name of Michal. No one ever suspected that Chef Michal was a wolf in sheep's clothing.

"Michal was a very nice guy and he made wonderful desserts. I never once thought he was the assassin. I mean, he was handy with a knife, but that was for cutting his fabulous hummingbird cake, not killing people," said one of the sous chefs who worked at the Royal Palace.

In a double tragedy, which has rendered Terrowin effectively leaderless, a fire at the Royal Ascension School's Royal Residence Hall killed all current Royals and their professors, including wiping out the Ascension class. At approximately 3:22 a.m. the blaze was seen surrounding the Royal Residence Hall. Firefighters responded immediately, but their efforts could neither contain nor extinguish the fire. Witnesses recount the terrible blaze from which no one escaped:

"The Ascensions tried to climb out their window on the top floor, but the fire was too hot. There was nothing we could do for them," said Fire Chief Pendleton.

The only remaining Royal is Sultan Assassin Kass. Assassin Professor Xalvador also survived this terrible tragedy and will be returning to the Capital to conduct funeral services for the king and queen and their administration, and also for the Royals who succumbed to the flame and smoke.

$\mathcal{C}$hapter 46

The night of the fire at the Royal Residence Hall, King Richard was in the Capital anticipating a quiet evening with his mistress. As the queen, his protector, advisor and the queen's lover prepared to sleep in their suites, tucked away in the Palace, an unanticipated, undetected danger had infiltrated their most sacred sleeping quarters. Assassin Leonardo, a master of disguise and master chef, had taken more than a year to secure a position within the Palace as a pastry chef, under the name Michal. He'd killed the previous pastry chef as part of his scheme to enter into the king's chambers and had since been catering to King Richard and his innermost cabinet with impressive desserts. The king's favorite, rum-soaked pound cake.

As he prepared the daily specialties, he waited for the day when he would be able to complete his life's mission. He could not poison him, for that would expose him to capture. For over two years he worked diligently, filling the bellies of King Richard, his queen and all their guests with his delectable desserts.

Prior to the night of the fire at the School, Assassin Leonardo received an anonymous note instructing him to meet at midnight, outside the walls of the Palace. The very night the fire would be set at the School. The note threatened to expose him and his scheme as an assassin if he did not comply. So Assassin Leonardo secretly left the Palace to meet the unknown party.

They met down in a ravine, below the darkest side of the Castle.

"How did you get out without anyone seeing you?" said the mystery person—a man, wearing a mask.

"Well, that's pretty easy, as long as I'm wearing my official uniform, no one in the Castle asks questions, and there's always a gap in the security, so I just climbed over the wall. But, what is it you want to help me with?"

"How close are you to killing the king?"

"Well, I am on the inside, so there's that, but I'm still trying to figure out how to escape after the deed is done."

"I see."

"So, you're here to try to help me with my mission? You have any ideas? Hey, who are you?"

"Yes. I have ideas." At that moment a knife was plunged into Leonardo's innards, killing him instantly as it thrusted upward, bursting his heart. "Just keep quiet as you die," Professor Xalvador said.

Xalvador took Leonardo's clothes for himself and left his body there, in the dark, for someone to find later.

Xalvador climbed most of the way up the Palace wall, wearing the official chef's uniform, and waited for the patrols to pass by before pulling himself over the top of the wall. He made his way to the kitchen, where there was a delightful assortment of cookies, pies and cakes. He piled two plates with cherry tarts, pecan tassies, vanilla drop cookies and a few slices of an especially scrumptious looking pound cake and walked down toward King Richard's mistress's suite.

The guards stopped him as he approached.

"The king has requested some desserts for the lady," he said.

"Where is Chef Michal?"

"I'm his apprentice, Gustave. He's downstairs. I could get him if you want, although, it took longer than usual to make this for the king and I'd hate to make him wait any longer."

"Straightaway," and the guards opened the door to the room. They both were sleeping under the blankets of a magnificent bedroom suite. Xalvador placed the dessert tray down by the door and walked over. He pulled a sword from beneath his clothes and stood at the edge of the bed, watching the two sleep nestled together.

"It's the wrong king, but you will have to do." Xalvador thrust his sword into both of them simultaneously and covered any noises they might have made with one of the large pillows on the bed. He wiped his blade on a coverlet and stopped to place the desserts on a little table beneath the window. He tucked the tray under his arm and walked out the door.

"Have a good night sir," said the guards as he walked

away.

"Not as good as those two! Looks like they may be sleeping in late tomorrow." The guards laughed.

Xalvador entered the rooms of the others all the same way. That evening he killed them all, the queen, protector, advisor and queen's lover. The entire current administration. Knowing that it takes about five hours by horseback to reach the School from the Capital, he set off in the early morning to meet Kass in the forest. He was beside himself with anticipation and did not know how he could wait that long for news of the fire, of his success. The king's body would not be discovered until dawn.

Chapter 47

When the Princes woke, they found their bodies were cuddled together, trying to keep warm. The fire was smoking, but not providing any heat.

They continued to head south, walking at a steady pace, eating the molar bread and drinking the last of Salil's water.

Over the next few days, the Princes followed the shoreline, stopping each night to make shelter and gather any edibles and water they could find. Along the way, there were several freshwater streams leading to the ocean. They sometimes caught fish and found clams, crabs and the occasional lobster. They ate seaweed from the ocean when they could find it. In fact there were many days where seaweed was their only meal.

Some days were good, most were bad. It was a game of ultimate survival for the Princes, and they were barely making it. But they kept walking farther and farther south.

Chapter 48

Two days after the fire at the Royal Residence Hall, Xalvador and Kass rode along in the first of a line of horse-drawn carriages exiting the School on their way to the Capital. Behind them were the bodies of the Royal students who had perished in the fire. Each Royal had his or her own carriage, which bore the name of their class and title in white letters on the black cloth of the coach cover. Large sprays of flowers lay on top of the coaches. And farther behind them were the remaining students and faculty, riding slowly in a procession.

It was an overcast day, with steely skies and a steady rain. Gloomy. A sign was posted on the outside gate entrance to the School, "Closed Until Further Notice."

"My dear Kass," said Xalvador, grabbing hold of Kass's hand. "It is our time at last. Everything I told you, everything we dreamed about for the past couple of years, is right before our eyes." Kass almost smiled beneath her mask.

"What about the Princes?" Kass asked, eager to go hunt them down.

"They are mere children. They won't get far. We must be patient. We are the last remaining Royals, and the country needs us now more than ever. Patience, my dear."

"Yes, sir."

It took them several hours to reach the Capital. People were lined up alongside the road, placing flowers on the horses' manes, on the doors of the coaches, even in the spokes of the carriage wheels as they arrived in the Capital city. White rose petals rained down, filling the street leading up to the Capital building, which was adjacent the Royal Hospital. Everyone was there waiting to pay their respects to the fallen Royals.

Xalvador's carriage stopped behind seven others that were already lined up on a red carpet in front of the Capital building. Those seven carried the bodies of King Richard and His Royal Cabinet. They were also covered with black cloth but did not carry their names, adorned instead with gold lining. A small gold crown was woven into the black cover of King Richard's carriage and there was one for the queen as well. Guards stood around the carriages in full salute. Enormous floral wreaths were along the side, facing the crowd.

Xalvador and Kass exited the coach and made their way up the steps. At the top, King Richard's parents, along with the parents of all Royals who perished, stood waiting to receive them. Most of the families wore black, some of the men had dark shades over their eyes, while some of the women wore black veils to cover their tear-soaked faces. They held up black umbrellas to shield them from the rain. Xalvador greeted the king and queen's parents first.

"King Richard's mother and father!" called the announcer as Xalvador approached them. The crowd applauded, not sure if the applause was appropriate, but wanting to show their appreciation.

"I'm so sorry for your loss, madam. Richard was a great and honorable king," he whispered to King Richard's mother.

She hugged him tightly and said, "Thank you. And thank God you survived. We all need your strength now."

On this ceremony went, with the announcement of each of the deceased within the Royal classes. The assassin's parents were not announced, but each assassin was announced and the crowd showed equal appreciation and applause.

"Prince King David and his parents!" announced the speaker. Xalvador and Kass greeted them. Kass kept repeating the same phrase: "I'm sorry for your loss." She would not shake their hands, and only lowered her head. This was not her arena.

"Prince Assassin Salil!"

In the crowd were Gabriel and Savanna, Salil's parents. They had been informed by messenger that Salil had been killed and were asked to come to the Capital to participate in the ceremonies. They wore modest clothing and seemed like any other concerned citizen in Terrowin. Upon hearing Salil's name, Savanna broke down in tears and Gabriel tried his best to console and comfort her. People offered water to both of them, and ladies used their fans to give Savanna some air while others shielded her from the rain. Most assumed from their reaction that they were Salil's parents, but no one said a word. They had just lost a child and people in Terrowin gave them the respect they deserved.

After greeting all the parents, Xalvador made his way back to the front of the stairs and turned to face the crowd of people gathered before him. The Terrowin flag was raised at half-mast. Umbrellas scattered around. Everyone waited to see what the last remaining adult Royal would say. How would he comfort them? He grabbed the megaphone and began addressing the crowd. "Citizens of Terrowin. A tragedy of monumental proportions has struck our country. My heart goes out to the all the families on the platform behind me. Your sacrifice and courage, and their sacrifice and courage, will not go unremembered. Today is not the time for speeches, but a time for mourning. So that we may all remember our sons and daughters, our brothers and sisters, our friends, teachers and students. Therefore, we will have three days of mourning in Terrowin. Followed by a funeral for King Richard and all the Royals we have lost."

Xalvador stopped at that moment. His voice cracked. He was almost sobbing. He put his hand to his eyes and covered his face. Kass had never seen this type of emotion from him before, and she rushed to his side more from instinct than out of concern. He hugged her. Took a deep breath and continued. "In three days, we will have a funeral for all our Royals. Thank you, and good day."

With those words, the crowd outside the Capital building began to walk past the carriages, throwing even more flowers on top as they passed by. Xalvador invited King Richard's family, along with the rest of the Royal Cabinet members' loved ones, to a reception dinner in their honor. Xalvador was humble and gracious during dinner with the families. A perfect host and gentleman. Afterward, he invited them to the Royal Palace, where they would be his guests until the time of the funeral. Kass joined them.

Chapter 49

The Princes continued their journey farther south along the shore, stopping every night to prepare a fire and eat whatever they were lucky enough to find in the immediate vicinity. They were not yet starving, but hunger invaded their bodies by mid-afternoon every single day. The molar bread long gone. They dreamed of being back at the School, enjoying the amenities they had grown accustomed to. They sometimes talked to each other, asking what they wished they could eat. Memories of cheesy pizza and peanut butter and hamburgers with thick slices of fresh tomato were conversation they had often. As they traveled farther south, the mountain range to the east slowly gave way to miles of grassy plains. And farther still, grassy plains gave way to rolling green pastures. The mountains returned and a lush rainforest ran parallel to the beach.

Most of the time, the ocean was only a kilometer or two away from the edge of the forest, where trees and plants grew wildly. Cedric decided that they would walk within the cover of this jungle, as it offered shade throughout the day and building materials for their camp each night.

At this point, everyone's shoes were tattered and flopping about with each step. Their clothes bordered on indecent, having worn thin and even ripped in some places. They tried their best to keep up their hygiene, but the luxury of clean water was something they had sparingly, and even then only in the loosest interpretation of "clean." At this particular juncture, they hadn't had a proper meal in three days and counting.

The entire group was restless after settling down for another night. "Does this Provins even exist?" asked Brandon. "We've been walking for weeks! Are you sure we're going the right way?" He looked over at Salil, still wearing her mask and the most presentable of the group.

"Well, I've never heard of it before," said Cedric.

"Those were Professor Walden's last words to me."

"I'm hungry, I can't eat any more of this seaweed and tubers! I'm not going anywhere until I have a proper meal!" David was whining again. He sat down and crossed his arms, with a pout on his face.

"Food, that's all you can think about. Typical. What about our clothes? A proper bed, and maybe sleeping some other place than outside. I swear, I can't take another night out here in this Nomans Land!" Nara's words represented the views of the entire group. They were weary from their exile and bone-tired from walking.

"Fine, I'll head down to the beach and see if I can catch

something for dinner," replied Tem.

"Salil, go with him," Cedric commanded.

They both went, neither of them happy about having to work alongside the other. As they walked down to the beach Tem spoke to Salil.

"I know you had something to do with this. With all of this. You may have everyone else fooled, but I know you. And when I find out the truth, I swear I will be the one to end your life before you can carry out any more of your deadly scheme." Salil did not say a word, she kept walking, ignoring Tem.

"Do you hear me?" Tem grabbed Salil's hair, pulled out his sword and held it at her throat. "Do you hear me? I should kill you now." He pressed the sword a little harder. Salil didn't move. She was scared and weak from all the walking they had done. She was tired. While others slept during the night, Salil mostly kept watch as long as she could and then slept for only a few hours as the sky began to lighten. Deep down, part of her wanted him to do it. Just end it right then. Death would provide a quiet relief from the daily struggles of life they were all going through. Her body, her spirit, she simply didn't have the energy to fight back.

Tem pulled his sword away from her neck and she collapsed on the forest floor.

"You just know, I'm watching you, Salil." A tear ran down the side of her cheek. She swiped it away, out of view of Tem, and they continued down to try to find clams while they still had daylight. Not saying a word to each other.

They returned to camp before dark to find everyone

huddled around the fire, excited to see them upon their return.

"Finally, you're back! What's for dinner?" said David.

"Nothing. We couldn't find anything."

"That sucks."

"Well, we could always try these." Salil pulled out a pile of worms she had managed to dig up on the return trip to the camp.

"Ewww. I can't eat those," Ava said, her face so scrunched up it was a wonder they could understand her.

"Never!" shouted Nara, as she crossed her arms, turned her back and kicked the ground rather impressively.

"Well, suit yourself. They have protein and will carry us until tomorrow."

"It's just a worm. Here, I'll have some." Cedric took a few of the worms and popped one into his mouth. He gagged trying to get it down, but finished the others off without production.

David and Brandon followed Cedric's lead and downed a few of the earthworms for dinner. "Come on Nara and Ava, just think of them as spaghetti. Spaghetti with marinara sauce!" David slurped another worm into his mouth. He found that he enjoyed teasing both Nara and Ava.

"Ok, maybe just one." Ava was the first to reply, which caused a natural sense of competitiveness to return to Nara.

"Give me a few of those!" Nara said, beating Ava to the last remaining worms. Ava tried to hurry past Nara, and there was a brief shoving match between them. Nara grabbed a couple and raced Ava to put them into her mouth. They both looked at each other as they ate the worms, trying to see who could finish first.

Ava finished and opened her mouth, to show Nara that she had swallowed hers. Nara, taking her last couple of chews, paused for a moment. Her palate was not accustomed to the taste of dirt and the feel of slime as she chewed. She tried to swallow, but her stomach would not allow the worms to enter. They were rejected, and Nara vomited in front of everyone. Ashamed, she ran off into the woods alone trying to find something to take the awful taste out of her mouth.

The boys laughed at the sight of Nara running in the jungle. "Bring me back a burger if you find one!" David yelled, laughing so hard it hurt his stomach.

Cedric decided that they would stay there for a couple of days. They made walking sticks and spears and washed their clothes in the stream nearby. Nara and Ava at first kept their personal appearance acceptable as if they were still at School, but soon those efforts subsided. It was futile. Washing their hair in fresh water was their only luxury and they were the first to call "dibs" on bathing in the nearby stream. Out of sight of the boys, of course.

"Salil, come join us for our bath," Nara would say.

To which Salil always replied, "No, you go, I can wait."

Chapter 50

The day of the funeral was designated a national holiday in Terrowin. People from near and far came into the Capital city. Leading the burial procession was a drum and horn band, playing somber beats as they made their way down the street. The black-covered carriages from the days before were replaced with white carriages, accented with gold. Eight horses, marching in side-by-side pairs, carried each of the carriages of King Richard and Queen Isis. The rest of the Royals were transported in carriages pulled by four horses each. The caskets of each of the Royals were carried behind their carriages, arranged with the Terrowin flag draped across one half. Citizens lined the streets, packed in for kilometers around to get a last glimpse of their country's beloved servant-heroes. Guards stood at attention in front of the crowds, dressed in full uniform as the carriages passed by.

Xalvador, Kass, King Richard's family and Queen Isis's family were all in the first carriage behind the caskets, and the procession after them reached back over two kilometers, with more than one hundred carriages following behind. Xalvador sat tall, well-dressed and confident looking. Kass was in a dark dress, still wearing her mask. She had never worn a dress before, but Xalvador made her wear one today. He told her it was for appearances. The sun was out on this day, and the gold around the carriage covers shined brightly as they made their way to the burial site. Some people threw flowers in the path of the carriages as their departed Royals passed by.

They buried each of the Royals in separate ceremonies. Groups of people followed behind the carriage of their departed family member or friend. Salil's memorial was one of the smallest, as were most of the assassins'. Still, they were given no less than a proper burial site. Gabriel and Savanna listened to the priest bestow blessings upon Salil and her family as they lowered her casket into the ground.

"Ashes to ashes, dust to dust." Savanna cried the loudest amongst the people around, giving everyone cause to assume that she was the mother. Savanna approached the casket, knelt down and touched the side of it. She spoke, "My little Salil. I hope you have found peace. Know that Mommy and Daddy never stopped loving you. You were our gift from God." She began to sob hysterically as Gabriel and the priest tried their best to console her. After a few moments, she composed herself and placed her one red rose on top of the casket. She turned to everyone staring at her and held her head up and wiped her face. Proudly she said, "Her name was Salil. She was our only child." At which point Salil's casket was lowered into the ground.

After the burials, everyone gathered outside the gates of the cemetery and waited for Xalvador to emerge. He was scheduled to lead the people back to the Capital building where he would give his final remarks to all of Terrowin. Xalvador finally walked outside the cemetery entrance. He, along with Kass, attended King Richard's funeral.

King Richard's carriage pulled in front of Xalvador and he was helped into the coach by several guards, along with Kass. They pulled away slowly and the people of Terrowin walked behind them, in the direction of the Capital building.

Xalvador had prepared for this moment for many months, and his heart raced as he went over his speech in his mind. He grabbed Kass's hand. "This is it. Are you ready?"

"Yes, I think so."

"Don't worry, everything will be fine. They are going to adore you." She smiled.

Upon reaching the Capital steps, Xalvador was helped down from the carriage, and with Kass at his side he walked up the steps to the platform. The stairs were lined with guards standing at attention. Xalvador turned around to find all of Terrowin in front of the Capital building and as far as the eye could see. They had sufficiently mourned, and now they waited to hear the fate of their country from a man who just years before was imprisoned for trying to kill the king.

Xalvador looked upon the people and grabbed the megaphone. He addressed them, "Citizens of Terrowin. Today as a country we mourn the passing of our most patriotic citizens. Children, teenagers, young adults and former Royals who all sacrificed their own self-interests, and eventually their lives, for our country. Terrowin will never forget their sacrifice." He went on:

"I must ask now, is former King Javier or Queen Tiffany Rose among us now? King Javier! Queen Tiffany Rose! Are you here? We need you now!"

The crowd went silent, everyone looking around to see if maybe King Javier or Queen Tiffany Rose were still alive. They had been missing for several months, and everyone assumed they were dead. No one stepped forward.

"My beloved Terrowin, I believe I stand before you as the highest-ranking Royal survivor, and I take this position most humbly and with a heavy heart." Xalvador continued his speech to the people of Terrowin, discussing their collective past, and how they, as a people, had overcome many tragedies throughout their history. He concluded his speech with the following words, "and as I accept the throne today, the need to hide my identity is no longer necessary. I remove our masks, and take my rightful position as King of Terrowin!" At first the crowd gasped at the sight of Xalvador and Kass standing there, masks removed. Then, without hesitation, a great roar went out, as they cheered their new king.

The ceremony concluded with the crown being placed upon Xalvador's head. Everyone knew—well, those versed in the Terrowin Constitution knew—that, in the event that the reigning King and all within his cabinet are no longer living, or are in any way unable to perform their duties, the Ascension King is to take power immediately. And, in the event that the

Ascension King cannot serve, the youngest former Royal over the age of twenty-four will take the throne until a new king can be inducted at age twenty-four. With former King Javier and Queen Tiffany Rose absent, Xalvador was the next successor in line. He had just orchestrated a coup that would last for at least twenty-four years, and none in Terrowin were the wiser about his scheme.

He settled into his new role as King of Terrowin with his protégée Kass at his side. Learning the extent of his powers and enjoying a never-before-seen level of extravagance in his lifestyle, which he felt was befitting the last remaining Royal. He and Kass enjoyed lavish dinners, State parties and hosting various important businessmen and local government officials from around Terrowin. After about three months of accompanying Xalvador to events where she was most uncomfortable, Kass had become thoroughly unsettled.

During dinner one evening, Kass at one end of the table, Xalvador at the other, in the king's dining hall, Kass asked, "Xalvador, my king, when shall I go and hunt down the others?"

"Ah, yes, the Princes. I almost forgot about them. Straightaway."

She had only been waiting for him to give the word. "I'll leave in the morning."

Xalvador walked over to her and stood behind her chair. "Take these. Something special for you that I made." He held out five small spheres, about the size and color of walnuts. She knew what they were. He then gathered her long blond hair and lifted it from her shoulders before gently twisting it in his hand. He held it aloft for just a moment, then tugged at it hard. He yanked her head back and whispered in her opposite ear, "Find them, and kill them all. Ok? Ok, my dear?"

His breath was hot. His lips so close to her flesh. But she was as strong as ever.

"Yes, my king."

$\mathcal{C}$hapter 51

The following morning, just before sunrise, Kass set off on horseback to return to the School and begin tracking the Princes. She was dressed in her assassin uniform, two swords hanging from each side, a bow and arrow on her back and bolas attached to her waist. Wearing her mask, she arrived. The School was abandoned. Grasses and weeds already grew wildly. It was eerily quiet as she approached the burned remains of the Royal Residence Hall. She dismounted her horse and went straight upstairs, into Salil's room. There she dug into the soil at the corner, exposing the hidden rock.

Kass lowered herself impatiently down into the hole and lit her lantern upon reaching the bottom. She looked at the mural of Rigor Mortisis with a hot sort of envy. She hated the fact that she had not discovered this passageway when she was a Prince Assassin. Seeing Salil's name written in black ink at the bottom filled her with a seething hatred. Right there, she vowed, "Salil will be the first one I kill."

She looked around and saw footprints leading down the

passage. She followed. When she reached the entrance of the cave, the sun was high in the sky. She carried a bag, stocked with enough provisions to last her several days. She thought about going back to retrieve her horse, but decided against it and instead hurried down the rope that led to the beach and set off on foot. On the shore she looked around, trying to decide which way they might have gone. South was her best guess, and she headed south at a steady pace.

As she walked, she studied the landscape around her. It made the most sense that they would sleep under cover of the mountains or forest, rather than being exposed on the beach. She found their first cave within hours of leaving the beach. The grassy beds and old ashes from the fire still remained. She knew she was more than three months behind them. As she examined the ashes, she concluded that they had not stayed there for very long, but it was enough for her to know that she was headed in the right direction. She kept walking south.

Chapter 52

The group slept that night as best they could on a belly full of worms. Tem was usually the first one awake, still fulfilling his duties to protect David. On this morning he woke to find Salil missing. She was up to something, he thought to himself. He grabbed his sword and followed her footprints into the jungle.

Her tracks soon disappeared. He tried to track her for almost an hour but lost all signs of where she might have gone. The trees and foliage were thick and he came upon a variety of unsavory creatures in his path. Centipedes, lizards and massive spider webs surrounded him. As he passed one large tree, a brown and black—very well concealed—boa slithered up and into the higher branches. After that, he unsheathed his sword and continued on, but now he was walking in stealth mode, trying to blend in within the jungle.

Salil was deep in the jungle herself. She found some type of animal tracks and was following them. She moved along, sometimes on the ground, sometimes in the tree branches. She was stalking her prey, although she did not know what it was just yet. She moved quietly, stealthily. Something skittered in the brush up ahead of her. She waited for a moment, hoping to be undetected. The movement continued away from her and she kept following. Closing in on whatever it was.

She hid behind a tree trunk, concealed by thick leafed plants in front of her. It was time. Now or never. She climbed the tree a ways up and saw movement in the thick bushes below her. Right there. She pounced like a leopard stalking prey from the treetops and drew her sword, ready to strike upon impact.

Her aim was true, as she landed right on top of Tem. "Kiaaaa!" Her sword drawn, ready to slash his innards when she hit the ground. Tem let out a scream. But her sword was already moving downward. At the last moment, she realized it was him and directed her sword right beside his head, striking the ground instead, missing his head by a few centimeters.

"Don't kill me, please!" Tem cried, his head grinding into the dirt and his arms stretched out wide with Salil on his back.

"Oh, it's you!" Salil pulled her sword from the ground.

"Get off of me!" yelled Tem. He realized he was still alive and tried to push Salil aside.

"Shhhh." She pushed his face back in the dirt and put all her weight on his head, ensuring that he could not move. "Something's out there," she whispered.

She tried to use the sunlight in the forest to discern what she saw, it was mostly shadows, but something was moving and now it was coming toward them both. Tem tried to move his head as he heard something in front of him, he wanted to see what it was.

The rustling in the brush became more intense as the thing was closing in on them almost at full speed. Tem finally was able to lift his head and saw a full grown wild boar running directly toward him, tusks clearing the brush between both him and Salil.

"Stay still."

"No, let me up! Let me up!"

"Don't move!"

"No, get off of me!"

The boar was just a few meters away and Tem was still fighting with Salil to let him up. At the last moment, Salil pushed his head down in the soft ground to get more leverage. With bent knees, she jumped up forward and upward, a frog leap, leaving Tem alone, the boar focused directly on him. Tem closed his eyes and braced for the impact, covering his head with his hands like they practiced in tornado drills at the School. Salil did a front somersault and landed right on the approaching boar, her sword coming down first between its shoulder blades.

"Kiaaa!" Her feet spread apart on descent, she mounted the boar, killing it instantly just a meter from a cowering Tem.

"Breakfast is served," said Salil.

"Yeah, I could have done that." Tem stood up and wiped the dirt from his face and clothes.

"Sure you could have."

Tem dragged the boar back to camp. The others were just

waking up. "Who wants breakfast?" Tem said as he arrived and dropped the boar in front of David.

"Woah! Bacon!"

"And eggs," said Ava. "Nara and I found eggs this morning while we were out walking."

"Nice job, Tem!" said Cedric. "That will feed us for a week!" Tem said nothing. Salil just walked over to the side and rested for a moment.

"I'll get it started," said Brandon. Brandon looked over at Ava, remembering she was a better chef than him, but she didn't object, as she wanted no part in dressing and prepping the boar. He separated out the legs for smoking, and the ribs they would have for dinner.

"Hey Nara and Ava, here's some breast meat for you. God knows you both can use some of this!" said Brandon, laughing as he continued to butcher the boar.

"That's not funny. But at least you found your long lost brother, you pig!" Nara replied, clearly frustrated at Brandon's antics.

Brandon continued to cut slices of the belly—although not cured, the slices of bacon from the belly would do just fine. He prepared everyone a breakfast of boar belly and fried eggs on flat rocks he heated with the fire. They ate off leaves gathered from the forest and enjoyed their time together, finally having a proper meal.

Cedric decided the group should rest there for a few more days and regain their strength. The boar would last them and he had no idea how much farther they needed to travel. They rationed out the meat and smoked some to bring with them on the next leg of their journey. Brandon was in charge of doling out the portions to the group over the next couple of days. He tried to get as creative as possible with his cooking and found some savory herbs for flavor.

Nara and Ava took full advantage of the stream by washing their clothes and bodies every day. Salil and Tem went down to the ocean to gather clams and the few crabs they could find. The group had enough energy that they were able to relax at the beach during the day and have full bellies at night.

Chapter 53

On the third morning in Nomans Land, while everyone was sleeping late, Brandon woke everyone up. "Hey, you guys, wake up! Wake up!"

"What is it Brandon?" Cedric was the first one to respond, sounding annoyed at being awakened before he was ready.

"It's gone. The ham. The smoked boar. It's all gone! Someone took it! Who took it?"

"Wait, what do you mean it's gone?" asked Tem, his suspicions already directed at Salil.

"I didn't take it," said David.

"Well, one of you did! That's all we have left and we agreed to save it for our next walk." Brandon was on the verge of crying.

"It had to be you Tem! You're always complaining about being hungry. And looking after David. You probably took it to give to David, while the rest of us starve out here!" Nara said, her pretty chin trembling as she started to cry.

"I did not." Tem's voice cracked.

"Did too."

"Did not!"

"Wait!" The sound of Salil's voice startled everyone. "Brandon, where did you leave the boar?"

"I wrapped it up in some leaves and hung it in the tree over there." He pointed to a big tree off to the side of their camp.

"Show me."

Brandon led the way over to a large tree with thick branches reaching high into the sky. One branch was low enough for Brandon to have thrown a twisted rope over the top of it and hang the smoked boar. The rope remained, but the wrapped package of meat was gone.

"Right here."

Salil looked around at the ground, checking for animal tracks. The only tracks she found were ones leading back toward their camp. She looked up into the tree but saw only branches. She climbed up the tree on the side where the boar had been hanging. She looked in the treetops, but still saw nothing. She made her way back down to the rest of the group and looked at each one of them. She walked around to the opposite side of the tree trunk. The ground had recently been disturbed. It was evident to her that something had jumped down from up in the tree before moving into the deep brush.

She went back around and whispered, "Be quiet. Cedric, take David and the rest of the group and head back to camp and pack up. Tem, you have your sword?"

"Yes."

"Come with me."

Salil pulled out her sword and Tem followed her. She found tracks leading away from the camp and followed them, slowly, cautiously, quietly. She was unable to tell what kind of tracks they were, but they were spaced closely together, almost like a mountain lion or some other large cat. The tracks seemed to disappear just a few meters into the foliage at the base of another tree. Salil circled in one direction and Tem in the other, around the big tree, but they could not find any additional tracks.

"That's weird, they just disappeared," whispered Tem.

Salil put her hand over his mouth, looked him in the eye, and pointed her sword up to the top of the tree before them. She had already concluded that if it was a mountain lion, it had surely spotted them and would pounce at any moment. She and Tem looked up slowly and saw what appeared to be a nest made out of twigs and grass and leaves in the branches above. Something was moving inside. They heard deep rhythmic breathing. It was asleep.

Both Tem and Salil readied their swords. She told Tem the plan and they backed away from each other slowly, a couple of meters apart, directly below the nest. Tem jumped straight up and slashed at the bottom of the nest, splitting it right down the middle. Leaves and pieces of ham fell down first, then the entire structure hit the ground. Salil was ready, her sword high over her head, poised to strike the beast dead the moment it reached the ground.

Thump. It landed. Salil moved in for the death blow,

sword over her head. Tem was at the ready to strike a second blow if necessary.

"Owww!" came a sound from under the fallen leaves of the nest.

Salil stopped. She replaced her sword. There, underneath the debris, was a little boy. He was wearing an assassin's mask.

"Jimmy?" said Salil.

Tem was breathing hard from all the excitement. "Little Jimmy? You're the one that took our meat? Where did you come from, how did you find us? You here to try to kill us?" His sword was still in his hand.

Salil smiled at little Jimmy, he was covered in dirt and looked like he hadn't taken a proper bath in weeks.

"Tem, gather up the rest of the boar and let's head back to camp. Come on little Jimmy, next time don't leave so many tracks!" Salil popped Jimmy on his head, right at the spot where he had fallen.

"Owww! Ok, ok."

Chapter 54

Tem, Salil and Jimmy walked back to the camp. The group had already packed their belongings and was ready to start walking again.

"Look what we found." Tem pushed Jimmy before the group.

They all knew him. Jimmy had to be the cutest little assassin in the history of the School. At least from the way he talked and walked, and the way his dark red hair was always bursting out the sides of his mask. David, Nara, Ava and Brandon were happy to see Jimmy. He looked frighteningly haggard and they immediately asked him if he was ok. The girls each gave him a hug.

"So, wait, he took our ham?" asked Ava, completely unaware of the far more significant questions posed by Jimmy's presence.

Cedric looked at Jimmy skeptically and asked the right questions. "How did you find us? And how did you escape the fire?"

"Do you have any more of that meat? I'm starving! I haven't had breakfast yet."

Little Jimmy sat down with the group and explained to them what he had witnessed the night of the fire. He was watching Kass from high above on the rooftop of the Music and Arts building, still playing his favorite game of hide-and-go-seek. He had been missing for a couple of days and relished the fact that once again no one could find him. He told them how he watched Kass "spread some powder around and around and around" the Royal Residence Hall. He recalled how she went inside, only to return and light the fire. He also shared the story of the firefighters' failed efforts to put the fire out.

"So, it was Kass who set the fire. But, why? Why would she do that? Why would she want everyone dead?" Cedric asked, as Jimmy chowed down on some leftover ribs Brandon had roasted the night before.

"Well, not her, maybe Professor Xalvador. I saw him and Kass meet in the woods after the fire. I followed her."

"Professor Xalvador?" Salil asked.

"Yes."

"What does he have to do with this?" asked Cedric.

"Well, after the fire, he and Kass went into our house. I snuck behind them. I couldn't hear what they were saying. But she stayed downstairs and he went upstairs. So, I followed him. That's when I found the secret tunnel!"

"What secret tunnel?"

"The tunnel for assassins! In Salil's room. I heard them

coming so I climbed down into the tunnel and hid. She almost found me. Anyway, I think he said that she was coming to kill you all."

"Kill us! Kass and Professor Xalvador? Oh my goodness!" Ava cried. Everyone in the group had their own internal reactions to those words. They all knew Kass and how dangerous she was. And Professor Xalvador, well, most students tried to avoid his classes, and knew of his assassin past.

"They know we're alive," whispered Cedric as he stepped away from the group, contemplating every possible permutation they might now be faced with.

"What else, what else do you know?" asked Tem. He grabbed Jimmy and stood him up. Fear had overtaken him.

"That's all. Get off of me!"

"Let him go!" David pushed Tem aside. "Cedric, what should we do?"

"We need to head south like Professor Walden said. Come on, let's pack up and head out. Try not to leave any trace behind. Also, Salil and Tem, you two should walk at the rear of the group, I don't want any surprises. If Jimmy can find us, Kass will surely be able to."

"Hey, wait, I haven't finished my breakfast yet," little Jimmy protested.

"It's breakfast to go. Come on, we must get moving," Cedric commanded, and with that the group, plus one, started walking again, into the unknown and farther south.

Chapter 55

They had walked almost a hundred days. The smoked boar lasted less than a week and they again went through a roller coaster of feast and famine, depending on what they were able to gather from the forest and the ocean. Salil and Tem did most of the hunting and fishing. Nara and Ava tried their best to gather any fruit or berries they could find, along with little Jimmy. Brandon and Cedric did most of the navigating and setting up of their evening shelters. They made additional water containers from the dried stomachs of animals they caught. Salil learned this skill in one of her early survival courses.

Little Jimmy tried his best to keep up with the group as they walked. Oftentimes Cedric would question him further to get any additional information that Jimmy might remember. To no avail, Jimmy just kept repeating what he told them the first time they met.

Now, while they marched, they constantly looked over their shoulders to make sure that Kass was not behind them.

They tried as best they could to cover their tracks, but any seasoned tracker could follow them because, prior to Jimmy's arrival, they had no reason to believe that anyone was following them. Salil, Tem and Cedric alternated keeping watch during the nighttime hours.

They walked farther south, again keeping close to the shore. They weathered storms from the ocean and warming heat of the day as they continued. Still no sign of Provins. At this juncture, it was almost a week since they consumed any protein because they had been traveling atop an old lava outcrop section of the shore. The blackened lava rocks, reaching hundreds of meters into the air from the shore, were remnants of a volcanic eruption long ago. The eruption had destroyed all life, only a few grass plants had started to repopulate the area. Rolling hills and crevasses surrounded their blackened landscape, the ground uneven with sharp rocks all around. In addition to their food shortage, it hadn't rained in a few days and their water was almost depleted. The sun was hot and the heat radiated from the rocks making it almost unbearable to walk during the day. But Cedric insisted they press on, continuing southward.

Fishing was impossible and the foraging trips yielded nothing. Tem gave most of his final share of water to David, who was now lagging behind with Salil. Nara and Ava looked after little Jimmy as best they could but hunger and, worse, dehydration was settling in.

After two days, the group was in dire need of water but there was still none to be found. They had stopped sweating, one first sign of dehydration and heat exhaustion, and their skin was baked from the sun. Their lips were peeling and cracking. They had no choice but to continue south as they dragged their feet, knowing that there was no going back and not much hope on the horizon.

Cedric looked to the sky, desperate to see clouds overhead. He looked back at David and little Jimmy, calculating that they had maybe one more day without water. It was his decision to press on. He figured that they must try to reach the end of this old magma field and find fresh water as fast as possible. Perhaps he had made a mistake.

David fell, out of exhaustion, and Tem rushed to pick him up.

"Don't touch him," Tem called to Salil when she tried to help David to his feet before Tem arrived. Tem, also weary from lack of food and water, could only muster the words. She took out her water canteen and gave David her last few drops of water, which she had been saving. As the water touched his lips, he looked up at her and simply said, "Thanks," with a scratchy voice. The group watched David for a moment, wondering if he would perish. They were all too weak to give any kind of support, instead they only thought about their own survival.

Cedric looked around him and saw nothing but black sun-baked lava rocks. The ocean crashed on the shore, seemingly teasing them. They were surrounded by water but there was none to drink.

"Come on, let's get to the top of that hill and find a place to rest tonight." The ground sloped upward on an incline that seemed to summit almost a kilometer away. Cedric hoped the top would give him a better view of his surroundings. He wished this desolate landscape would offer some relief.

With Cedric's words, the group moved forward, walking on auto-pilot, they simply followed the person in front of them, heads down, trying to escape the rays of the sun. David and little Jimmy doing the best they could. The group no longer worried about whether Kass might be following them. It was water and relief from the sun that occupied their minds.

When Cedric crested the hill he couldn't believe his eyes. Was this a mirage? "Hey, guys come look!"

The excitement in Cedric's voice gave everyone an adrenaline boost. They all started running toward him. When they reached the summit and looked downward, they could see a tropical paradise. The harsh obsidian terrain disappeared abruptly and gave way to a white sandy beach as far as the eye could see. The dense green forest appeared once again, with coconut, banana and even mango trees. It was the sight of the coconut trees that caught everyone's attention, as they looked ripe and would have life-giving liquid.

The Princes raced down the side of the volcanic rocks and ran out to the beach. Even little Jimmy summoned a fresh burst of strength upon seeing the beach. They all started running as they hit the sand, each trying to find the first coconut to open. Cedric let the others run ahead as he was taking an assessment of this new landscape. Salil lagged behind doing the same thing.

"Do you think this is safe?" he asked her.

"I hope so." They both made their way down to the others.

The Princes and Jimmy immediately grabbed the first fallen coconuts they could get their hands on, started opening them and downing the water inside. The sweetness overwhelmed their taste buds as they tried to open as many as they could, first drinking the liquid and then consuming the flesh. After the realization that they were no longer in danger of dying, they sat in the shade, coconut shells all around them, and just watched the waves crash softly on the quiet beach. There were fish swimming in the shallows. Tem thought he would try some fishing later.

Cedric decided that they would stay at this location for a few days to once again gather their strength. They had traveled over three months, and still no sign of Provins, or any people at all.

Chapter 56

After three days on the beach, the Princes and Jimmy regained their strength and started acting like children again. Tem had been surprisingly successful at fishing, and the girls found a nearby freshwater stream. Everyone had clean clothes and they made a sustainable camp, complete with a shelter made from tree branches, leaves and brush they found nearby.

One afternoon, Nara invited Salil once again to join her at the nearby stream. Salil finally agreed. Well, technically, she didn't agree so much as she just walked with Nara when she asked, without overtly responding in any way whatsoever. Nara went in the water first and Salil watched cautiously from the bank.

"Oh, come on in. You do know how to swim, right?"

"Of course I do."

"Ah, clean water! The things I've taken for granted all my life, I swear, Cedric better have a plan. Cause I'm not walking anymore out there into nothing." Nara dunked her head under the surface, leaning her head way back when she rose up to get the water out of her eyes. "Come on in, Salil. What are you waiting for?"

Salil finally decided to do it, to join Nara in her bathing, but she waded cautiously into the stream, fully clothed. When she was up to her chest, Nara swam over to her and splashed water in her face. Salil didn't flinch.

"No fair, you have that mask on!"

Salil touched her mask. She'd forgotten that it was still on. She splashed Nara back and caught her by surprise, causing her to cough and sputter. They both held their breath for a moment, unsure of how to proceed into this new territory. Then Nara whirled about, sending sheets of water impressively but rather ineffectively into the air with both her arms and Salil laughed—had she ever laughed like this before?—and fell onto her back kicking the water into Nara's face. Nara was losing that battle, but it no longer mattered as the girls played in the water without a care in the world.

They kicked and splashed and swam in circles and dunked each other for a little while before they were ready to get out. They sat together, side by side, at the edge of the stream, soggy but comfortable and happy, basking in the sun's rays. Nara started talking to Salil, who was just contentedly watching the slow-moving water. "You know, when we get back home, the first thing I'm going to do is go and cut my hair. Maybe color it. The sun has just done so much damage." She snaked her hand back behind her neck and lifted the mass of her hair in a practiced move, sweeping it over one shoulder and scowling at the ends before flinging her arm out and letting it all fall down her back. "I'm sure they will tell me that it all has to be cut off." She pouted. "Imagine that. Me? Cut all my hair off? Well, I'd rather be caught dead than to walk around with shortened hair. It just wouldn't be queenlike."

Salil didn't say a word. Nara took this as agreement and continued, "Oh, well, I guess you don't really care about those things. I don't mean that in a bad way. Please don't take that wrong. I mean, you're always so, so tough." She reached out her hand toward Salil's hair. "Have you ever had your hair permed? Or colored?"

"No, I haven't."

"Well, you should try it one day. When you look in the mirror after, it's like you're looking at a different person, a new you. That is, if you like what they did to your hair. But, with that mask over your face all the time, I guess you just can't really be bothered with such things."

"Not really."

"You know you could take that mask off."

"What?"

"Well, we aren't in Terrowin anymore. And once we go back, you'll have to put it on again. Why not take it off? For now." Nara positioned herself behind Salil, who was just sitting there, acting as if she wasn't listening to Nara. But in reality, she was thinking hard about what she said.

"I mean, we are alone here. None of the boys. No students or professors. And especially not Ava. Just me and you."

Nara slowly reached toward the back of Salil's head and held her hands there. Salil was still just sitting. Nara began to gently unclasp her mask. Salil jumped and moved away from her just the slightest bit.

"Oh, relax." Nara was completely unperturbed. "Just this one time, ok?" She laid her hand on Salil's shoulder to calm her.

Salil's breathing quickened when Nara touched her, her chest rising and falling visibly. She was still not comfortable with human contact that was not intended to brutalize her. "Ok. It's ok."

Nara removed the mask and placed it on the ground beside them. Her fingers at the nape of Salil's neck, she drew them slowly upward and untied her hair, long black straight hair that tumbled down to her waist. Salil did not turn around or move at all. Nara spoke.

"See, I told you it's not so bad. And look at your hair! Wow, if I had hair like that I could do so many things with it." Nara placed her hands on Salil's shoulders and drew her fingers across that plane and back up her neck, through her thick hair towards her scalp and then pulling, combing Salil's hair through her hands gently, all the way down. She repeated this motion several times, neither one of them speaking. Salil tried to meditate at this moment, remembering her training, thinking controlled breathing was the answer, but this was different. She found she enjoyed Nara's company, and after a few moments allowed herself to close her eyes and just listen to the sounds around them. A bird in the distance. The water cresting ever so slightly against the shore. A frog off in the tree to her right, and several dragonflies and mosquitoes buzzing about. She heard all of these things clearly, and even managed to extract Nara's voice from the other sounds.

"Salil, do you hear me? Hey!" Salil had missed Nara asking her to turn around.

"Hey, I said I want you to turn around. Let me see your face. I mean, it's only fair, you've seen all of us." Salil tried to return to her cold unemotional self.

"No." She stood up from Nara, her back still turned, her mask in her hand.

Nara stood up with her. "Hey, wait." She touched her shoulder. "Just trust me, ok? I want to see you."

Salil tightened her grip on her mask. She had never heard anyone speak to her in such a way. A normal child in a similar situation would recall memories of a mother's warm calming voice, a father's gentle embrace. Feelings of love, admiration, protection, hope, trust. All emotions she had never experienced. The feelings were unfamiliar, even overwhelming, and her mind was still processing whether or not she enjoyed them. Her eyes started to burn and swell with tears. She could not understand why. Before she had only cried when she was angry, or the time Kass had broken her nose in the advanced fighting class or when Tem put his sword to her neck.

She felt no hostility toward Nara, yet her eyes watered anyway.

Nara reached out and pulled Salil toward her, trying to turn her around to face her. Finally Salil relented, defenses down, and allowed herself to be turned around. Her head was bowed down toward the ground, she could not look directly at

Nara. Nara placed her hand under Salil's chin, lifting her head ever so slowly and gently. Salil felt exposed and vulnerable without her mask, but she trusted Nara at this point. Or at least that's what her feelings were telling her.

Once she was looking straight ahead Nara spoke, "See, you are so beautiful." Salil's eyes were full of tears, ready to spill over and pour down her face. She just looked at Nara, blinking, trying hold the tears back. But one slid down the side of her cheek. Nara lifted her hand and wiped it away.

"You're not alone anymore, Salil."

She reached to give Salil a hug. Salil's feet did not move. She had never been this close to a person she wasn't trying to put in a chokehold in sparring class. She didn't know what to do, she just stood there, her arms at her side, while Nara gave her a hug of reassurance. Salil's eyes remained wide open, her breathing increased and she could feel Nara's heart beating against her chest. She just stared into the woods, unresponsive but filled with unknown emotion.

Chapter 57

Salil heard something rustle in the bushes close by, startling her, causing her to jump back and quickly put on her mask. She was not ready to have anyone else see her without it. She turned to Nara and hissed, "Shhh," trying to figure out what was moving in the brush. They both ducked down trying not to be seen. Salil didn't know if the others were simply coming to collect water or bathe, or maybe it was an animal or something far worse, like Kass.

Salil walked slowly toward the rustling, and Nara stayed right behind her as best she could, making way too much noise for Salil. Soon they heard voices, more than one voice, and not the likes of David or little Jimmy either. These were adult voices, several of them.

"Hey dude. We caught some gnarly waves today. Yeah, and little Stowie finally got his hanging ten right today!"

"I know, massive! And the ollies, dude you killed it today."

There were at least five young men, not more than twenty years old, walking with surfboards headed into the dense forest away from the beach. They were shirtless and tanned and muscles protruded from their bodies, so perfect it was as if they were sculpted out of marble. They walked barefooted with long and wild hair. Some had twisted their hair into locks, which reminded Nara of braids she once had done during a birthday celebration years ago.

The guys were walking adjacent to Nara and Salil, who were concealed in the bushes along a barely discernable path that Salil had not noticed before. They stayed quietly hidden as the men walked just a few meters from where they were hiding.

"Stowie!" shouted one of the men, who paused after walking by the girls.

"Stowie, where are you dude? Come on, we can't be late for din again, you know how Moms is!"

Salil and Nara stayed perfectly still, not knowing anything about these men, their instincts telling them to remain hidden. The older guy walked backwards, looking off in the distance apparently trying to find this Stowie. He walked closer to them. Salil grabbed her sword with one hand, ready to strike at these strangers. Nara put her hand over her own mouth, desperately trying to conceal her heavy breathing.

The guy stopped right in front of them. Salil strengthened the grip on her sword.

A boy, no more than fourteen years old, managed to sneak up behind Salil and Nara and was watching over Nara's shoulder as she remained crouched down behind Salil. He watched with them for a few seconds, as they watched the men, neither of them aware that he was behind them.

"Hey, now, what would you two chickies be doing here?"

A startled Nara dove to the left, well, more like slipped, trying to get away. Salil turned quickly and drew her sword. She held it with both hands pointed at the older boy.

"Woah. Slow down there lady," he said with a smile on his face, kind of mocking her. She attacked him, trying one of her favorite moves, sure to inflict a mortal wound. He moved more quickly than she, to avoid the blow, and as her sword passed his body, he performed a perfect counter-move, which trapped her wrists and flicked the sword from her hands.

"We won't be needing that," he said, as he tossed the sword away. "And why don't you just calm down little lady?"

Salil was furious, intent on showing this boy her true martial arts skills and prepared to attack him. He smiled at her.

As she lunged toward him, she felt a hand grab hold of her collar from behind and lift her up in the air. Her feet now off the ground, she was suspended in mid-air and started kicking and swinging wildly. But the strong hand would not let go.

"Get off of me!" she yelled.

"Help! Help!" Nara's cries echoed throughout the forest.

"Quiet down little lady, no one is going to hurt you. Chill."

"Let her go!" Nara cried.

"Relax little one."

"Stowie. What are you doing?" said the man who was now holding Salil away from his body, still with one hand.

"Nothing. I just saw these two girls here, watching us walk

by and I only wanted to say hello." He tossed his head to fling the hair back from his face. "Hello!" He waved to Salil, who was still frustrated and angry with him for disarming her so easily.

Tem, Cedric, Brandon, David, Ava and little Jimmy came running toward Nara's cries for help. Tem had his sword out, and Cedric and Brandon came with spears they had made long ago for hunting and encounters like this.

They stopped when they saw Salil still suspended in air. Tem stepped forward, pushing David behind him. Brandon ran over to Nara while Cedric stood still, understanding that these were grown men and a fight would be futile. Little Jimmy stood behind David and Ava, his mask still on.

"More little ones," said one of the guys, smiling, surprised by the presence of these children. He was not threatened by Tem or his sword. "Who are you and where did you come from?" he queried.

Cedric spoke up. "Hey, can you put her down first?"

"Oh, sorry about that dude. Little one here with the mask has a hella attitude problem. She needs to take a dip and relax." He put Salil down slowly and she walked over to the rest of the group, but not before she defiantly snatched up her sword.

"We are just travelers. We mean you no harm. We were just passing through, and looking for a place called Provins." Cedric did not want to reveal too much information to these strangers. He learned at School that information was power, and he did not want to share more than he had to at this particular juncture with these strangers.

"Provins? Why do you want to go there?" asked Stowie.

"Well, we were told it was a place we might find shelter and be among friends," Cedric said, hoping for some additional information.

"Yes, we know Provins. But where are your parents? Y'all a little young to be out here all alone," the older one said.

"Dead. All of our parents are dead," said Cedric.

"Sorry dude. How long ya been traveling?"

"Over one hundred days." The man looked shocked. Children alone for that long. He felt sorry for them, as did the rest of the men, but was also a little impressed at their resolve.

"Man, you guys have some big ones to be traveling alone all that time. Come, let's go, we'll take you to Provins."

"Ok, can we go and retrieve our belongings?" asked Cedric.

"Sure dude. Relax. No rush."

After returning to their camp, they walked with the men and Stowie for almost thirty minutes along the narrow path, deeper into the woods. The Princes said little to these men, still trying to determine whether to trust them. There were five of them, and the boy Stowie. From listening to their conversation, Cedric determined that Stowie was Manchild's little brother, but only by a few years. Manchild was the strong guy who picked Salil up as if she were a ragdoll. No wonder they called him Manchild he thought, maybe it was just a nickname, but that's what the others called him. There was also Seahorse, Tailwind, Honeyboy and Springtime. Odd names, but that's what they were called.

Stowie lagged behind, trying to make small talk with the group as they marched forward. He made his way between Salil and Nara. "So, you were really gonna cut me something deep with that sword of yours, were ya?" he asked Salil, who didn't respond, much less look in his direction or acknowledge that she'd even heard him.

"And you," he laughed as he turned toward Nara. "The look on your face! Priceless!"

"Hey back off!" Brandon stepped up, getting between Stowie and Nara. This was one time Nara didn't mind Brandon trying to play the knight in shining armor role.

"Well, anyway, you'd have never cut me. I mean, imagine, me getting cut by a little girl like you anyway. My boys would tease me ten ways from Sunday!"

"Well, maybe she won't be the one to cut you," said Tem.

"Oh, come on mate. Cool your britches. I'm just teasing her. Is she your girlie, bro? I mean, no offense, if you dig chicks with masks who carry swords and all, who am I to protest."

"Salil? No way! She's not my girlie."

"Ah, Salil is the masked warrior's name. I'm Stowie."

"And I'm David. This is Nara, Tem, Cedric, Ava, Brandon and James, but we call him little Jimmy." Stowie turned to little Jimmy.

"Ah, little Jimmy, another one with a mask, just like Salil." He bent down, "So, is she your girlie, bro?"

"Ewww. No way!"

"Well, no worries. We are almost there. Gonna cause a lot

of fuss, the eight of you. We don't get many visitors around
here."

"Where is here, by the way?" interrupted Nara, annoyed at
Stowie.

"Here is our home." Stowie led them out of the forest, and
upon exiting the tree line they looked out on an entire village
set forth in a large clearing. It was probably best described as a
city, much similar to their Capital, but built with wood and
leaves rather than stone and rock.

They had finally reached Provins.

Chapter 58

The people of Provins existed for hundreds of years in this same village. From infancy, every citizen was taught the five tenets of life as declared by Morris Grotisi, the Father of Provins.

> *Tenet No. 1. Thou shalt not kill.*
> *Tenet No. 2. Every boy and girl shall have free*
> *will to decide his or her own path.*
> *Tenet No. 3. Don't worry, be happy.*
> *Tenet No. 4. All people are created equal.*
> *Tenet No. 5. Shower the people with love.*

Following these five tenets, the people of Provins evolved into a community where caring for everyone and sharing with everyone became the norm rather than the exception. People lived lives that outsiders might probably describe as being on a perpetual vacation. People did not have careers, they didn't worry about paying the rent, or buying property. They never thought about collecting material wealth. Instead of trying to build a bigger house than their neighbors, they helped their neighbors build their house. No one went hungry. And no one yelled or fought out of anger.

There was no formal education system for children. Instead, they learned by modeling the behaviors of the adults around them, trial and error, and were eventually taught in a more structured fashion by mentors as they matured. Kids were not made to do things they did not want to. They were not forced to eat their vegetables, or go to sleep at a certain hour. If a baby cried, everyone around would try to help, to stop the baby from crying. Everyone pitched in, and everyone offered to help.

There was no king or queen in Provins. Instead, they had a Council of Elders, which was made up of the most senior members of Provins. Anyone could serve on the Council of Elders once they turned sixty, if they wished to do so. The Council did not so much govern as it did listen to disputes that might arise and offer high-level advice to the parties involved. The sessions frequently concluded with music, drinks and dancing as a way to remind the people of Tenet No. 3: Don't worry, be happy.

Several words that you, or I, or the Princes use on a daily basis no longer existed in Provinian-speak. Greed, jealousy, envy, hatred, deception, stealing, lying, cheating, bribery, gluttony, murder, betrayal, arson, rape, child abuse, adultery, incest, threaten, and the list goes on, simply did not exist in their language. These people were as close to the kumbaya as anyone could get!

But, Provins was not without its fair share of problems and controversies. The live-free-or-die culture of Provins made it the world leader in accidental children's deaths. Drowning whilst surfing was a leading cause of death, followed closely by cliff diving and tree climbing accidents. Almost every kid, girls and boys, in Provins can show you one or two "wicked scars" from some broken bone or gash they received surfing, playing sports or falling from a tree they had no business trying to climb at four years old. But aside from this, the people of Provins lived in harmony with their surroundings, happy and content.

One thing that struck the Princes as they looked out to see the citizens of Provins in their daily lives was how athletic and strong looking everyone appeared. The men and boys walked around without shirts, biceps and pectoral muscles pulsating out of their tight-skinned bodies. The women were no less spectacular looking. Toned, tall and tanned, they walked around in shorts that seemed way too short, with a variety of tops showing off midriffs and shoulders and leaving nothing to the imagination. It was all enough to make even the most open-minded Terwinian blush. To strangers it might appear that they were showing off their buff bodies, but their way of dressing really just reflected the carefree society of Provins.

Oh, and the color and complexions of people! The skin tones ranged from a sun kissed vanilla bean hue to deep dark double chocolate coloration and every shade in between. All seemingly even-toned and smooth-skinned. You could almost take any five women and men in Provins and put them on the cover of the highest-rated modeling magazine!

The hairstyles were equally impressive, showing the creativity and artistic expression of each individual. Boys had mohawks, faux hawks, flat tops, mop tops, dreads, twists, pompadours, fades, shaved heads, and some just let their hair grow wild, out of control, like Stowie. Girls were equally expressive, with bobs, curls, ponytails, pigtails, french braids, flips, cornrows, chignon twists, 'fros, messy buns, pixie cuts and long beachy waves. Both sexes, male and female, used berries and barks and natural flora to formulate dyes of every color to stain their hair, some sporting one color, others integrating several. Someone even had rainbow colored hair!

The Princes looked out at the city, which seemed to go on for several kilometers in a horseshoe-shaped valley. Far off to the east lay recently-planted fields of vegetables. Cattle, sheep, chicken and pheasant farms were set out to the north, and to the south were what appeared to be various factories and merchant stores. The stores were arranged like a strip mall, or so it appeared from the hill where the Princes were standing.

Just below the opening where they'd emerged from the forest was an enormous athletic complex and stadium. There were football fields, swimming pools, weight training equipment, beach volleyball courts, a rock climbing wall and basketball courts, all surrounding the stadium that was empty at the moment but looked as if it could host the entire village for a big game. There were several groups of children and adults engaged in various sporting activities. Some were playing beach volleyball, some were on the football fields. There were two groups of people just off to the side in open fields, one group looked like they were practicing some form of martial arts. Their movements were slow, deliberate and fluid. Another group was just sitting and meditating.

As they made their way past the athletic fields, everyone stopped what they were doing to greet Manchild and his companions.

"Good day Manchild! How was the surf today!"

"Hey Stowie, what's cooking dude! Who are your new friends?"

"Welcome to Provins!"

A little girl, no more than six years old, ran up to the group. Her hair was dyed dark purple, seemingly colored from fresh blueberries, and she had a wild handful of yellow dandelions. As the Princes passed her she handed each one a flower and said, "Welcome to Provins. I'm Mercury." When she reached little Jimmy she repeated, "Welcome to Provins, I'm Mercury," and winked at him with the brightest six-year-old, missing teeth kinda smile. Causing him to run and hide behind Nara, blushing.

More people lifted their hands in greeting as the group passed. Nara was the first to accept all the attention, responding with her practiced wave. Brandon wasted no time fitting in, surrounded by all this exposed skin. He waved to a group of girls playing volleyball as they passed. "Hey there! Hello!"

"Hi! Welcome to Provins!" the girls yelled back.

"Come on, this is great," said Brandon to the rest of the group. "And you know what they say, when in Rome..." With that, off came Brandon's shirt. He tried to flex his muscles as he passed the girls.

"Ugh, he can be such a dog sometimes," snarled Nara.

"Come, y'all must be tired and hungry. We'll find a place for you to crash, and tomorrow you'll see the Elders," said Manchild.

More and more people came to greet them as they walked farther into Provins. Soon there was a crowd waiting for them, lining the main street leading to the living quarters. Others followed behind, almost like a parade. The entire village stopped what they were doing and joined the crowd. Late arrivals were jumping up to get a glimpse of the Princes, all the while smiling and greeting them with warm voices. Everyone wanted to have a chance to welcome the new visitors to Provins.

People were handing them fresh fruits, skewers of grilled meats, arepas, sweet cakes and flowers. Leis of tropical flowers were placed around each one's neck, unlike anything that grew in Terrowin. Smiles were abundant. David and Cedric shook hands with so many people their knuckles and elbows started to hurt. Salil tried to stay in between Nara and Ava so as not to have anyone touch her, but even she could not escape the warm welcome of the people of Provins.

Manchild walked them to the heart of the village where several housing units were built along the main road. He dropped them off, boys in one unit and girls in the other. "Ok, little ones, dinner starts in like an hour or two. It just depends on when things are ready, no rush, ya know. Our village is your village. Go around, holla at some folks. If you want to go shopping for some new gear," he said, thinking how over-dressed and shabby they all were, "you can head on over to the mall. And snack shops are always open if you want to grab a munchie before din. Got it? Ok. I'll be back later."

"Hey, wait, we don't have any money so how can we possibly go shopping, um, dude?" Nara said, with more than a drop of sarcasm.

"Money, what's that? Everything here is free, little fry. Chill. No one uses that stuff anymore. Although, we have pictures of money, I think, in the Museum. I think?"

"Free?"

"Yeah, everything. Enjoy!"

"Awesome!"

When Manchild and Stowie left the group, Cedric called everyone for a meeting in the girls' room.

"Ok, so this is Provins?" asked Tem.

"Yes. They seem like good people," Cedric replied.

"I like them so far," David said. "Stowie is funny."

"And kinda cute too, isn't that right Salil?" Brandon teased, looking over at her.

"Shut up Brandon," Salil shot back.

"But listen everyone. The fact remains that Kass is still out there, somewhere, looking for us. Tem, I want you to stay with David at all times. Brandon, you stay with the girls, don't let them out of your sight. In the meantime, I'm going to try to find out as much as I can about this place. And remember, we are not to say a word about where we came from or our positions. As far as they know we are travelers, and we should just keep it that way. Got it?"

He paused to make sure he had everyone's attention. "Any questions?"

"What about me?" asked little Jimmy.

"Oh, you, ummm." Cedric had not really taken into account that little Jimmy was part of their group.

"Don't worry, we'll take him with us," Nara offered.

"Aww, I wanted to go with the boys!" Jimmy protested.

"Fine, but I think the mall has a candy store, and we were thinking of going there."

"Really! Hmm. Ok, I changed my mind. I want to go with you!"

No one else in the group had any questions and Cedric's words had brought them back to reality for a moment.

"Ok, let's go check out this place. We will meet back here before dinner. What is everyone going to do between now and then?"

Nara and Ava looked at each other, and together they said in unison, "Shopping!"

Chapter 59

Everyone except Cedric went shopping at the strip mall. The girls even managed to get Salil to go with them. They all selected new clothing, something that would be appropriate to wear in Provins. Brandon and Tem walked around shirtless, chests exposed and a bit puffed out. The girls found outfits that were suitable for Provins, Nara's a little more conservative than Ava's. Well, a lot more conservative, considering that Ava looked like she was about to go swimming, in a two-piece bathing suit. Nara wore a one piece suit, but she also had a skirt made of fabric wrapped around her waist. Salil found a new martial arts uniform at one of the stores, it was white and lightweight, and short-sleeved. David thought he was a little too skinny to walk around without a shirt on, and Cedric thought it was just improper. David found a light-colored polo shirt and new shorts. Little Jimmy found some clothes more befitting an eight-year-old kid headed to the beach, still wearing his mask, sticky smudges on his face after making his way through the chocolate shop. Freshly showered, with their new outfits and a much needed visit to the hair stylist and manicurist, the Princes looked once again like Royal children, Provins style. Nara and Ava even managed to dye their hair with hues of strawberry.

That night, the Princes and little Jimmy had dinner as honored guests of Provins. They enjoyed a feast that rivaled their best dinner celebrations at the School and ate until their tummies were full. Stowie and Manchild introduced them to several of the Elders in attendance and many of their friends and family. Stowie tried to make small talk with Salil during dinner. He wanted to find out more about her, but this proved to be a difficult task.

"So, why do you walk around with a mask on?"

"It's tradition."

"And what's up with the swords and bow?"

"Protection."

"You know, here swords are outlawed, and you're making a lot of people kinda queasy wearing those things. No need to have swords here, dude, since there's no killing in Provins. Tenet No. 1 and all."

"No killing?"

"That's right. No killing, since the time of our great Father, Morris Grotisi."

Stowie explained the five tenets of Provins to Salil, which at least seemed to get her attention, although she mostly listened while he spoke.

"Don't worry, be happy, what does that even mean?"

"Well, that's an easy one. It's like, dude, look around you,

you have family, friends, all you can eat, shelter and games. It's like, relax, go catch a wave, everything's just super!"

"What if someone doesn't have a family?" she replied, her thoughts going back to her own existence in Terrowin.

"No family? Come on, we're all family here. It's not just moms and dads, it's friends, and we are all friends here! All family and friends!"

"Sounds nice. So what if someone tries to kill someone here?"

"Oh, like ya did today with your little sword?"

"Yeah."

"Well, don't get it twisted. We learn how to defend ourselves, we just don't use weapons. But we train how to disarm someone with a weapon, like I did ya today." He laughed remembering their first encounter. Stowie started demonstrating the techniques to Salil with his arms waving in the air. "Too easy. I must admit, I had my doubts if it would work against someone with a real sword."

"What do you learn, what's it called?"

He started executing more moves, trying to show off. "Projitsu, an ancient form of kick ass combat handed down by our Great Father!"

"Could I learn it?"

"Heck yeah, we have classes four times a week! We can start tomorrow."

Finally, Salil thought, she could continue her training. Somehow, while she didn't miss being at the School and some of her classes, she did miss working out and practicing in her room. Her legs felt stronger from all the walking she had done, but she hadn't practiced much hand-to-hand combat in a while, except for killing that wild boar, which in her mind was kinda cool.

"Thanks."

Salil went with the rest of the Princes and Jimmy to have their first peaceful night's rest in a long while. For one night, they tried to forget about the fire, forget about Kass and forget about Terrowin.

Chapter 60

They were awakened early the next morning before most people in Provins were up. Manchild was there to retrieve them.

"Come, we must go now, the Elders want to meet with you."

Brandon was still half asleep as he walked. Rubbing his eyes, he remarked, "I thought old people slept late."

They all replied at once, "Shut up Brandon!"

They walked into a building, close to where they were staying. It looked like all the rest of the houses, similar to their units.

When they walked in they saw six Elders sitting at a long wooden table. Three women and three men. One of them reminded Cedric of Professor Walden. He spoke first. "Welcome children. Please join us for breakfast." He stood up and walked over to them. "I'm Elder Morning Sunshine. I think you met my sons Manchild and Stowie." He shook their hands. "Welcome to Provins."

David was the first to offer his hand. "Thanks for having us here. I'm David, this is Nara, Cedric, Tem, Ava, Brandon, Salil and little Jimmy. Boy, we haven't eaten and slept like that in months, many thanks!"

The other five Elders came and introduced themselves to each of the Princes. There was Chocolate Love, Sky Blue, Moonlight Walker, Star Fish, and Humming Bird.

"Well, great to have you. Please, have breakfast."

Set out on a table was an array of fruits and vegetables, boiled pheasant eggs and smoked boar sausage along with pineapple juice, coconut water and hot tea and coffee. They each made themselves a plate of food and joined the Elders at the table.

"So, how did you find us?" asked Elder Morning Sunshine.

Everyone looked at Cedric, knowing he was the spokesperson for the group.

"After our parents died, we decided to leave, and one of our teachers told us to find a place called Provins."

"How old are you?"

"Well, we will soon be thirteen, except little Jimmy who will turn nine."

Sky Blue, the oldest female Elder interrupted. "Will you stop interrogating these wonderful children! Listen, we already decided that you can stay here and be a part of our family. But, we have just two small requests. First, the swords of Salil and Tem and Salil's bow and arrow, well, there's no use for them here, because we don't have anything to worry about. They cannot wear them, it makes the people nervous. Second, the masks. You two have to remove your masks. I mean, we are all family here. Oh, unless we have a parade or festival, then lots of us wear festive masks. It's so much fun!"

After last night's feast, little Jimmy was convinced that this place was even better than Terrowin. He removed his mask right away. "No problem. It's true, we can go to the store and get chocolate and candy any time we want? And have food any time? And swim? Play football?"

"Yes little Jimmy. Any time you want."

"Sweet! I'm so gonna like it here!"

However, it seemed to Salil that they were singling her out of the group. First her swords, and now her mask. Everything she had been taught and trained to do was being challenged and questioned. She was conflicted. Cedric tried to intervene.

"Great Elders, where we come from, it's tradition that she wear her mask, at all times, no exceptions. Could you allow us this one indulgence?" Cedric tried his best to be diplomatic, trying to preserve their way of life whilst not offending the Elders.

Sunshine responded, "Little Cedric, we understand. But you are in Provins now, no need for masks and no need for swords. Don't worry, be happy."

David interrupted, "Hey, it's no big deal, I've seen her with her mask off, just yesterday at the water with Nara. Her long black hair and teary little eyes!"

"Shut your mouth David!" Nara said in Salil's defense. She shot David of look of exasperation. Nara walked over to Salil, and put her hand on her shoulder. "Salil, it will be all right."

Salil felt comforted by Nara's words and the touch of her hand. She simply said, "As you wish." She removed her mask, and with that the Princes (and little Jimmy) were accepted into Provins.

Chapter 61

The Princes had been enjoying life in Provins for almost two months. For the first time in their lives, they were behaving like almost-thirteen-year-olds should act. They had been there so long that the thought of a murderous Kass tracking them was pushed farther and farther into the backs of their minds. The group started going separate ways, each finding different activities within Provins to occupy their time. Brandon spent most of his days playing sports, trying to impress the girls. Nara and Ava tried their hands at designing different clothing, which might be more appropriate for them to wear. Although, Nara mostly directed, while Ava was the creative talent behind their production.

Tem still followed David around. David liked to spend his time among the Elders, especially Elder Morning Sunshine. He enjoyed his company for the most part, but David's constant questions about everything could sometimes get annoying. Sunshine indulged him as best he could.

Cedric spent a lot of his time walking the perimeter of

Provins alone and studying many hours in the libraries and museums. Their history and culture fascinated him, and before long he knew many of their customs, traditions and superstitions.

He learned that Morris Grotisi had come to Provins a long time ago, before the "Darkening." Prior to Grotisi's arrival, the people of Provins were both tribal and nomadic. He unified the tribes and established the five Tenets of Provins. He was also the founder of Projitsu and preached that fighting should only be used for defensive purposes, without weapons.

Cedric also learned that the people of Provins had been almost completely annihilated after the eruption of the nearby volcano Mount Himalua. As Grotisi was aging, Himalua erupted in a violent explosion, sending dust and ash so far into the atmosphere that it rained from the skies, down over the region for almost two weeks after. Then came the lava. For thirty days and thirty nights, lava spewed forth from the great mountain, consuming everything in its path and destroying almost half of Provins, all that lay to the north. The Darkening followed the eruption. The sun did not show its face for almost half a year, nothing grew and the people of Provins almost perished. Were it not for the fishing vessels that brought back nourishment from the ocean, Provins would no longer exist. Cedric recalled a similar reference in Terrowin history, they called it the year without a summer. Temperatures remained cool throughout that summer and days were hazy and dusk-like.

Cedric learned that Provinians, despite their laid-back

appearance, were great fishermen and navigators of the ocean. They had a massive fishing fleet and, as far as he could tell, were even more advanced than the people of Terrowin in their seamanship. Although, they were forbidden to fish to the north of Provins, always heading farther south or due east. For good reason, to the north lies Mt. Himalua, and history told of countless people who ventured into the Blackness, never to be heard from again.

Salil spent most of her time with Stowie, learning Projitsu. She was a good student, but the moves did not come naturally to her. She had been taught mostly offense, her sword and bow her friends. The rhythmic movements, which seemed dancelike at times, did not come easily to her. Oftentimes she would find herself at the end of some arm- or leg-locking position, in pain as her opponent applied pressure to indicate that he or she had executed the move properly. Stowie seemed to take great pleasure in submitting Salil to these various positions during practice.

They practiced with wooden swords to learn how to disarm an enemy wielding a real one. "Come on girlie Salil, try again." She was one of the best swordspersons there, so she attacked Stowie using moves she learned at School. This time he ducked under it, and pushed her arm away causing her to spin around. As she spun, he grabbed her hair and yanked her head to the ground, executing a simulated death blow to her exposed neck as she lay on the floor. Her frustration grew with every counter-move he executed.

Stowie began to taunt her. "Salil, you know, you're too

serious! Let go, man. It's too easy, you're too predictable. Let me tell you a secret about a person who has a sword," he said, dodging another one of her attacks.

"What?" She tried to strike him.

"They always want to use the sword!"

"Kiaaaa!" she attacked. This time with a straight thrust, which appeared to go through his body. He paused and looked down at the sword. His eyes widening like he was in pain, then weakening in such a way she was terrified he might die.

"Stowie, I didn't mean it! Are you ok?"

He grabbed the sword, which was between his left arm and side, and used it to pull her closer to him. With a pained look in his eyes, he placed one hand on her shoulder and quickly moved in close to her.

"Got ya!" he laughed, and swiftly planted a kiss on Salil's cheek as he fell away toward the ground laughing.

Salil backed away from him and touched her cheek with the opposite hand. Without saying a word, she dropped her sword and ran away as fast as she could, headed to her cabin.

"Hey, wait, where ya going? I was jus playin!" Realizing he might be in trouble he shouted to make sure she could hear him, "You won't tell my dad will ya?"

When she reached the cabin, she grabbed her swords and mask and ran all the way to the beach and the black rocky cliffs from where they first entered Provins. She climbed the rocks and sat alone, watching the waves crash, waiting for the sun to go down and the stars to come out.

Salil put her mask back on her face and tried to remember

the times she walked down her secret passageway alone. She tried to remember the lines written there on the wall. *Assassins Walk the Path Alone.* Now, she wanted to return to her life as it was before. Things were simple then, they made sense to her. Train. Study. Fight. Before they'd left, her mind was at peace, beginning to accept her fate and even relishing the fact that she, as an assassin, was somehow special or different from the others.

Provins was a strange land for her, alien. Too many people, too happy, and way too much touching. She had never felt so confused in her life. She wanted to return home and resume her training. That was all she had known growing up, and that was all she wanted to accept at this moment. She closed her eyes and tried to remember the breathing techniques of Professor Glinda. In, hold, release. In, hold, release.

"Hey! You sure do run fast!" It was David. He was out of breath, struggling from the climb. "What are you doing up here?" he asked. She didn't respond to him. "Well, it's a nice view. Mind if I sit here with you?"

"It's a free country," she said rather stoically.

David sat beside her and didn't say a word for a few moments. Salil did her best to ignore him.

"Salil, do you miss home? I mean, do you miss School?" He asked her.

She looked over at David, surprised that he might be having the same thoughts as her. "Yeah, sometimes."

"Me too. Don't get me wrong, I like it here, but I miss all

our friends and professors. I hope everyone's ok."

"Well, at least you had friends at School."

David didn't respond to that comment, he knew exactly what she meant. "Do you think we can ever go back?" he asked.

"I don't know."

"Well, when we do, it will kinda suck, you know, you having to try to kill me and all when we're older."

"Maybe."

"Yeah, but you know, you do have friends. I'm your friend."

She did not reply.

"I remember the night of the fire. I was scared. I didn't want to die just yet." David struggled to keep his composure. He was maturing, but none of them had ever spoken of the horror they shared leaving the School the night of the fire, never having a chance to reflect on the events of that night.

Salil looked over at David, tears welling up in his eyes.

"What about Kass?" he asked. "You think she will ever find us and kill us all?"

"Maybe." That was the only word that came out her mouth. She wanted to try to console David, but she had never consoled anyone in her life. In fact, she really didn't understand what she was feeling, but looking into David's teary eyes and hearing his voice crack, she started feeling those things again. Emotions. She wanted to help him, but she didn't know how. She said the first thing that came to her mind, without thinking, she placed her hand on top of David's.

"David, I won't let Kass kill you. I'll kill her first if I have to."

David rubbed his eyes with his hand, wiping away the tears before they fell from his eyes, regaining his composure. Remembering he was almost a teenager.

"Come on big guy. We better get back before Tem starts worrying about you."

"Yeah, and you and Stowie! Kissy, kissy, kissy!"

"Shut up!"

Chapter 62

Salil was still adjusting to having her mask off in Provins, and after her talk with David she worried more and more about whether Kass would eventually find them. One evening, a few days later, Stowie visited the girls' cabin. Salil was still annoyed by his kissing antics and hadn't returned to the Projitsu class since.

"Hey! How you doing, no worries right? We're going for a history lesson tonight, I think y'all should come," Stowie said. Salil had been spending more time with Nara and even told her about Stowie's kiss.

"Oh, here's loverboy. So, now you want to make nice, huh? Thanks for the invitation. Now byee!" She waved her hand at him dismissively.

"Oh, come on, it's fun! Trust me, everyone will be there."

"Get out, Stowie! Now!" yelled Nara, in the most annoying voice she could muster. And let me tell you, that was pretty high on the annoying scale.

Stowie walked a few steps away, then popped his head

back in the door with a winning smile. "It'll be fun."

Nara threw a cup at him, which crashed against the door, prompting Stowie to run away quickly. She told Cedric about the history lesson, though, and Cedric thought it would be good for everyone to attend. He gathered their group and they all headed to one of the big structures in the middle of the village. It resembled a teepee, one of the building styles the Princes learned about in their own history. Terwinian ancestors had used them as dwellings before building wood cabins and stone castles.

When they walked inside, crowds of people were milling about, it seemed as if the entire city was there. A huge wood fire burned in the middle, sending up stacks of smoke to the top opening. Most people sat on bleachers arranged around the perimeter. Families and friends sat together, kids and toddlers on the floor in front of the bleachers. Mothers held infants with their husbands by their sides. Young lovers sat beside each other, holding hands and sharing drinks of fresh coconut, pineapple and kiwi juices, with tiki umbrellas and crazy straws.

There were bowls being passed around that appeared to be made of coconut shell halves, but they might have been some kind of wood. They were all different, sanded smooth, some carved with intricate designs, some studded with shells, or adorned with dangling beads and feathers. Smoke rose from the bowls, and there appeared to be a sort of ritual wherein one person cupped the vessel at about chest height for the person beside him and wafted the smoke with one hand while the other person leaned forward and inhaled deeply before leaning back, eyes closed for a few moments. Then that one would take the bowl and do the same for the next person. By the time the Princes arrived, there was standing room only and they made their way to the front to sit among the children on the floor. There were no bowls being passed down there.

Stowie found the group and invited himself over to sit next to them. Everyone seemed like they were enjoying themselves. Drummers were positioned on one side, playing rhythmic tunes, as the last people made their way in. Standing in the middle was Elder Sunshine. He raised his hands and everyone immediately stopped talking. He was ready to begin. He started with a prayer. "Blessed be Provins, and all those within." The crowd hummed, just a slow buzz that felt almost electric. "Let us remember the five tenets of Provins. Tenet number one."

The Provinians chanted in unison and recited each of the tenets, beginning with "Thou shalt not kill."

Once they were finished, Sunshine began. He was telling a story to the people and they all stayed quiet, except for the occasional cry of a baby or squawk of a toddler. He told of the founder of Provins, Morris Grotisi, a man who had come from the north and author of the five tenets of Provins. Sunshine was a great orator and told the story using the full range of his voice and his body, for full dramatic effect. It was clear that the people had heard this story many times before. But for the Princes it was all brand new, and little Jimmy really enjoyed listening to the man change his voice as the drums chimed in at various moments.

Cedric was loving the fact that he had previously read about these moments in Provins history and knew most of what was going to happen:

"Firestorm! Firestorm! Firestorm!" the group of people chanted three times and then went silent as they waited for Sunshine to continue.

"A firestorm rained down upon Provins for thirty days and thirty nights! The forest set ablaze all around us." He threw a handful of dust onto the fire, prompting it to flash higher for a few seconds with a great whoosh. Then, he poured out a stream of water on the fire, leaving it smoldering, the room darkened with just a red glow remaining, giving enough light to see inside the room.

The people whispered: "The Darkness, the Darkness, the Darkness."

"The Darkness came upon the land, which tested our faith in the five tenets. We had been taught to share all we had with our neighbors, even if it were our last, but we never actually expected to be down to our last. Don't worry, be happy. But how could we be happy when those around us were dying from starvation and disease? People who had food, did not share with neighbors who had none. People who had shelter, turned away those who were homeless. People who were living, offered no comfort to the sick and the dying. The Darkness tested our faith in our Father and his tenets.

"The Father! The Father! The Father!"

Little Jimmy was so entranced he started repeating the

words with the others after learning the first phrase. He managed the last two, "The Father, the Father."

Sunshine was a master storyteller, and by now the entire room was enthralled, waiting for his every word. Even the Princes were amazed by the presentation. All eyes were upon Sunshine. No one stirred.

"But our Father, Morris Grotisi, reminded us that at times like these, even during our darkest days, especially during our darkest days, we have to remain firm in our beliefs. He was dying, his own body in the grips of plague and starvation that had already taken so many of our people. Yet, still he found strength, he wanted to look upon the lava flow with his own eyes. The great Father journeyed toward the mountain, slowly, his old body withering with each step. When he reached the cliffs, which were once covered with trees, he saw that barren black rock had overtaken our land, had taken our people, there was inhospitable Blackness as far as the eye could see. Lava continued to flow underneath the hardened crust. The ocean hissed, steamed and boiled at the point where the hot molten flow met the cool waters off our shore."

Sunshine continued, opening his eyes wide, "He saw with his own eyes!"

People in the crowd began to nod and some called out in response.

"With his own eyes, brother!"

"Tell it!"

Sunshine dropped to the ground, "And fell down on his knees,"

"On his knees!"

He crawled forward about a meter and collapsed, "...too weak to continue any farther.

"He pointed to the north," Sunshine flung up his hand as the people started the low hum, "to the land now scorched black! There, on his knees," Sunshine rose back up to his knees, "he pointed to the place from which he came unto Provins."

The crowd chanted in unison, "The Prophecy! The Prophecy! The Prophecy!"

Sunshine stood tall. "Our great Father warned us, oh yes he warned us, that people will come. People will come! From the north! Be wary of them." He paused for effect and looked around. No one made a sound. Then he whispered, "For their ways are not our ways."

The crowd whispered in response, building to a crescendo as they recited: "Their ways are not our ways. Their ways are not our ways. Their ways are not our ways!"

Little Jimmy, filled with joy and a happiness that was unfamiliar to him, found himself drunk with jubilation. This was an energy he had never felt before. The whole building was vibrating. He was so excited from hearing the story and watching the performance and chanting with the people that he jumped up in front of everyone and proclaimed, "That's where we came from!" He hopped up and down with something like ecstasy. "We came from the north, we walked the Blackness and we almost died!"

Cedric put his head down upon hearing Jimmy's words.

The energy within the room seemed to disappear. Shock and awe descended upon the group.

Someone yelled out, "Be wary of them, for their ways are not our ways!"

At that all the Provinians turned their backs to the Princes and chanted in unison, "Their ways are not our ways. Their ways are not our ways. Their ways are not our ways."

Then people started walking out of the building, not looking at any of the Princes or at little Jimmy on their way out. Stowie stood up in disbelief and walked over to Elder Sunshine. The Princes scorned. Were they to be banished? They walked together back to their sleeping quarters, none of them saying a word.

When they arrived back, Nara was the first to speak, "Cedric, do you think they will kick us out? Where will we go?"

"I don't know. Let's just sleep on it and discuss it in the morning."

"I was really starting to like it here," she said.

"Don't worry, be happy, I will talk with the Elders tomorrow," David said to everyone's surprise. They looked at him a little differently. He actually seemed as if he could be royalty in that moment, the leader he was taught to be, who they hoped he might be.

"I'll go with you," said Cedric.

"No, Elder Sunshine has his morning walk very early and I usually walk with him. I got this. We should get some rest. Shower the people with love! Goodnight." At David's words, everyone in the group readied themselves for bed.

Chapter 63

David woke early the next morning and was waiting on Elder Sunshine to exit his cabin. The sun had not yet breached the horizon and most in Provins were asleep at this hour.

"Good morning," David greeted Sunshine.

"Ah, little David. Good morning to you also." They walked together, taking their usual route. "I'm sorry about what happened last night, but you have to understand our people and our ways. Even though we are filled with love, we still have our superstitions and beliefs."

"Yeah, tell me about it."

They walked and talked for a while, stopping at one of the merchant shops to pick up a cup of coffee for Sunshine and hot chocolate for David. David started talking about his life in Terrowin, and their own beliefs and the declaration of the wisemen. He told him about being the future king and about the fire and Kass pursuing them.

"David, I know all about Terrowin. It took me a moment to figure out that you all were Royals."

David stopped in his tracks. "Huh? You know about Terrowin? How?"

"Well, I am one of the direct descendants of a Royal." He paused and started drawing in the dirt with a stick,

M-O-R-R-I-S G-R-O-T-I-S-I

"Better known in your country as—" he took his stick and started drawing a line from each letter,

R-I-G-O-R M-O-R-T-I-S-I-S

"So, wait. Rigor Mortisis, the great assassin of Terrowin, founded Provins?" David shook his head in disbelief. "That's deep. But why don't the others know?"

"Well, it's a family secret, and only those directly descended from him know this part of our history. When he left Terrowin he was a man without a soul. He never wanted to be an assassin, but he was programmed to be a killer from the day he was born. After he killed the king, he hated himself, his childhood and Terrowin. He hated life itself and contemplated ending it all. The pain was too much, and he arrived in Provins a sad and broken man. Until he fell in love."

"Always a girl there to change a man, in our history too."

"Yes, and having never felt feelings of love, security and happiness, he wanted to change who he was and how he lived."

"So, he went from assassin to saint?"

"Well, he became a better man. And was able to start over again in life. But before he died, he told his wife about his life in Terrowin. About the Royals and how they were raised. He swore her to only reveal this to his descendants and no one else. So, when you children first arrived, I kinda figured that maybe you were from Terrowin. Salil and little Jimmy's masks confirmed my belief."

"Ohh."

"And it took me a few days, but I figured out that you were king and the positions of the others. Boy, you're going to have your hands full with that queen of yours Nara."

"Ugh. Don't remind me." Sunshine laughed. "But I assure you," David looked at him in all seriousness, "we mean you— and your people—no harm."

"I know that, but my people believe so strongly in our way of life, it has kept us happy and safe for hundreds of years."

David thought about what he might do to convince him. "Just give us until spring and we will be on our way, we need some time to figure things out."

"Ok, I'm sure we can work that out. But what about this assassin that's coming after you all?"

"Tell your people none of that, no need to alarm them. We will handle it, out of sight from Provins. If she ever finds us at all."

"Little King David, you are wiser than you appear."

"Thanks, I tried to learn as much as I could in School."

"I'll have some work to do to convince the others, but I think this will turn out just fine. I always enjoy our morning walks and conversations. We should continue these."

Later that morning, Sunshine spoke with the other Elders of Provins and they agreed that the Princes and little Jimmy could stay. David spoke with Cedric, Tem and Salil about the deal he'd struck with Sunshine. He also told them a little more about the history of Provins and the story of Rigor Mortisis and Morris Grotisi, which Salil paid close attention to. Cedric seemed almost annoyed that David had access to information that he was not privy to, despite having spent all that time studying the history of Provins. But at the end of the day Cedric accepted that David was the Prince King, and part of him was even impressed with the little guy.

David, Cedric, Tem and the Elders agreed that Tem and Salil would take turns keeping watch outside the forest leading to Provins. If Kass was going to come, she would come from the north, the same way they had traveled. And if she was as good as Rigor Mortisis, the Elders did not want her to so much as enter the village. At first, Tem objected to leaving David unprotected. He needed some assurances that David would be safe when he was away. And he still did not trust Salil enough to leave her alone in the forest waiting to meet up with another assassin from Terrowin. The Elders assured Tem that David would be safe within the city and that they would be responsible for his well-being. Salil only agreed to stand guard if she could have her mask and her swords while she was on her watch.

By lunchtime, word had spread throughout Provins that the Princes would be staying and there was no need for alarm. People accepted the Elders' wisdom and resumed their daily routines without a care in the world.

Chapter 64

Over the next few weeks, the Princes and Little Jimmy settled, once again, quite comfortably back into daily life within Provins. Salil did not object to being on watch, she knew her own life was also in danger. Both she and Tem took turns watching the forest just north of Provins. Salil preferred the night shift, as it offered her some solitude and escape from the people of Provins, and she could sleep during the day, oftentimes avoiding contact with people for days at a time. Sometimes Stowie would wander the forest looking for her at night and just sit with her. At first she pleaded with him to return to the village, but he wouldn't listen. Finally, the thought of having him around, in the event that Kass did show up, began to sound better and better.

Salil had another reason for wanting Stowie around. He was a descendant of Rigor Mortisis, and Salil wanted to know more about the man who she now believed had saved her life. In a sense, Stowie, Manchild and Sunshine were like her family, the family that she'd never had. She talked more than usual and asked many questions. About him, his family and what he knew of the great Father. Salil felt a strange connection to Stowie somehow, especially after learning his heritage, it was almost brother-like.

"So, this Kass person. You know her?"

"Yes."

"And you think she's coming alone, to kill all of you?"

"Yes."

"Come on, one against seven, no worries little Salil, you can handle her! And, if she shows up while I'm here, she betta watch out. I'll take her sword, just like I took yours!"

"I wouldn't be so sure."

"Oh, please. What's one girlie gonna do?"

"Shut up Stowie! You don't know Kass. She is a killer. She's much more advanced than you or me. I'm not sure I can stop her." Salil's memory took her back to the Advanced Fighting Class, where she fought Kass. It was no contest, and she was still afraid.

"Well, you don't have to do it alone. We're all family now."

Salil looked over at Stowie, still certain that he did not fully comprehend the threat that Kass presented.

Chapter 65

The days grew shorter and there was still no sign of Kass. The people of Provins were anxious to celebrate the Festival of Light and Love holidays, it being the most festive time of year for them. People scurried about, trying to figure out what gifts to give their family and friends. Now, in Provins, it's customary to give gifts to everyone you know, not just immediate family. And, there is no ranking or hierarchy on the type of present you would give to someone. Meaning, a mother would give her child the same sort of gift she would give to a neighbor's child. So, since most Provinians knew a lot of people, shopping starts early and continues right up until the Provinian Lovefeast. Almost everyone can expect to give and receive at least fifty gifts.

The idea of shopping for someone was foreign to the Princes. During holidays and birthdays, the State always gave the customarily mandated gifts to each of them, according to their status. But the girls took to shopping quite easily. Except Salil. Heck, the only gift she'd ever received was the one from her parents, which still remained unopened. But Nara and Ava dragged her along to the shopping district anyway.

"Do you think David would like this, Salil?" Nara asked, holding up a pair of shorts and matching basketball jersey.

"I'm not sure. Do you think he would look good in a jersey?"

Nara and Ava stopped in their tracks, looked at each other and burst out laughing. "Oh, my goodness! Salil is alive, she's alive! You made a joke," said Ava.

"Huh? What did I say? Stop laughing at me."

"It's ok Salil. We're not laughing at you, but at the sight of David wearing this! His skinny little arms!"

Salil thought about what Nara said. She smiled and said, "A-ha!" which was pretty close to a laugh for her.

Meanwhile, the boys were having a very difficult time at the shopping thing.

"Cedric, are you sure it's customary to give a gift to everyone you know during the holidays?"

"Yes, David. That's the custom here, and it would be offensive and rude not to follow their traditions."

They were shopping in the girl's bathing suit department. Brandon and Tem whispered to David, out of earshot of Cedric. He nodded at them.

"Well, can't you just get everyone's gifts for us? You're the smart one," said David, holding up a two-piece bright polka dot bikini and shaking his head.

"No way. No amount of flattery will get you out of this one. None of you!" said Cedric, pointing to Tem and Brandon, who obviously thought Cedric would take care of this for them if David asked.

"Dude, but you're the intellectual and stuff," Brandon said.

"Uh-uh. No way. Besides, there is no amount of intelligence that makes shopping for girls easy."

"Dude, I mean, I don't need your help, shopping for the girls is easy for me."

"Thanks for making my point for me," Cedric said drily.

"You should help these guys though, for real," he motioned to Tem and David. "But I'm good. Here look, I had fifty of these made." Brandon showed the guys a photo of himself, skin oiled with coconut like the locals did, striking a bodybuilder pose that showed off his muscles, with a local provinirose clenched in his teeth. It was inscribed, "To My Dearest_____, With Love, Brandon."

"See man, and I left the space there to put in the name of the girl I'm giving it to. Smart, eh?"

"Hell yeah, dude! That's hella awesome. Wish I had thought of that! You don't mind if I copy yer idea, do ya?" Stowie said.

"Genius Brandon, just genius," replied a sarcastic Cedric.

"No problemo brother!"

David walked away from the boys, Tem followed him. "So, Tem," he said, "getting things for Nara and Ava, easy stuff. But what do you think I should get Salil?"

"Salil? Ummm, I'm not sure."

"What did you get her?"

"Well, I know she likes killing things, so I made some new

arrows for her bow, and I even put her name on them."

"That's a cool idea. Nice. Yeah, I wanted to get her something good, but I have no idea."

David walked over to the jewelry store. There was a wide variety of necklaces, bracelets and earrings. There was silver, gold, different colored pearls from local oysters and various gemstones mined right there in Provins.

David approached the counter and inspected several items. He had already picked out a pearl necklace for Nara, something befitting a future queen. Ava also received a necklace, but hers was a little less glamorous, the wires twisted around semi-precious blue and green stones. He understood the Provinian ways, but he was a Royal, and he knew his queen should never get something less extravagant than his lover.

"Excuse me, what's that bracelet there, the one with the black and blue pearls?"

"Oh, this one here? Well, this is a traditional friendship bracelet. Years ago, it was customary to give such a bracelet to anyone you considered a friend. That way, people who might know someone you know could immediately identify themselves as a friend. So for years people walked around wearing various bracelets from different friends. If you came across a stranger, you simply looked to see if you had a similarly patterned bracelet, and if so you were immediate friends. Well, it was something like that."

"Cool, I'll take two of those."

David kept one for himself and planned to give the other to Salil.

The Terrowin Times

KING'S MASKED MILITIA KILL 24, Hundreds Detained

Last night, 24 people were killed, dozens were wounded and hundreds more were detained by the King's masked militia, who responded with deadly force, in an effort to contain the growing protests in Terrowin.

Yesterday's protest centered around the King's latest controversial decision to cancel the Birthing Holidays this year. Over 50,000 Terwinans occupied Terrowin Square in response to the cancelation.

King Xalvador has enacted several questionable decrees since taking the crown and citizens have been quietly objecting to his policies, i.e. closing the Ascension School permanently and creating a masked militia.

Growing dissent in Terrowin reached a boiling point last night, when a peaceful protest turned deadly. The militia, after several stern warnings asking the crowd to disperse, opened fire, killing thirteen men, seven women and four children. Three of the women were pregnant. After opening fire, chaos ensued and the militia started handcuffing and detaining protesters.

Unconfirmed sources report that over two hundred men, women and children were being held inside the Birthing Hospital. A facility once used to care for the future king of Terrowin appears now to be used as a detention center.

Citizens are fearful. "The masked men just opened fire! We were unarmed. There were arrows and rocks everywhere," reported one citizen who refused to give his name. "How could he cancel the Birthing Holiday?" asked one pregnant woman. "Me and my husband planned to give birth to a Primo. It's tradition! Who will be our next king?"

In response to the protests, King Xalvador increased the militia's numbers in the Capital, imposed a 5:00 p.m. curfew and decreed that there shall be no groups of more than two people congregating in public.

Anyone caught violating these laws shall be subject to immediate arrest.

$\mathcal{C}$hapter 66

The end of the year Provinian Lovefeast celebration included a great festival held on the field of the football arena. Tables and chairs were set up on the grass, and food was all around. Music played and dancing started early in the evening. The moves were strange to the Terwinians, but some of them had the courage to try to learn. Of course, Brandon and Ava caught on quickly and they were soon leading others, sharing dance moves they had learned in Terrowin. Even little Jimmy joined in. Tem insisted that he remain with David that evening, which meant Salil was on watch.

Dinner was to be served at eight. Lanterns were lit all around the arena, and a special table for the Elders and their guests was set up at one end of the stadium. Hundreds of pheasants were slowly roasting on an enormous rotisserie, scenting the air with herbs and spices. Pheasant was the traditional main course, but other local favorites included grilled shrimp, devilled pheasant eggs, mango and mint chutney, sushi of all types, pigs-in-blankets, a variety of fish from the ocean (some of which the Princes had never eaten), butterscotch pie, coconut-banana cream pie, kiwi-frosted tropical mint cake, pound cake, chocolate buttermilk cake, chocolate whoopee pies, lemon-rosemary bars, peanut butter fudge, huckleberry cookies and, really, cookies of every flavor known to Provinians. The delicious aroma-filled air made everyone's tummies growl with hunger and excitement.

Off in the forest, Salil was keeping watch, high in one of her favorite trees, overlooking the stream where Nara had first removed her mask. On this night she wore her mask and the bracelet that David had given her just hours before. He told her it was a "friendship" bracelet. She actually liked looking at the bracelet and thinking that maybe, just maybe, she had some friends. And David seemed nice enough.

She brought along her pouch, which held the unopened letter and gift from her parents. She debated with herself about opening them up this night. She held the letter in her hands. Her talks with Stowie, spending time with Nara and being with David had given her a new feeling of belonging. As she studied the people of Provins, how everyone was family, she hoped that maybe her parents might somehow feel the same way about her. No, not hoped. She knew it, in some way she felt it deep in her bones. But she was still hesitant. Just as she began to open the envelope, Salil heard some rustling in the woods. She quickly stuffed the letter in her pouch.

She turned around to get a glimpse of what was moving through the woods. The moon was full, which made her vision a little better on this particular night. She tried her best to conceal herself up in the branches. Leaves crackled off in the distance, footsteps heading in her direction. Salil readied her bow and arrow, aiming and tracking. She waited for a clearing to get a perfect line of sight.

Her breathing slowed. She was not scared, she was focused. She knew. She knew it was Kass, she had finally found them and was making her way toward Provins. Salil would not let her friends down. She pulled back on the bow even farther, feeling the tension in the wires and ready to release upon first sight of Kass.

Patiently waiting, remembering that she had to release between heartbeats, she slowed her breathing even more, which slowed her heart rate. Then, clumsily walking out of the bush, was Stowie.

"Stowie, you idiot. You almost got shot! What are you doing here?"

"Hey lady, relax. No one should spend tonight alone. I wanted to come say what's up. You know, and give you a little love."

"A little love?"

"You know a gift, a present. Come on, yo. Here just take it."

Stowie climbed the tree and handed Salil a wrapped present. It was a picture of Stowie, posing in a football stance and holding a ball, with the words, "To Salil, all my love, yo!"

Salil smiled when she looked at the picture. "Thank you, Stowie."

"No doubt, Salil."

They both sat there, without saying a word, listening to the music off in the distance.

It was almost an hour before dinner and some people took their seats within the open stadium, waiting for festivities. Provins most definitely hosted the grandest of parties. The entertainment consisted first of a marching drum band. Now, not the kind you see at a typical American football game, where they march in unison, stiff like robots. The Provins marching band was more akin to a Caribbean festival band. The men and women wore elaborate outfits adorned with bird feathers, animal hides, body paint and skimpy outfits made of grass and golden straw.

Bright colors were the theme, and hair colored in exotic shades flowed in all directions to the sounds of the music. Several drummers led the way, both male and female, beating on different-sized drums, some big, some bigger, some with their hands and others with drumsticks. One drum was so big that it took five people to carry it, while the drummer was hoisted above on stilts, bashing away with both hands using huge mallets. Now everyone knew it was time to party, the real music was about to start. People stood up in the stadium, clapping their hands in rhythm with the drums, some started dancing in place and others joined the procession after the drummers passed them.

Following the drummers was a series of people carrying and playing various types of instruments, shakers, flutes, horns, castanets, tambourines. It was all heavily orchestrated, but with the effortless feeling that came from everyone appearing to do their own thing as the accompanying music complemented the drummers. Behind them were the singers, better described as chanters. These were men and women who would occasionally holler out in unison various sounds, which would prompt the audience to follow in suit. "Heeeeyyyyyy, Yooooo, Aalllriight!" Following the chanters, were a series of adults and children all dancing together, a pre-choreographed set. Hands in the air, bending from side to side and jump-spinning in the air.

There were a few floats that followed the dancers, one for the Elders, who stood on a platform and danced with each other. David and Tem joined the Elders on their float, David fully participating in the festivities, while Tem stood around watching, smiling. Another float carried young children, dressed in costumes and face paint, all dancing ecstatically.

Brandon and Ava joined the chanters when they passed them and started following along. The procession circled the entire stadium, and it seemed as if almost everyone had joined in following the marching band. The Lovefeast had begun.

Chapter 67

Salil and Stowie could hear the drummers and the chanting from their perch high in the tree. "We're missing the best part of the festival right now. But it's cool yo. I'm here wit ya, girlie," said Stowie.

"Yeah, sounds like fun," replied Salil, still trying to focus her attention on her watch.

"You know, I hope y'all get to stay in Provins, cause—" At that moment, a bolas came flying through the trees and hit Stowie square on the side of his head before he could even react, knocking him out instantly. He fell from the tree and landed hard on the ground below.

"Stowie!" Salil yelled as she tried to catch him before he fell. He lay there below her, unconscious.

Another bolas came crashing through the branches, but Salil heard the rustling as it passed through the leaves and was able to move her head in time. She knew it. Kass had found them.

Kass walked the same path as the Princes, through the

Blackness, and had arrived the day before. She set up camp on the outskirts of Provins and even managed to get inside the perimeter last night while they all were sleeping. She scouted the village from within without ever being detected. She'd thought about killing Tem the night before when he was on his watch, but she had other plans in mind.

Kass approached Salil, who was climbing down the tree to check on Stowie before intercepting her enemy.

"So, you finally made it here," Salil said in a bored voice, looking directly at Kass.

"Yes. I did. Now it's time for this to end."

"Wait," said Salil, trying to buy some time, still not wanting to face Kass again. "Why did you and Xalvador do it? Why kill all the Royals, King Richard surely is onto this scheme?"

Kass laughed. "King Richard and his cabinet are with the rest of the Royals. Dead."

"King Richard? Dead?"

"Yes."

"So, who is running Terrowin—Xalvador?"

"That's King Xalvador. Come on, it's time for you and the Princes to join the rest." Kass drew her sword and Salil hers.

They walked in a circle, opposite each other, in a clockwise motion, swords out in front. Kass attacked first, she rushed in and executed a few moves with her sword, chopping down and swiping across close to Salil.

Salil blocked every one of the moves, a spark flashed with the last collision of the swords. But she could feel Kass's superior strength with each blow. Kass attacked again, with almost the same series of strike combinations. Salil blocked them all again, but Kass executed a front kick at the end of the series, which Salil was not expecting. The kick found its mark, hard on Salil's chest, sending her flying across the woods where she landed in thick bushes.

Salil picked herself off the ground and rubbed her chest. The kick hurt.

"Professor Glinda isn't here to protect you this time."

"Kiaaa!" Salil ran at Kass, swinging her sword and executing her own series of spinning techniques as she came forward. Kass's eyes opened wide, she was genuinely surprised at the ferocity of the attack. But she blocked every one of the moves. The last blow was blocked close to Kass's body, and now they were standing almost face to face, swords in a stalemate clash. They looked at each other, breathing heavily. With her opposite hand, Kass grabbed Salil, ensuring that she could not get away. Salil struggled to move away for a second, her attention only focused on Kass's sword. Salil pushed a little more, and with her opposite hand swung and punched Kass in the face, causing her to turn away and let go of Salil. The punch opened up a small gash, just above Kass's eye, and blood started trickling down her cheek.

"Yeah, we're not in class anymore," Salil said, backing away from Kass, still holding her sword out in front.

Kass touched the spot where Salil had hit her. Seeing her own blood she calmly stated, "No matter, you and all the other Princes will be dead soon. It's inevitable."

"Let's see you try it. Your ways are not our ways!"

"It's already starting, and you can't do anything about it. Grrr!" Kass moved forward again, swinging her sword at Salil, this time a little harder, a little fiercer. She swung at her head, Salil would duck. She swiped at her feet, Salil would jump over. They went back and forth, Kass clearly in command of the fight, though not landing any clean blows with her sword. Salil tried to counter Kass's moves and swung her sword low, lashing at Kass's ankles. Kass saw it coming, but instead of jumping over Salil's blade, she stepped on the sword with her foot and held it pinned to the ground.

Salil was helpless, she struggled to release the sword from Kass's foot to no avail.

Kass drew her sword over her head, poised to strike down on Salil. Salil still struggled to remove her sword from beneath Kass's foot. She whimpered against her will. Kass started to attack, full-on ready to stab Salil in the head. As the blade flashed toward her, Salil managed to grab the other sword from her side and put it up to block the incoming blow. Salil had one hand on the sword still pinned to the ground and the other hand on her sword protecting her head, but Kass found another opening. She kicked Salil directly in the face, knocking her back. This strike drew Salil's blood and left her breathless. She dropped the sword beneath Kass's foot and stumbled back, pinwheeling her arms, her remaining weapon dragging the ground as she tried to regain her balance.

Kass took out her second sword and moved in, ready to finish Salil off. She approached, this time twisting and spinning and swinging both swords at Salil. Salil did her best to block the blades but they were coming too fast, one after another after another. Bang! Clank! Bang! Clank! Slice. Salil was not quick enough. Kass's sword tasted the flesh deep within Salil's shoulder. Salil dropped her sword to the ground. Stumbling backward, touching her shoulder, she could feel the blood rushing down her arm in streams. It was a deep wound.

"It's over. The great little Salil is defeated."

She kicked Salil's sword away and dropped one of her own on the ground. Satisfied and confident that she could finish Salil off with just one blade. Salil backed away slowly, holding her shoulder. Kass stalked her like prey once again, slowly, deliberately. She faked an attack, Salil jumped backwards. Kass laughed, she was enjoying this. Salil's mind raced as to what to do. She looked up to see if there was a branch she might jump to, and around for a tree she might climb, or a stick on the ground she could use. Anything. There was nothing.

Kass moved in for the kill. Instead of backing away, Salil moved forward, focused on nothing but Kass's sword. Kass's momentum already indicated a coming sideswipe thrust (to deliver the final blow to her torso area) and she could not stop the sword, already in its swinging motion. Salil was just quick enough to meet Kass's dominant wrist, catching it with both hands and, using her momentum, she flipped Kass over her back, still in control of the hand that held the sword. As she flipped Kass over, Salil used her own body in tandem and they both ended up on the ground. When they stopped rolling, Salil had Kass in an arm-bar technique, she used her hips to force pressure to Kass's elbow. Kass tried to resist with all her strength, but it was her one arm against Salil's two legs and entire body. Salil lifted up and grunted with all her might, trying to break Kass's elbow. The elder assassin released her sword and Salil did a backwards roll, kicking it far away as she landed back on her feet.

Kass struggled to get up. Dirt covered them both and Kass rubbed her elbow, relieved to be out of the arm-bar. Salil stood there, she was not going to quit. Kass looked at her with loathing and said, "I don't have time for this." She started coming forward, this time only with punches. She punched and punched at Salil as hard as she could, knowing that she was still much stronger than her younger counterpart. Salil did the best she could to block the flurry of pummeling. Bam! One landed on the shoulder where she was cut, which sent excruciating pain through her body. She slumped over, grabbing her shoulder. That's when the next blow hit her flush on her temple. Salil never saw it coming.

She was down, barely conscious. To her it seemed she'd lost her hearing. She couldn't see where Kass had gone, and everything around her was moving in slow motion, as if she were on a time-warped dream-speed spinning tea cup ride. Kass went to retrieve her sword. Salil made it to her knees, still dizzy from the blow to her head. She spotted Kass in the distance, walking toward her, sword in her hand.

"Salil! Where are you? Salil!"

Someone was approaching. Kass, not knowing who it was,

stopped, and then took off running into the forest. This fight could continue later.

"Salil! Where are you?" It was Stowie, stumbling out of the brush and toward Salil's battered body. "Are you all right? What happened?"

Salil was so happy. She was alive! She hugged Stowie and said, "She's here. She's here." She kept repeating it.

He held her for a moment, looking around and yelling for help. But no one was there, everyone was at the celebration. "Come on, you're bleeding, we gotta get ya some help. Can you walk, yo?"

"Yes." Salil retrieved her swords, bow and pouch and they walked together, back to Provins. Along the path they saw one of the village's many pet dogs. He was dead on the path. Thick white foam came from his mouth. Stowie didn't have time to stop, as his primary concern was getting Salil some help. "Come, we must get back quickly!"

Salil turned her head to take another peek at the dead dog. Then she hurried along behind Stowie.

Chapter 68

Back at the stadium, dinner was about to be served. Volunteers were handing out plates of food to all those who were seated, half a roast pheasant and all manner of side dishes. Music continued to play and some revelers were still dancing in the middle, they simply took their plates and continued to whoop it up, grabbing their pheasant by the drumstick and twirling it around in the air as they gyrated their hips to the music. The local spirit, auga ardente distilled from sugarcane, was flowing and everyone was having a great time.

David was seated with the Elders and the rest of the Princes were close by at another table. Brandon had taken Nara and Ava to dance a little in the middle of the stadium. Ava was clearly the better dancer, but Nara tried her best to find some sense of coordination. Tem and Cedric, neither being dancers, just watched. Brandon came back over to their table, Nara on one arm and Ava on the other.

"Yeah! That's what I'm talking about. A par-tay! Whooooo

hooooooo! Love for everyone!"

The girls were just laughing at him. Everyone was allowed to have some fun this night. When they sat down, their plates of food were already on the table. Of course, Tem and Cedric would not dare eat before David started eating, so they waited patiently and without question.

"Yo, I'm starving right now. My queen, I am your little puppy dog tonight." Brandon got down on all fours and held his mouth open for Nara. "Feed me."

"Brandon, you are sooo crazy!"

"Woof, woof! My lady!"

"Ok, ok. Here."

She dropped a potato into his mouth.

"Oh, come on, do you two really have to do this right now?" said an annoyed Tem.

Brandon gobbled up the roasted potato quickly and begged for more, sticking his tongue out and panting.

Nara seemed to be having some fun and Ava joined right in, both of them taking turns feeding puppy dog Brandon.

When the plates were served at the Elder's table, Sunshine stood up and hushed the crowd by banging a gold gong on the table. "People of Provins! Love to us all! On this holy night, let us remember friends who have parted this world, and others we have found this year. Let us remember our great Father, and the ways that have brought us a lasting peace." He continued blessing the food.

Off in the woods adjacent to the stadium there was movement, too far away for anyone to notice.

"Let us be thankful for this bounty of food and the hands that prepared it. And so it is!"

The stadium responded, "And so it is!" With that, everyone started eating.

David grabbed his roast pheasant and was about to dig in. He paused, pheasant in his hand. "You know, I'm glad we are here, Sunshine. Thanks for your hospitality."

In the distance, where there had been movement in the woods, tension was being applied to a bow, poising a sharpened arrow. Aiming directly at David's chest.

David looked at his pheasant, he maneuvered it so that he could take his first bite from the crispy skin-covered breast. The arrow in the distance was released, headed directly for David.

When the arrow struck, the pheasant in David's hands went flying away, pierced and impaled on a wall off to the side. After the release of the arrow, two more came flying. Then Salil and Stowie ran from the woods, Salil, bow and arrow in hand, shooting at the pheasant the people were holding. Stowie was yelling as loud as he could, "Stop, don't eat the pheasant! Don't eat the pheasant!"

But many people could not understand what he was saying. Breasts, drumsticks and wings exploded out of people's hands from Salil's arrows. When they reached the stadium, people were running all over the place, ducking under tables, unsure of what the commotion was. Salil and Stowie ran past a small child, holding a pheasant leg, and Stowie smacked it out of his hands. He ran around the stadium, telling people the pheasant was poisoned and trying to stop anyone else from eating it.

Tem had gone to David immediately after seeing the arrow and shielded him with his body. He knew it, it was Salil all along. When she was close enough he drew his own sword, ready to attack her.

"Wait! Kass is here. The pheasant has been poisoned. You didn't eat any right?" she said between taking deep breaths.

"What, Kass? Poisoned? Where is she?"

"I don't know, but we have to get everyone out of here now."

Ava, Nara and Cedric ran over to where David was sitting.

"What. What's poisoned?" asked Nara.

"The pheasant! The pheasant! You didn't eat any yet, right?"

Nara and Ava's faces showed the horror, as they both looked in Brandon's direction. He was still at the table, both his hands clasped around his neck. He was having trouble breathing, and a thick white foam was coming out of his mouth and down his chin. Nara ran to him first as he fell out of his chair.

"Brandon! Brandon!" She bent over him and lay down at his side. Holding him in her arms.

Ava stood beside her crying, "No, no, no."

Brandon's body convulsed, he couldn't get air into his lungs anymore. Nara just held him, crying, trying to comfort him in any way possible. When she looked up, David, Cedric, Tem and Salil were all standing beside her and Ava, watching

Brandon die. She looked around the stadium, and the scene was something out of a zombie apocalypse. Provinians young and old who had consumed pheasant before the warning lay sprawling on the ground, going through the same horrific death throes as Brandon. Mothers embraced their children, husbands their wives. No one who ate the pheasant was immune. That night, Kass managed to kill more than a thousand Provinians with the poison she had stirred into the marinade the night before. Stowie's father, Sunshine, was among the dead.

Tem and Cedric helped carry Brandon back to their cabin and laid him on his bed. A white blanket was placed over his body.

"David, we can't stay here," said Cedric.

"I know, let me go talk to the Elders."

"Wait, where are we going to go? Isn't Kass out there? Wouldn't we be safer here?" Nara asked. "She's going to kill us all!" A fresh set of tears streamed down her face, both for Brandon and for fear of her own life at the hands of Kass. Ava just sat by the bed where Brandon lay, crying softly.

"Salil, do you know where she is? Oh, look at you! What happened? Quick get her some bandages," Tem said. David rushed and found some towels and gave them to Tem, who wrapped her shoulder and tended to her. She barely flinched when he pressed towels against her shoulder to slow the bleeding.

"I don't know where she went, Tem."

"It's ok. Hey, thanks for saving David tonight. You saved a

lot of people tonight."

"Yeah, but what about Brandon?" Salil bowed her head, turned and walked away, unable to look at his lifeless body.

"Wait here everyone, I'm going to talk with the Elders." David walked out of the room.

Chapter 69

There were several men standing at the entrance to the suite where they'd first met all the Elders for breakfast. People were gathering there in vigil, lighting candles and saying prayers. Some whispered at David as he walked by, he could only ascertain parts of what they were saying. "The Prophecy," "This is all their fault," "Their ways are not our ways!" The men allowed David to pass, sensing it might be better for him to be inside than outside amongst the people.

Inside, Sunshine lay still on a marble table. Candles were on the floor surrounding his body. Stowie was sobbing, seated with his legs crossed, along with Manchild, their mother and several other extended family members all in the same position. David paused, then walked over to Stowie. He sat down next to him in the same manner, joining the family circle in vigil. He put his hand on Stowie's shoulder, "I'm sorry for your loss. Elder Sunshine was a great man." Stowie did not acknowledge David, instead staring straight ahead. David then said, loud enough for everyone to hear, "I'm sorry for your loss.

We're all sorry." With those words, he jumped up and rushed out of the room. He returned to his cabin and ordered everyone to pack up, they were leaving at dawn.

The Princes tried to sleep that night, but none of them could, their thoughts on Brandon, the people killed from the poison and Kass. Only little Jimmy was able to shut his eyes for a few hours. David whispered to Cedric, trying to make sure none of the others could hear him, "Cedric, where will we go?"

"I don't know David."

"I wish we could go home. Maybe King Richard could help us if we went home."

"King Richard is dead," said Salil as she got up and walked over to the door.

"King Richard? Dead?"

"Yes, Kass told me, it was her and Professor Xalvador. We are the last of the Royals, and she's coming for us. I don't know that I can stop her."

"King Richard is dead, oh my goodness. What will we do? She will kill us all!" Nara had heard the conversation, another round of fear consuming her.

"No, she won't. Salil, you don't have to do this alone." Tem said, as he got up from his bed.

"Yeah, that's right, there's still six of us, she can't beat us all if we stick together," David said, trying to rally his people.

"Well, one thing's for sure now. With King Richard dead, Xalvador has taken over Terrowin. We can't go back home. We can't ever go back," Cedric said, as he remembered the Terrowin Constitution's stipulation for succession of power.

Knock, knock, knock.

Tem went to answer the door. It was Stowie. "The Elders want to talk with David." His face still showed signs of heavy crying.

Chapter 70

David returned to the Elders' suite where the remaining Elders awaited him. Sunshine was his only ally, most of them had wanted to banish the Princes the moment they discovered that they had come from the Blackness. David approached the council.

"First, let me say that I'm sorry for all that has happened tonight. You all have my deepest condolences."

Sky Blue replied. "Thank you young David, one day you will be a great leader for your people. But your ways are not our ways, and we must ask that you and your friends depart immediately."

"I understand."

"We will provide you with horses and provisions to last about two weeks."

"May I ask, we cannot go home, where in your wisdom shall we go? We have never been so far from home."

The Elders whispered amongst themselves for a few moments.

"Our history tells us of a people to the east. Beyond the mountain range. We do not know how far, nor have we ever seen them, for their ways are not our ways. But we remember stories of our Elders, which spoke of magic and sorcery that is beyond our comprehension. Maybe they can help you out."

"Are they friendly?"

"We do not know. I'm sorry. You must leave this dawn."

"Thank you great Elders for your hospitality and wisdom. Again, we are sorry for your losses, we never meant for any of this to happen."

"Go in peace, and may your travels be safe."

David was about to walk out. Then he stopped and turned back around. "One more thing. Well, actually two. Can you give our friend Brandon a proper burial, with honors? He was a great friend and it would comfort us to know he will be taken care of. And also, can little Jimmy stay here with you? If me and my group must die, let us die fighting, but little Jimmy should not be put to that test at his age. Let him grow up as a Provinian and be happy."

The Elders conferred, considering David's requests.

"Brandon shall receive a proper burial, with honors as you wish. And little Jimmy may stay with us."

Sky Blue spoke, before David left the room. "David, can you ask Salil to join us for a moment?"

"Sure."

David returned to his cabin and informed Salil that the Elders wanted to speak with her.

Salil entered their suite, with her mask still on.

"Please remove your mask, little Salil." She complied.

"Salil, Provins owes you a debt. Without your wisdom and quick thinking, many more of us would be dead today. We wanted to say thank you." The Elders stood up and walked over in a line. Each one then embraced Salil, separately. She could not return the gesture, but instead fresh tears started forming, the emotions within her erupting like Mt. Himalua. She was thinking about Brandon, the people she'd seen dying and those she helped save.

At the end of the line, Sky Blue grabbed Salil's hand and bowed down before her. "Salil, your courage, bravery and compassion reminded all of us of the stories we've been told about our Father, Morris Grotisi. When he arrived in Provins he used his sword and fighting skills to create peace and unite our people. We see that same spirit in you. We want you to have his sword, so that it may protect you and give you the courage to fight your enemies, as well as the compassion to save your friends." She handed Salil his sword. It was lighter than her own and the craftsmanship was beautiful.

"Thank you," were all the words she could muster.

Chapter 71

In just a few hours the sun would rise over Provins. The Princes prepared for travel, this time east, again into the unknown. They mounted their horses in the dark, leaving little Jimmy asleep in his bed, and made their way toward the fields in the east end of Provins. The horses walked quietly and none of the Princes spoke as they departed. When they reached the edge of a field of drying corn stalks, a group of Elders and other people were waiting to see them off and wish them good luck.

Salil had hoped to see Stowie, but she could understand that he might be still grieving the loss of his father. When she didn't see him there, she felt guilty that maybe Sunshine's death was somehow her fault, her mind replaying the events over and over as she thought perhaps she did not do enough to save more people.

The Princes paused by the group of Provinians sending them off. Mercury, the little girl with purple hair who had greeted them the first day with dandelions, was also there. She handed each of the Princes a green clover and wished them good luck. It was time to depart. Tem was in front, followed by Cedric and then David, Nara, Ava and Salil. They headed into the cornstalks, the horses walking at a slow trot.

"Hey, wait, wait for me!"

Stowie was riding a horse in full canter toward the departing Princes.

"Wait! Wait for me!"

The Princes stopped and turned around. He reached them. "Hey, y'all gonna leave without telling a dude goodbye? Heck, I thought we were friends!"

"Stowie, you can't come with us. This is our fight," Salil said to the surprise of everyone.

"Well, I'm going with ya whether ya like it or not. That Kass killed my dad, and hundreds of others!"

Cedric interrupted. "Stowie, people will die, and we may have to kill. Tenet number one of Provins, Thou shalt not kill. Can you handle that?"

Stowie thought a moment. "Hmm, well, ok, I won't kill anyone, but I owe that Kass a bop on the head. She hit me something hard ya know!" He was rubbing the still-swollen lump on the side of his head from the bolas. "Oh, come on, can't I go?"

Cedric looked to David.

"Ok Stowie, come on," said David.

"Yeah, mate!"

"Here, you might need one of these." Salil threw him one of her older swords and they trotted off around the inner horseshoe of Provins and into the forest, headed east.

The seven of them cautiously waded into the woods and toward the mountains, constantly looking around them and up in the trees for any sign of Kass. They mostly stayed quiet, with only the occasional grunting from the horses echoing through the forest. The air was cool this morning and fog had settled into the valley below the mountain as the sun tried to burn its way through the mist.

They walked about an hour east of Provins, in terrain that was still familiar to Stowie, the mountains off in the distance. Then, a rustling in the trees caught the attention of Salil and Stowie.

"Aww, not again!" Kass's bolas found Stowie's head once more, knocking him off his horse. Almost simultaneously, Kass came flying out of the forest, swinging from a vine, headed toward David. Like an eagle swooping down to catch a rabbit, Kass grabbed David with one arm and yanked him off his horse. She landed in stride, dragging David with her as she disappeared in the thick deep brush. Salil took her bow and arrow and drew back, but she did not trust her aim, not wanting to hit David.

Nara and Ava screamed, causing all the horses to get agitated. They both were thrown down from their mounts. Tem dismounted and ran toward where he had seen Kass disappear.

"David!" he called as he ran, his sword drawn.

"Tem, no! Wait, Tem! Wait!" commanded Cedric.

Tem stopped, not sure whether to listen to Cedric or

continue after David.

"What are we waiting for, she's getting away! David! David!"

"It's a trap. If you go in there she has the advantage. She will take us out one by one. We have to stick together! And, we need you."

"I have to save David! David!"

Cedric grabbed Tem. "Think about it Tem! If she wanted to kill David he would already be dead. No, it's divide and conquer. Think about it."

Ava and Nara were now with Stowie, who was still unconscious. They were huddled over him, trying to wake him, looking around for Kass. Salil had slipped behind a tree, giving her some cover. She was listening and peeking into the forest, trying to determine the whereabouts of Kass.

"Ok, we'll go together. Keep quiet. She knows where we are, but we don't know where she is."

"Quiet, everyone." Cedric went to Nara, Ava and Salil. "Ava and Nara, I want you two to stay here by Stowie but not in the open. Salil," he pointed up at the trees, indicating that he wanted her to survey from above. She nodded and handed Cedric her other sword, then disappeared up the first tree she saw. Nara and Ava looked at Cedric with disbelief. Leave them there, alone?

Cedric pointed to Tem, and they both went into the bushes exactly where Kass had taken David. They went quietly, with their swords drawn in front. Tem led the way.

After a few failed attempts to wake Stowie, Nara and Ava

looked around the forest and realized they were both alone and exposed. "Stowie, come on, please wake up." Tears ran down Ava's face as she shoved his body. Ava whispered again, "Stowie," loud enough to try to wake him, but soft enough so as not to reveal their exact position. The horses were still on the path, milling about, oblivious to the danger around them. Then Nara heard some movement in the opposite direction from where Tem and Cedric had disappeared in pursuit of Kass.

"Shhh." Nara held her finger up to her mouth. They heard the faintest walking sounds, heading in their direction. They left Stowie, still unconscious, stayed low and crawled underneath a patch of brush, hoping they would not be discovered. It was Kass, and she was dragging David along. His hands and feet were bound and his mouth gagged. She had not seen Nara or Ava. The girls were able to see both her and David's feet come to a halt, just a few meters or so from them.

"Now, let's see if your friends will come to you, future king. Call out for help!" Kass ripped off the binding around his mouth and held her sword to his neck.

"Call for them, I said!"

"Tem! Cedric! Help me! I'm here. I'm here!" With the last "I'm here," he could barely control himself and he wept, knowing that he was leading his friends right into Kass's trap. She pushed him against the side of a large evergreen tree and ordered him not to move. She waited for Cedric and Tem.

On cue, they both came running from the forest in David's direction. Nara and Ava were still hiding in the bushes off to the side.

"Kass, just let David go. You don't have to do this," Cedric pleaded with her.

"After I kill Tem, you're next."

"Cedric, let me handle this." Tem moved forward. He was almost the same height as Kass and looked as if he were just as strong. He came forward, his sword drawn. He was focused, concentrating only on his patriotic oath to protect David with his own life if necessary. He was not afraid. He was fast and furious, striking at Kass with all his might. She blocked most of his blows, and dodged a few. They clashed, swords extended, each pushing against the other, testing each other's strength. Kass was surprised at how strong he was. Tem was equally surprised at her strength. She pushed him back while executing a spinning kick to his midsection.

Nara and Ava, seeing an opportunity, ran over to David, who had not moved from the tree Kass pushed him against. His feet and hands were still bound. They started to untie him. Kass, without missing a beat, took out her bow and arrow, turned and shot one arrow right above David's head. Deliberately missing him, but sending a message to the girls whom she considered no threat at all.

"Don't touch him."

As she moved towards a staggering Tem, still trying to regain his balance from the kick, Cedric approached from the side. She saw in her peripheral vision and blocked his oncoming attack, skittering backward to avoid the direct force of his strikes. Tem regained his balance and joined. It was now two against one. Both Tem and Cedric took up opposite positions on the side of Kass. Nara and Ava, struck with fear, simply could not move. David tried his best to wiggle out of his bindings, to no avail. Kass was holding them both at bay, using a series of spinning and jumping techniques to confuse the boys. She would attack Cedric moving forward, knowing that Tem would move in from behind. She thrust her sword behind her to deflect his blow, while executing a kick to Cedric's face. She was clearly better than both of them and it would only be a matter of time before she disarmed and killed them both. Although, together they were putting up a good fight.

They were all breathing heavily, dirty from falling on the ground, and they paused. "Enough of this," said Kass, and she pulled one of Xalvador's spheres from her pocket and quickly ignited it. It was made from the same experimental fire powder and exploded in front her, separating Cedric and Tem with a great wall of fire. David, Ava and Nara were now behind her. After lighting the fireball, she walked directly toward the three of them. It was clear, she was coming to kill David. He fell to the ground, still trying to escape his bindings. Kass stood over him.

"Goodbye King David," she said sweetly as she lifted her sword over her head, ready to strike. The blade dropped. Ava cried out, "No, not David!" and threw herself forward, pushing David aside, taking the death blow for herself. It didn't matter to Kass, another Prince gone. She looked at David.

Nara screamed out, "No! No! No!"

Around the fire, from opposite directions, both Tem and Cedric came running toward Kass at full speed. Kass stopped her assault, looked at both of them and ran directly at Cedric, calculating that he was the weaker opponent. She jumped in the air and did two front somersaults, knocking Cedric's sword out his hand with her own blade while in midair, and double kicking him in the chest. He flew back into the bushes. Kass turned her attention to Tem.

She walked straight for him, confident, knowing that this was it for him. She took out her second sword. As she got closer, she started spinning, swinging the swords at all different angles. Tem tried his best to block the ones he saw and dodge the ones his blade was unable to connect with. He tried a counter-move with his own sword, but Kass saw it coming, and using both her swords caught his one blade and twisted. Tem lost his grip. Kass kicked him in the groin. He cried out and dropped to one knee, knowing his fate was sealed. With both swords in her hands, she raised one, ready to pierce his spinal column. She paused with the blade lifted, and before she could strike an arrow whistled out from the trees and struck her right shoulder, lodging deep inside her.

Kass looked up to see Salil there, another arrow pointed right at her chest. Salil's hands shook. Blood started soaking through the bandage from her previous wound. Kass wondered whether she would actually release the arrow. But Salil controlled her breathing and drew the arrow back farther, with enough movement that Kass knew she was serious and would not miss the second time.

"Shoot her! Kill her!" yelled Tem.

Kass stopped her attack, broke off the arrow in her

shoulder and walked slowly toward David and Nara. She said nothing as she mounted one of their horses and took off. All the time, Salil's arrow focused on her target.

$\mathcal{C}$hapter 72

Nara ran to Ava, who was barely breathing. Nara tried to stop the bleeding. Tem went to David and untied him. Cedric limped out of the bushes. Salil stayed in the tree, watching Kass disappear into the forest. Stowie was regaining consciousness.

"Owww, man. She did it again!" he said, shaking his head.

Another sound caught Salil's attention. Coming from off in the distance, opposite where Kass was headed.

"Hurry, up, get David out of here," she hissed from the tree branches.

Nara still tending to Ava, cried out, "Help me, she needs help. We can't just leave her here!"

All except Nara knew that it was just a matter of time before Ava would die. Cedric spoke, "David, we must get out of here. We have to leave."

"No! I'm not going to leave her here to die like this. Not like this," Nara protested through tears.

"Tem, get David out of here," Salil said. "Cedric, you and

Stowie go with them. I'll help get Ava and we will catch up with you."

"Ok, are you sure?"

"Yes. Go now, someone is coming!"

David, Tem, Cedric and Stowie mounted the horses and rode off, away from the approaching sounds.

"Come on, let's get her on a horse." Nara and Salil carried Ava to one of the awaiting horses and gently lifted her up.

"She should go back to Provins," said Salil. "Maybe they can help her before it's too late."

Nara looked at Salil and hoped that maybe she spoke some truth. She nodded with a face that was swollen from crying. Salil turned the horse, with Ava's body slumped over it, toward Provins. She smacked it hard on the hind side, and the animal took off running down the path they had come from, in full gallop back to Provins.

"Come, we must hurry," said Salil. They ran to the one remaining horse and were about to mount when several metal spears came ringing out of the air and landed all around them. Encircling them, like a net. Then, twelve menacing men on black horses, wearing black bear fur, faces painted black, with tiger skins and heads draped across their own faces approached the two girls, cutting off anywhere to run. Salil drew her sword. The men drew their swords in unison.

Salil thought better of it, she put down her weapon. They were caught. Captive.

About the Author

JERRY CANADA grew up in Long Island, New York, and attended SUNY Stony Brook, where he studied psychology and served as student body president. A two-time All-American in track, he still holds university records in multiple events. He earned his JD and graduated with honors from UC Berkeley School of Law (Boalt Hall.) A former prominent trial lawyer, second-degree black belt, high school track and field coach and passionate world traveler, Canada has been telling stories and working with kids all his life. He currently lives in Raleigh, North Carolina; EXILE is his first novel.

COMING IN 2015

The Tales of Terrowin

Book Two

CAPTIVE

Jerry Canada